HIDDEN IN MAGIC

IN MAGIC SERIES
BOOK ONE

KJ WARAWA

MYSTIC
CITY
PRESS

AUTHOR'S NOTE:

I wrote *Lost in Magic* several years ago but I've always felt that it didn't quite live up to its potential. I've finally had a chance to rewrite it, and *Hidden in Magic* is the new and improved story. You'll see some differences in the plot and character backstories, although the overarching storyline is the same. I hope you enjoy this reimagined and refreshed version of Meredith and Jack's story.

CHAPTER ONE

*J*ack Knight braced himself to crush the heart of the only woman he would ever love. Weeks of sleepless nights and internal debates left only one option.

Calling on his magic, he summoned cold, spreading it throughout his body. It numbed everything—a trick he hadn't needed in years. But years earlier it had been the only way to survive each day. Sometimes each hour. His magic wasn't just a part of him; it defined him. Staying with Meredith any longer would mean compromising who he was —something he'd sworn never to do.

He'd done this to himself—waited too long to break things off. Hell, he never should've come back to Blue Mountain, Colorado, after college. But he had. And by the time he'd been back a year, Meredith had sucked him into her orbit, forcing him to shove aside the promise he'd made never to compromise. Then Meredith turned eighteen, and he made love to her for the first time. She'd been too easy to love, and he'd fallen fast.

Jack lowered himself to the bed's edge and watched her

sleep. He could still remember the first time they'd woken up together. Her long, dark curls fanned across the pillow, gleaming in the early morning light. The moment she'd opened her eyes and smiled at him, he'd known he wanted to wake up beside her every morning for the rest of his life.

The desire to crawl back into bed with her now and ignore what he had to do yanked at him. He wanted nothing more than to take her into his arms and have his way with her body, making her scream out in pleasure. Then they would spend the day talking, laughing, and making love some more.

But he wouldn't. He couldn't. If he didn't end it now, he'd compromise who he was at his core. Even if he could live with that, he couldn't force their future children to do the same.

He brushed her hair from her face and whispered, "Mer, Bubbles. Wake up." Leaning in, he kissed her cheek.

"Hmmm."

He chuckled at her sleepy response. Most mornings she woke fast, ready to take on the day, but he'd kept her up late last night. "Time to wake up."

She opened her eyes and smiled. "Morning."

Her voice rasped with sleep, low and sexy. It threatened to punch through his resolve. But he had no choice. He had to leave, even though he didn't want to. For the thousandth time he cursed his bloodline and everything it had taught him.

He leaned down and brushed her lips with a ghost of a kiss. That final taste would have to carry him for the rest of his life. He stood and crossed to the chair in the corner of the room. If he didn't put some space between them, he might lose his nerve.

He grabbed his boots and focused on tying the laces.

She sat up in bed. "You're already dressed… Oh God, am I late for class?"

He glanced at the digital clock. "No, it's only six."

"Then why are you dressed?"

"I'm leaving." The words hurt more than he expected, and kept hurting.

She hesitated, as if his body language was already telling her something was wrong. Or she'd sensed him pulling away the last few days. "You don't mean to do a quick errand or to see a friend, do you?"

"No." He stood, wishing he had something to keep his hands busy. But he couldn't conjure something to hold. He'd already taken all his belongings, which had migrated to Meredith's house over the years. He'd removed a few things here, a few there, until there would be no trace of himself left behind. Nothing for her to see and remember when he walked out her door for the last time.

Meredith pulled her knees to her chest and wrapped the sheet around her like protection. She hated feeling powerless, though she always gave every piece of herself to those she loved. And he was about to rip away every ounce of control she had left. Maybe not as much as what she'd lost twelve years ago when her family members died, but it might be close.

"I don't understand. You said once your master's degree was done, you'd take some time off before looking for full-time work. Is that what you're doing?"

"I'll find work. Just not here." His throat tightened, dry and useless.

Her eyes held so much emotion, even in the dim light. The kind of depth that could suck a man in and make him want to stay forever. And damn, he did want to stay. But if he did, regret would come.

Screw the distance. He had to touch her one last time. He

crossed the room in three long strides and pulled her into his arms. She stiffened at first, then her entire body relaxed and melted against him. He wrapped his arms around her, tucking her close, and letting her warmth seep into him. Her strength, her softness, her beauty, had always reached places in him he thought had died with his mother and brother.

Those places would die again when he let her go.

He soaked in all her affection and love and held on for as long as he dared.

She tilted her head back to meet his eyes. "I thought you loved me. I still don't understand. Please don't go."

The desperation in her voice cut deep. But what lay ahead loomed too stark to ignore. He traced her cheek with his knuckles to feel her softness one last time, then pulled back before his willpower crumbled into a burning pile of ash at his feet.

"I do love you. I'll always love you, but I can't stay. We don't have a future together."

Tears filled her eyes, but she blinked them away. It was another fragile grab at control. "None of this makes sense, Jack. We *could* have a future together. We've even talked about one. If you loved me, you wouldn't leave."

The lump in his throat had become a boulder. He had to leave now or he'd lose his courage and destroy both their futures. "I hope you find someone who gives you everything you've ever wanted and deserved, Bubbles."

Jack walked out of the bedroom, closing the door behind him, but not before he heard Meredith's final words.

"That was you, Jack."

He leaned back against the door, shut his eyes, and listened to her sobs. The sound shredded his heart the way he'd shredded hers.

"You're finally leaving?" a familiar voice asked.

Jack looked up and pushed away from the door. "I have to, Elise."

"You could have found a way to tell her the truth." Meredith's mother studied him with a hard look, as if she could see into his soul. He didn't know if she had a magic specialty, but if she did, he doubted it would be that.

"I doubt it. But even if I had, that would have made you the bad guy."

"I know," she said with a sigh that seemed to carry the weight of the last twelve years.

"Elise, you know I never agreed with what you did. I don't think I would have made the same choice if I were in your position—but we'll never know. And even if I had been willing to make you the villain, my magic wouldn't have let me tell her."

"No, but we always have choices."

And Jack had to live with Elise's choice. "Are you ever going to tell Meredith the truth?"

"No. I told you when you asked me the first time, my sisters and I made peace with what we did."

"Then you've given me no other option." He stepped around her, then paused. "Will you do me a favor?"

"Depends on the favor."

"If one day you decide to tell Meredith and her cousins the truth… let me know first. I'd want to be here for her."

"I can do that."

Jack gave her a single nod and walked away, leaving the love of his life behind.

CHAPTER TWO

Eight Years Later

Jack picked up another box to unpack when someone knocked on the door. "It's open, Damon," he called loud enough for his best friend to hear.

"Not Damon," Ben Davis said as he walked into the apartment, shutting the door behind him.

Jack greeted his boss and long-time mentor, standing to shake his hand. "Coming to make sure I'm really here to stay?"

Ben gripped his hand but hauled him into a quick back-slapping hug. "Something like that. I had to see it with my own eyes."

"It's real." Jack gestured to the boxes scattered around his living room and covering the surface of his dining room table. "For now."

"You promised me a year."

"I know. But now that I'm back..." He shrugged. "I'm not

so sure." Jack was practically on pins and needles waiting to run into Meredith. He'd only seen her from a distance since he walked out on her eight years before.

Not that she ever knew. Being apart from her had been hell. He had lasted a short, pitiful six months before he had to see for himself that she was alright. He'd flashed to her university and stayed in the shadows as she walked to class with her cousins.

During that six months, she'd lost weight, and some of her light had faded. He'd been responsible for that. But he hadn't changed his mind. He still believed he'd done the right thing by walking away.

From that point on, he only allowed himself to get a glimpse of her once a year. It was the highlight of his year and the worst kind of punishment all rolled into one. If it wasn't for his best friend, Damon Stone, giving him regular updates on how Meredith was doing, he might have slowly gone insane. Either that, or rushed back to her, confessing why he left and begging for her forgiveness, but his reasons for leaving in the first place wouldn't have changed.

It took two years for Damon to inform Jack that the day he'd wished for and equally dreaded had arrived—Meredith had gone on a date.

"Why?" Ben asked, pulling Jack from his memories.

"What?"

"Why are you second-guessing the move back here?" Ben took a box off the couch and placed it on the floor before taking a seat.

"What if Elise doesn't go through with it?"

"She will, or she wouldn't have told you she was going to tell the Little W's the truth. She told me too, so I can't see her backing out now."

Jack's lips twitched up at the name he hadn't heard in

years—Little W's. Fiona, Damon's mom and Elise's best friend, had started calling Meredith and her three cousins by the moniker shortly after the fire that claimed the lives of seven members of the Williams family. Fiona claimed *Little W's* was easier than saying Meredith, Rowena, Jo, and Reece, or any combination of the names.

"I think it's time we drop the *little*."

Ben chuckled. "You're probably right."

Remembering the reason for mentioning the nickname, he sobered. "I know she said she was going to tell the truth, but why now?"

Ben shrugged. "She didn't tell me, but I'm guessing it has something to do with Beatrice. Maybe her sister's death has her feeling her mortality and she's worried what will happen to the Lit— the W's if she dies without them knowing the truth."

"I get that she's the only remaining sister, but Lillian died years ago and her death didn't cause Beatrice or Elise to waver on their decision."

"I wouldn't be so sure, Jack. I think the sisters have second-guessed their decision almost every day for the last twenty years." Ben yawned and a mug of coffee appeared in his hand. "Hope you don't mind."

"I could use one myself." Jack sank down into the armchair opposite Ben and conjured himself a cup of steaming java. He smirked. "Or something stronger—later. I might need it."

"Look, I know you were willing to flash back and forth from Phoenix every day indefinitely, but I'm glad you moved back."

"I don't know about indefinitely—six months wasn't too bad. If New York wasn't too far to flash to Blue Mountain in a single trip, I might have tried to convince you to keep me there."

Ben took another drink of his coffee before disappearing the mug and standing. "I don't think so. Your place was always here. And I don't mean the FBI field office here in Blue Mountain, I mean here so you can set up a new North American Council. It's time."

Jack opened his mouth to respond and then shut it. He wasn't sure what to say because if Meredith didn't forgive him, he wouldn't stay, whether he was destined to establish the council or not.

A knock on the door prevented him from having to come up with a response. "Jack?" Damon called as he walked in. "Oh, hey, Ben. Am I interrupting? I can come back."

"It's fine. I'm leaving."

Damon grinned. "Did you come to make sure he really moved in?"

Ben gave Jack's shoulder a squeeze as he walked by. "I wouldn't have believed it otherwise. I'm happy you're back, Jack. Stella is too. We'll both see you both tonight." Ben disappeared, flashing away.

Damon looked around. "I'm with Ben. I had to come and see for myself. Want help unpacking?"

"Sure. I had movers pack up everything in Phoenix and thought I'd sort it as I unboxed. I should probably get rid of some shit..." He wasn't in the mood to unpack and act like this was a brand new, fun adventure when he just wanted to see Meredith.

"Vet as you go." Damon walked into the kitchen and opened all the cupboard doors. "Ready?"

"Sure." Jack walked over to the dining room table and opened the first box. "The plates and bowls can go in the cupboard on the left."

Damon stepped back as Jack used his magic to lift the dishes from the box and sent them to the cupboard. Once they were stacked quickly and neatly, Damon shut the cupboard door.

"Cutlery?" Damon asked, opening a drawer.

Jack found the correct box and sent the tray organizer into the drawer first, followed by the cutlery. Each piece landed precisely in the correct spot. "I'll take the other utensils, bowls, and small appliances if you tackle the pot and pans. They go in the bottom pull out drawers."

"Right. On it."

They had everything in the kitchen unpacked and put away before moving on to the bedroom and then the living room, where they were sitting twenty minutes later, each with a beer. He might not remember where they'd put everything, but all the boxes were gone. Anything not in the right place was a minor issue.

"Are you ready for tonight?" Damon asked.

Was he? Jack had asked himself that question a hundred times in the past week since Elise had called him. At first he'd been so sure, he hadn't hesitated to tell her yes. But now that the time had finally come, he was nervous to see how Meredith would react. He could still picture Meredith sitting on her bed, grasping the sheet around her as he broke her heart. She'd always been kind and loving, but he wasn't so sure that would still extend to him.

"I don't know," he answered Damon honestly. "When I first left, I never thought this day would come. Then, I wanted it more than I wanted anything else."

"And now?"

"I still want it. I've never stopped loving her. You know that. I just don't know what my reception will be."

Damon laughed, a full-body, belly laugh. "It will be shit. Meredith will give you the cold shoulder. Hell, Jo and Rowena will too. Reece might not take as long to come around, but the women? You're going to have to work your ass off to earn their forgiveness."

Jack wasn't afraid of hard work. His only hope was that it would eventually pay off. No matter how long it took.

MEREDITH WILLIAMS GAUGED the distance to the door. If she vaulted from her chair and ran, could she make it before her date noticed? Option A: bolt. Option B: spill coffee down her shirt and bail. She leaned toward Option B—even if it burned.

She shouldn't continue to torture herself this way, but she couldn't seem to stop either. It wasn't that her latest date was a bad guy. He was successful and seemed nice, but, like all the others, there was no chemistry. Each time she went on a date with a new man, the minutes dragged on endlessly until she could make a plausible excuse to leave.

Forty-five minutes later.

She pulled into a spot in the back lot of her family's restaurant, The Magic Plate. With her back to the restaurant, she took in the Rocky Mountains in the distance—a view she never tired of—and drew in a deep breath.

Living close to the mountains, but in a city big enough to have everything she could want, Blue Mountain, Colorado, gave her the best of both worlds. And two years ago, when she'd taken on her dad's dream of turning the family's buildings into a community, she knew no matter when she found love—if she ever found it again—it would have to be here.

At least the business side of her life was going well. If only her love life could fall into place. She exhaled as disappointment settled in her chest. She had been so sure this time would be different. His dating profile had seemed perfect and their phone conversations, although brief, had given her such hope. All day her anticipation climbed higher. By the time she reached the coffee shop, her body pulsed with excitement.

He had arrived first and stood to greet her with a warm smile. They shook hands and, instead of letting go, he gently tugged her toward him and kissed her cheek. Pleasant. That's what she'd felt—pleasant. Like greeting an old acquaintance to catch up. Not even a hint of sexual tension flowed between them. She'd heard that chemistry grew with some couples, but it hadn't been that way with her. The last time she'd felt a heart-pumping, body-tingling, sexual desire for a man, it had hit her like a bolt of lightning.

From the moment Jack walked back into her life after finishing college, her seventeen-year-old self knew he would be her future. For two years she'd loved him more than she thought possible. He'd been her friend years earlier, but when he returned to Blue Mountain, he'd become her everything. When they'd finally made love shortly after her eighteenth birthday, she knew she would never love another man.

Meredith had given him more than just her body; she'd trusted him with her heart and soul.

Then he left. Jack walked out of her life and her heart shattered.

For the next two years she'd lived in misery waiting for him to come back. With encouragement from her family, she'd finally found the strength to pick herself up and start living again. She finished her degree, gained work experience, and began dating.

The problem? Dating was a double-edged sword. Her hope rose with each date, thinking the man could be the one to make her forget Jack. Then, when he wasn't, memories of

Jack bombarded her thoughts. All her unanswered questions about what she'd done wrong and why he left threatened to swamp her each and every time, crushing her again.

"No. I won't think about him," she told the empty car. No one had swept her off her feet yet, but she wouldn't give up hope. One day she would meet a man who would make her swoon again.

She grabbed her purse off the passenger seat and got out of the car. She entered the restaurant through the back door. The familiar scents of garlic and rosemary wrapped her in comfort after the disappointment from yet another dud of a date.

Jo and Rowena—two of her three cousins—sat at the small table at the back of the kitchen. Each woman held a half-filled glass of wine, and an empty bottle sat on the table between them.

Meredith dropped her handbag on the stainless steel counter at the back wall before sitting in the third chair. "All right, hit me. Tell me you warned me and I waved you off. Get the sisterly shaming out of your system." In preparation for the post-coffee-date-gossip-slash-grilling-session, she plucked Jo's glass from her hand and took a drink.

"Hey, that's mine. Why didn't you take Rowena's?" Jo asked, raising a pierced brow beneath her purple bangs.

"Because these little inquisitions are always your idea, so I'll drink your wine until you finish interrogating me. I suggest you hurry while there's still something left in the glass."

Rowena laughed. "I told you she figured it out a long time ago, Jo."

Meredith swirled the wine in the glass. "Well, it's not every day you both hang around the restaurant kitchen drinking wine. Uh… the drinking wine part is normal, but you usually do it in the restaurant, not back here."

"We were hoping you had a good time," Rowena said.

Jo eyed her glass in Meredith's hand. "But we weren't laying bets on wedding bells in your near future either."

Meredith drained the glass. "He ordered me a latte without asking, then explained index funds like I was five. After that he answered a call from his *assistant*," she said using air quotes. "The name on the screen said Mom."

"Ouch." Jo grabbed herself another glass and added more wine to all three, emptying the bottle. "Parental codependency and mansplaining finance? Classic."

Meredith forced a shrug. "Same as always. Decent on paper. Zero spark." All because the bar was set by a man who walked out without looking back.

Jo straightened. "This isn't an interrogation, not this time." Her smile disappeared. "This is a support group."

"What's wrong?"

Jo and Rowena shared another glance. When Rowena nodded at their cousin, Meredith's stomach knotted. "Jo, tell me."

"Your mom closed the dining room early and invited the usual group. And… an extra guest."

Cold prickled down Meredith's spine. "Who?"

Rowena eased closer. "Jack."

Glass halfway to her lips, Meredith froze. Eight years—eight birthdays, eight Christmases, eight million failed attempts to forget. If Jack had loved her, he wouldn't have left. End of story. There's no forgiving that. "Why didn't my mom tell me?"

"Maybe it was last minute." Jo took the glass that Meredith still held in mid-air and drained the rest of the wine. "I'll get another bottle."

Meredith turned to Rowena. "Did you know he was back?"

Rowena twirled strands of her long blond hair around

her finger. "No. But Auntie Elise said he's been commuting here from another field office for the past six months. And since when do we all get together on a Thursday?"

"We don't," Jo said as she returned with another bottle. After pouring, Jo lifted her glass and turned toward Meredith. "This impromptu dinner could just be because Jack is back, but I got a sense that Aunt Elise wants to say something."

"What makes you think that?"

"Just a feeling." Jo took another sip of her wine before meeting Meredith's gaze. "Your mom's been acting weird lately. I… I chalked it up to my mom…"

Rowena reached over and gave Jo's arm a squeeze. Their aunt Beatrice, Jo and Reece's mom, had died just under two months ago from a strange illness.

"Auntie Elise has been withdrawn, and that's to be expected," Rowena said. "But tonight, I got the same feeling as Jo. Your mom hesitated like she wanted to say more, then turned away."

"We're here for you, Mer," Jo said. "We can stall, help you sneak out—"

"Not happening." Meredith set the glass down. "He broke my heart, not my spine. I'm not hiding."

"That's our girl." Jo picked up her phone from the table and looked at the screen. "Dinner should be soon."

Meredith held her glass out to Jo for another top-up as she stood. "Just keep my mom from orchestrating a Hallmark moment."

With her free hand, she smoothed the skirt of her cranberry-colored business suit—professional yet feminine, an hour ago, woefully flimsy battle armor now—then inhaled the kitchen's comforting medley of spices. Showtime.

She walked into the main dining room with her cousins following close behind. Someone had pushed several tables together, creating a cozy family-dinner setup. At one end, her mom stood beside covered platters, chatting with Stella and Ben. Damon stood at the far side, a bespoke suit framing his large build, talking to Reece.

Near Damon, Jack leaned against a support beam. His hair was shorter on the sides with the top still long, a few ends brushing his forehead. A dark Henley stretched over broader shoulders, yet the slight tilt of his head—his quiet I'm-listening pose—hadn't changed. A trace of stubble cut across a jaw she once memorized by touch.

He laughed at something Reece said. The sound rumbled through her. He shouldn't get to look like he belonged. He'd left that privilege behind.

Stella spotted Meredith first, calling her name. Conversation faltered like a melody cut off mid-note.

Jack turned, his piercing gaze locked onto her, not shocked, just… hopeful. Painfully hopeful.

The room held its breath.

Meredith rallied every scrap of composure. "Mom," she called, voice even, "you forgot to mention tonight's guest list." She nodded at Stella and Ben, then zeroed in on Jack. "Welcome home."

Her cousins scattered, giving her and Jack a bubble of tense silence. He took one cautious step toward her.

Eight years narrowed into a single heartbeat.

"It's… good to see you," he said, his voice even deeper than she remembered.

"That's surprising," she said—before her filter kicked in.

For a fraction of a second something like pain flickered across his face, before he smiled. "You look as beautiful as always. Time has been good to you, Bubbles."

Meredith almost melted at the familiar nickname she hadn't heard in years. *No melting.* At least not for Jack. Not anymore.

"Thank you." She turned away and took control—like she had with her life and business for a long time. All by herself. "Mom, let us help." As if they'd read her mind, her cousins flanked her, forming a barrier between her and Jack, and helped her remove lids from dishes.

Ignoring Jack, Meredith turned to Stella, needing normalcy. "Where are the boys and Joel tonight?"

"Nate had a late class. Joel stayed late to work and Travis already had plans with friends."

"Plans with friends or a date? That boy has charm in spades." Reece blew on his knuckles and rubbed them on his shirt. "I must have rubbed off on him."

Jo elbowed her brother. "See, Stella, I knew you shouldn't have let Reece babysit."

Stella laughed. "Well… he's not wrong. Travis is charming."

"Don't tell him that." Jo shook her head and chuckled. "His ego is big enough already."

"Meredith," Jack said and lightly touched her arm.

She turned to face him as the group continued to joke behind her.

"I owe you—"

"Nothing. You owe me nothing, Jack. Because it's too late."

A muscle ticked in his jaw. "I am sorry. If I could've told you, I would have. I left because—"

"Because you didn't love me enough to stay." Her anger rose bright and sharp. "Walking away was your choice."

Her mom came toward her, but Meredith held up her hand to stop her. "Mom, let me finish."

Jack exhaled, steadying himself. "You think I stopped loving you, Bubbles, but I never did. Letting you believe that was safer for you than the real reason."

"Safe?" Meredith's laugh rang brittle. "Destroying me was safe? You crushed me, Jack."

"I never wanted that."

"So you say." She pressed her palm to her chest. "And I survived."

Silence stretched.

"If you've got your food, take a seat," her mom called out, cutting through the tension between them.

An hour. Maybe two. She'd survived years, she could survive a dinner. What were a couple more hours?

CHAPTER THREE

"We should sit down." Jack gestured to two empty seats at the end of the tables. What he really wanted was to carry her away so they could be alone together.

"Ah… I'm going to sit by Rowena."

He waited for her to fill a plate, then got his own. As much as he wanted to tell Meredith everything, until Elise confessed to the spellbinding, nothing had changed. He couldn't force Meredith to talk to him.

Meredith didn't spare him a glance as she took her meal and sandwiched herself between Stella and Rowena, shifting to give Stella more room.

Having no other choice, Jack took a seat at the other end of the tables, with Ben beside him and Damon sitting across from him.

"You need to be patient." Ben pitched his voice for Jack alone.

"I know, but now that I've seen her again, it doesn't feel that easy."

Waving his hand in a casual-like gesture, Jack used his magic to create a sound barrier to prevent being overheard.

"I came back because Elise said she was going to confess. What if she doesn't?"

Damon leveled him a hard look. "Then you'll have another decision to make."

"You think it's that easy?"

"I didn't say it would be, but do you want to lose another eight years with her?"

Jack didn't respond, the answer obvious. His friend knew the time apart had been hell for Jack.

They ate in silence for several minutes. Now and then Meredith's laughter reached him, like smoke from a faraway fire: no heat, just the awareness of it. Jack forced his gaze to his plate, his muscles tight with the effort it took not to look at her.

He sawed off another bite of tasteless steak, the ticking clock in his head growing louder. If Elise didn't confess soon, the night would slip away. He didn't know how much longer he could sit there and pretend he didn't want to whisk Meredith away.

"Ben, did Elise say anything more about why now?" Damon asked.

"No, but Frank is worried and I've always trusted my brother's intuition."

Damon nodded. "Maybe telling the W's is the right call. But is Elise just going to blurt out that we're all magics and the W's are too? And that their moms spellbound them twenty years ago? She thinks they'll be okay with that?"

"I doubt it, but since Beatrice and Lillian have both died from the effects of what they did, Elise is worried that she doesn't have much time left. I don't think Elise or her sisters expected a threat after they bound the W's. But now, Elise wants to make sure Meredith and her cousins can protect themselves if the threat becomes real, especially since Lillian and Beatrice aren't here to protect them."

"Is Elise sure the binding's effects killed her sisters?" Jack asked.

Ben pushed his plate away. "As sure as anyone can be without proof. But when she does confess to the spellbinding, don't let on about the effects. Elise will tell them when she's ready."

Jack avoided looking Meredith's way by watching his glass as he swirled the last of his wine around. He wanted to look at her forever. She was beautiful—inside and out. People gravitated to her. She came across as organized and confident, but Jack knew Meredith had more than her fair share of insecurities and anxiety. He'd had the privilege of seeing the real Meredith. Her vulnerability made her even more attractive to him.

Finally, he looked at Ben, his friend and mentor. "Meredith isn't going to take it well. She'll be angry and upset at what she's been denied—stripped of control over her own life. And Jo? She'll probably lose her shit when she realizes they lied. Although I think Rowena and Reece may take it in stride."

"I agree. So brace yourself. You may have to help them pick up the pieces. You, more than anyone else, should understand what it's like to disagree with a parent's decisions."

Jack dissolved the sound barrier and exhaled. That was the understatement of the century. The real question was whether Meredith could forgive him.

SHE COULDN'T TAKE it anymore. Sitting so close to Jack twisted her up inside. Part of her wanted to march over to him and demand to know why he had walked out on her. To understand why he'd crushed her heart and walked away like she meant nothing. She wanted to look him in the eye and finally get an answer.

But another part of her, equally as strong, had the urge to walk into his arms, rest her head against his chest to hear his heartbeat, feel his arms around her, and pretend the last eight years didn't exist. Beg him to pick up where they'd left off.

Meredith refused to do either. Instead, she held back and forced herself not to look in Jack's direction.

Dinner dragged for what felt like forever and she was ready to hightail it out of there. She loved her biological family and the friends that had been adopted into it, but being so close to Jack was torture.

They'd been through so much in the last month that it was amazing everyone was enjoying dinner and getting on with life like nothing had happened. That's what people did, though. At least, her family always did.

She watched her mom chat with Jo and Reece. Her mom laughed at something Reece said, but her smile didn't quite reach her eyes. There was a hollowness to her features. Grief had worn her down.

They'd lost Aunt Beatrice so recently, which made her mom the last one of her generation. Maybe on the surface it looked like they'd all moved on. But the loss had carved deep beneath the surface, and no one at the table could pretend otherwise.

Meredith had spent years asking herself why her family suffered so much loss. Answers never came, only more grief. More empty chairs at the table.

If she closed her eyes, she could still see the black lines visible under her aunt's skin during the last couple months of her life. She couldn't remember when she'd first seen them. They'd been subtle at first, like a trick of light. But once noticed, impossible to forget. Her mom and the doctor hadn't seemed surprised. As if they'd known to expect them.

Each week the lines darkened, multiplied. They'd been thin as threads at first on her aunt's face, then winding thick beneath her skin, snaking down her neck and chest. No one ever named the illness—black, insidious parasites that eventually took over her body.

When Aunt Beatrice finally exhaled her last breath, the lines vanished. Gone without a trace.

The memory raised a shiver across Meredith's shoulders. Something about her aunt's illness had never sat right. As though some piece of the truth still hovered just out of reach.

Reece and Jo had demanded their mother receive a second medical opinion. They'd pleaded with their mom and Meredith's to seek help, but both had refused. End of story. No one else was to be called.

So they'd waited. They'd watched. All helpless as whatever had claimed her aunt ran its course.

Another loss. One more in a long line of so many.

"What do you think, Mer?"

"Hm?" She turned toward Rowena. "Sorry, just woolgathering."

"Stella and I were talking about having a big extended family dinner soon with Damon's family, Stella and Ben's full family, and some others from the restaurant. It's been so long since we've gotten everyone together."

"Uh, sure."

Rowena chuckled. "Well, don't sound so excited."

"Sorry, I've just got other things on my mind."

"Like a certain FBI agent?" Jo piped in. "And I don't mean Stella's husband."

"Let it go, Jo," she said more harshly than she'd intended,

but she'd had a long day. Work had been hectic, then a bad date. And now she had to endure Jack's presence. He tried to pretend that he wasn't watching her by looking at Ben and studying his glass, but she knew he was. She knew every one of Jack's mannerisms and tells. At least she used to. Until the day he'd walked away.

"Sorry, Mer. I'm sure him showing up out of the blue is tough." Jo looked contrite, and Meredith gave her a small smile.

"Meredith, tell us how the building's renovations are going," Stella said after giving Jo's arm a small squeeze. "I haven't had a tour inside any of the finished condos yet, and I'd love to see them."

Stella's not-so-subtle change of topic was a balm to Meredith's frayed nerves. They spent the next half hour talking about her plans for the business. "I found some amazing tiles for the bathrooms—" Meredith looked up as Reece came toward the table holding a large platter of desserts. "Oh my god, I'm going to be in a chocolate coma."

"Oh yum. I'll take the chocolate pasta one, please. Does it have your chocolate hazelnut cream sauce?" Rowena asked Reece. "If no one else wants it, I mean," she said as she looked at the others for confirmation.

"Yes, it does, and I've got more in the kitchen if anyone else wants the same thing." Reece grinned. He was in his element.

"Oh yum," Rowena repeated as she took the decadent-looking dessert from her cousin.

"I'll take the molten chocolate lava cake and not worry about a chocolate coma." Meredith leaned back as Reece put it in front of her.

Reece gave his sister an enormous chocolate brownie, then took the platter around to everyone else. He had everyone's favorites.

"Delish," Meredith said when she finished chewing a bite and looked down the table to Reece.

Reece held the empty tray under his arm. "Thanks. By the way, I heard part of your earlier conversation. Your talk about contractors made me think about how the construction is going with my bakery, which made me think of desserts."

"How is it going?" Rowena looked at both of her cousins.

"I'm starting to see the design take shape, but I'm sure M could bore you with the details."

"Hey," Meredith laughed. "Jo, swat him for me. You're closer."

Everyone laughed as Jo reached over and smacked her brother's arm.

"Ouch." Far taller and twice as broad as his tiny sister, Reece rubbed his arm in mock indignation.

"I like details, so sue me. The bakery should be ready late fall, along with two other storefronts to rent out." Meredith turned to Rowena. "Which reminds me, I also have a few office spaces that will be ready shortly after. Have you thought about what you're going to do with your psychology practice? Now that we've gotten Reece's Pieces here almost ready to move into his shop, I can focus on you."

"Oh, it's going to be like that, is it? The nicknames are coming out?" Reece leaned toward Meredith, a sly grin lighting up his face. "I could mention—"

"Okay, okay, you two." Rowena chuckled, putting her hand up between the two of them as she'd done hundreds of times over the years. "See what I have to deal with?" she asked, leaning over to Stella.

Once the teasing settled down, Rowena picked the conversation back up. "I'm actually not sure what I'm going to do." Her voice took on a serious tone. "I transferred most of my clients to my partner when I came back for Auntie

Beatrice and since my partner hasn't built up her client base yet, she was happy to take them. I've been thinking of coming back permanently, but I'm not sure yet."

"We'd love to have you here permanently. I'll keep one office open for you," Meredith said, then turned her attention to Jo. "What about you? You staying?"

"Don't know. I had my post-doc student take my fieldwork for the summer. I was supposed to go back a few weeks ago at the start of the fall semester, but I wasn't ready. Next semester, I guess. But it's not like I'm far away, and you all come up to Denver a lot anyway."

"You're right, I just like having you close."

Stella asked Jo a question about work and Meredith sat back and listened as the conversation carried on around her. When everyone finished their dessert and after-dinner drinks were served, she figured she could skip out.

Meredith caught Jack's gaze and saw Damon elbow him in the ribs. She'd had enough. It hurt too much to be around him. Whatever her mother wanted to talk about could wait.

Meredith whispered an excuse to Rowena and got up from the table. She'd brought her purse from the kitchen earlier, so she grabbed it off a side table and headed for the front doors. A few minutes of fresh air would do her good.

She kept her eyes aimed forward as she made a beeline for the doors, refusing to look back at Jack. As the door clicked shut behind her, someone crashed into her.

She flew backward, smashing into the brick wall.

A scream ripped from her throat.

Rough stone tore her cheek as she slid to the sidewalk.

Pain flared sharp and fast.

CHAPTER FOUR

*J*ack watched Meredith get ready to head out and everything inside him urged him to follow her, but he didn't. He could tell she was already irritated enough with him. And if Elise didn't follow through with telling the truth, he might never be able to make things right.

Damon leaned forward. "Ben, did Elise say anything about changing her mind?"

"No, but I'll get Stella and we'll talk to her. Maybe she just needs a little support." Ben headed toward his wife.

Jack glanced back to Meredith as she reached the door. He would give her enough time to get into her apartment building before he left.

He lifted his glass for a drink when Meredith screamed, the sound so loud it reached inside the restaurant. Jack was on his feet instantly.

Ben headed him off, grabbing his arm. "Don't. Don't flash. We don't know what's out there."

He was right. What a rookie mistake. They could be heading into anything. Jack knew better, but this wasn't work, this was Meredith. He ran toward the door, Ben and Damon right behind him.

"Elise?" Jack heard Ben throw out, but Jack didn't turn around.

"We've got it in here. Everyone is safe," Elise called back.

Jack finally got his wits about him, his magic right at his fingertips as he scanned the outside. "I sense three plus Meredith." He flung the restaurant doors open and prepared for the worst.

The scene before him played out in slow motion. His FBI training took over as he assessed the situation in detail and with emotional detachment. Meredith was sprawled on the sidewalk about fifteen feet away from him, unmoving, blood on her face. Three men raced toward her, all magics, but Jack didn't recognize any of them. "Ben, take the right; Damon, left."

Jack thrust his hand forward and threw up a protection shield around Meredith as he flashed the few feet to the balaclava-clad man in the middle of the trio. Jack yanked the guy's shoulder back, throwing him to the ground and away from Meredith.

In a heartbeat, Jack slammed the man against the pavement. "Who are you?" He grabbed for the attacker's balaclava, but his fingers sliced through air. The guy had flashed away.

Jack cursed and sprang to his feet. The thug landed in front of Meredith, reaching for her once more. Jack held his power; if the man deflected a magic bolt, it would strike Meredith instead.

Jack drew his Glock and fired, aiming for the man's shoulder, high enough to avoid Meredith where she lay on the ground. The bullet thudded into a barrier and dropped to the ground. The asshole had the balls to turn and grin at him.

"Jack, look out!" Damon's voice tore through the chaos.

Jack spun around just as a glint of metal caught his eye—a dagger. His instincts took over. Throwing himself sideways, the blade sliced the air where he'd been only a moment before. He dropped low, his leg coiled, hitting the thug hard at the knees, driving him down with a grunt.

On instinct, Jack lunged forward to grab the man, but he disappeared mid-reach.

Surging to his feet, Jack scanned the area. Empty. The thug he'd tackled must have flashed away.

A groan pulled Jack's gaze to Damon's feet where another attacker lay sprawled. His face bloodied, his chest rising and falling. Still alive meant an opportunity for interrogation.

Jack's eyes locked on the third man, the one who'd been after Meredith. He and Ben were locked in a brutal clash of magic and shields.

Ben ducked low, dropped his shield, and fired a bolt of energy straight into the man's chest. The impact launched the guy backward, slamming him into the brick wall of The Magic Plate. Ben rushed forward as the man crumpled to the sidewalk in a heap. Two sets of cuffs shimmered into existence. Ben snatched one and tossed the other to Jack.

Recognizing the branding on the metal indicating they were the magic task force ones that prevented magics from flashing, Jack slapped them on the still-unconscious man at Damon's feet.

"Good job for a civilian." Jack grinned at Damon.

Damon's lips curved up at Jack's teasing. "Civilian, my ass, I'm magic. And…" Damon wagged his finger between the two downed men. "What happened to you, Mr. Hot Shot? Ben and I got our men."

Jack sighed. "He flashed before I could detain him."

"Jack!" He spun toward Meredith's voice. She shoved at the walls of the protective bubble around her, panic flaring in her eyes. "What is this? Get me out! What's happening?"

Jack disintegrated the protection around Meredith and kneeled in front of her. "There's blood on your face. Where do you hurt?"

Meredith touched her cheek, then stared down at the blood smeared on her fingertips. Her body swayed.

Jack caught her before she fell, lifting her into his arms and cradling her gently against his chest.

"It's okay. Let's get inside the restaurant. Ben?"

"I've got this. Damon and I'll watch these guys until a clean-up crew comes for this little mess. You take care of Meredith."

If only she'd let him once her shock wore off.

MEREDITH BURROWED her face into Jack's neck, breathing in his scent, the woodsy smell so familiar. It felt right.

No! It was wrong—he couldn't waltz back into her life after years and expect to pick things back up as if the years apart hadn't happened. She struggled in his arms. "Jack, put me down."

"No, you're injured." He adjusted her in his arms, holding her more securely as he carried her toward the back of the restaurant. "Elise!"

He could have saved his breath. Her mom had already rushed over and hovered as Jack shoved a table aside and placed her on a cushioned bench.

Her mom's eyes widened. "You're hurt and bleeding! Jack, what happened?"

"Three guys jumped her when she walked outside."

"Mom, I'm fine. I think I just scraped my face and bumped my head."

Her cousins joined them. Rowena handed Elise a cloth napkin. "Mer, what happened?"

Meredith looked up and noted the concern etched on Rowena's features. "I'm not sure. As soon as I stepped outside, some men came at me, but I'm fine. Really, everyone, I'm okay." She didn't know who the men were, but she'd been lucky she wasn't hurt worse than a few scrapes.

Jack finally released her, but he didn't go far. He sat beside her. His thigh felt warm against her leg, even through their clothing. As much as she had loved the feeling of being back in his arms, she couldn't forget the reason she'd walked out of the restaurant in the first place. Jack wasn't a part of her life anymore.

She moved her leg an inch, just enough to avoid touching Jack's. Childish? Maybe, but she needed to get back on solid ground. Making a quick glance in his direction, she saw what looked like hurt cross his features before he pasted a small smile on his face.

Her mom shoved the table further away and stepped in close. "Let me look at you." She dabbed Meredith's face with a cloth like Meredith was five again and had skinned her knee while playing.

"Mom, stop. I'm fine." Meredith pushed her hand away and turned to Jack. This time he would give her answers when she asked questions. "Jack, who were those men? Why did they—?"

"Jack, what happened?" her mom cut in.

Meredith studied her mother. Her voice sounded strange. Not fearful exactly, but tight, maybe edged with nerves.

Jack didn't even glance at Meredith, his gaze fixed on her mom. "Elise, the cat's out of the bag."

"I know," she replied. Meredith heard the soft give underneath the word. Resignation. For what, Meredith didn't know, but something was coming.

"Yes," Jack pressed. "You have to tell them."

"Tell us what?" Jo and Rowena asked in eerie unison, like synchronized parrots.

Meredith raised her eyebrows at Jack. "What was that out there? Some sort of magic trick? You, Ben, and Damon looked like you had lightning coming from your hands. And that bubble thing? What the hell was that?" The more she replayed the scene in her head, the more the questions stacked up. Nothing made sense but she got the feeling Jack knew.

"Bubble thing? Meredith, what are you talking about?" Reece looked as confused as Meredith felt.

All three of her cousins stared at her as if she'd lost her mind. She was beginning to feel like she was caught in a tennis match—gazes darting from face to face, everyone talking but no one telling her the score. She turned back to her mother, but she avoided meeting Meredith's eyes.

Meredith's panic climbed up her throat. "Someone answer me!" Her words came out harsher than she'd intended, but she wasn't getting answers and the longer no one filled her in, the closer she came to imploding.

"Elise, it's time."

Meredith started. She hadn't noticed Stella come up beside her mom. Stella gave her mom a quick hug, visibly steadying her.

Her mom's shoulders dipped with a visible exhale and she looked like every bit of the grief from recently, and maybe even before, settled on her. "You're right. Reece, get a bottle of the good stuff. We're going to need something stronger than wine and coffee."

Meredith's stomach dropped. That didn't sound dramatic, it sounded ominous.

"Elise, before you start, maybe deal with Meredith's injuries?" Jack's voice was low, grim. "Unless you want me to, but let's do it the fast way. She might have a concussion."

The fast way? "Jack, what are you talking—" Meredith turned toward Jack, forming a protest, when her mom waved a hand in her direction. A strange sensation moved across the side of her face and her mind became clearer, like someone had swept away the throbbing in her head. She raised her hand to touch her forehead. No pain.

"Holy shit. Aunt Elise, what did you do?" Jo's voice boomed through the room.

"What? Jo, what happened? Mom, what did you do?"

"I healed you," her mom said quietly. "I'll explain—"

"Explain?" Meredith felt her heart rate speed up. "What the hell is going on? I don't know what's happen—"

"Meredith, stop. I said I'll explain. You and your cousins need to finally know. Just give me a minute. Reece, please get that bottle."

Stella touched Elise's arm. "I've got it. You just sit. Relax for a minute."

Elise nodded and sat on the closest chair.

Meredith froze. Her palms itched like they needed to grip something, anchor herself. More questions swirled in her mind and her mom looked fragile—worn, like one more question might break her.

When Damon and Ben came in and everyone had a drink in hand, the room fell silent. All eyes turned to her mom.

She took a deep breath and her gaze met Meredith's, then swept over her nieces and nephew. "I'll explain everything, but please, no interruptions until I'm done. I have a lot to tell you."

"Aunt Elise, you're making me nervous," Jo said, her voice not laced with her usual confidence. "I get the feeling this has something to do with the strange disease that killed my mom. Oh my god… it killed Aunt Lillian, too, didn't it?"

Jo's hand shook as she lifted her glass, whiskey splashing the sides, before she put it down. Meredith clasped her own hands together, knowing if she looked down, they'd be shaking too. She'd said she was fine, and physically it was true, but inside? She was a basket case.

She forced her focus on her mom. Although she was always serious, it looked as if her face was paler and graver than it had been earlier.

"Yes," her mom said on a long exhale. "Twenty years ago, when your fathers and siblings died in the fire, we knew it wasn't an accident. You see, we're not normal humans. We have something extra. Magic."

Meredith stared. She must have misheard. "What?"

"Holy shit!"

"Is this a joke?"

"Oh my god!"

"Enough!" Her mom's voice cracked like a whip. "I said I'll explain, but you all need to stop interrupting. I know it sounds like something out of a book, but it's real. I didn't think I'd ever tell you the truth, but I can't hold it in anymore." She looked down into her lap. "Where do I start?" she murmured, as if talking to herself.

"Elise, how about I help out with the history?" Jack offered. When her mom nodded, he stood and walked around the tables to face them all.

Meredith blew out a long breath, forcing her breathing to slow. She stared at Jack, bracing herself for the punch line because there had to be one. Magic wasn't real. It had to be an elaborate prank, but she couldn't understand why.

"When people were first created, everyone had magic. They were born with it," Jack said and paused. His gaze drifted over her cousins before landing on Meredith. His eyes held no humor, no teasing. Only truth.

A chill slid down her spine. She knew every one of Jack's expressions and this one said he believed what he was saying.

"Many of us still have magic. The essence of it is inside us. We pull energy from our surroundings to use it—cast spells, conjure items, heal, telepathically talk to each other. I won't go into the details now. I know this is a lot to take in." He held out his hand. The glass that had been sitting on the table next to Meredith's floated over to him. He gripped it and took a sip.

Meredith gasped. "Holy cow!" she whispered.

"Cool!"

"Oh my god!"

"Shit."

Her cousins' voices registered, but her vision stayed locked on the glass in Jack's hand. Her body refused to move. It was like she'd been glued to her chair.

"That was just a little demo," Jack said, his lips twitching into a small smile, before he sobered again. "Like I said, everyone used to have magic. But as humanity evolved over the centuries, people turned to other beliefs and abandoned their magic, especially during the witch trials of the 1500s and 1600s. People suppressed their magic just to survive. In those families, magic faded with each generation and non-magics became a thing. Magics began to hide their abilities."

"And now?" Meredith almost couldn't believe what she was hearing.

"Now, we keep magic secret. If non-magics found out what we're capable of, we could be captured, experimented on, or worse. Magics marry magics, and most magics are not drawn to non-magics. Some believe Mother Nature made it that way to protect us, but no one knows for sure. Today, only a tiny percentage of people are born with magic, but with billions of people in the world, that means that there are still lots of us."

"Jack."

Everyone turned to look at Reece as he spoke. "I saw Aunt Elise heal Meredith. I saw a glass float. But I…" Reece shrugged. "Those things could be explained as magic tricks. I don't know how and I didn't see any strings, but… I can't wrap my head around this."

Jack nodded, then turned to Damon. "A demo?"

The two best friends looked almost smug. They stood side by side at the front of the room. "Watch."

Jack and Damon both disappeared. One second they were there—then they weren't. Meredith's breath hitched. "What the…"

"Believe us now, Reece?" Jack and Damon reappeared at one end of the tables, each holding a drink.

"Okay, Jack and Damon, thanks for the demo," her mom said, her lips twitching into an almost smile. "Let me take over from here." The men touched glasses; each took a drink and sat, Jack next to Meredith.

Meredith didn't laugh. If they were telling the truth, she had magic inside her. She'd been born that way. Then why didn't she know about it?

Her mom continued, unaware of the turmoil swirling inside her daughter. "Our families come from strong magic bloodlines. Three brothers marrying three sisters amplified our powers. Likely made our children even stronger too."

"Then why don't we have magic?" Meredith asked, gesturing to herself and her cousins. She wanted her mom to say their magic disappeared due to an accident, but if it had, wouldn't her mother have told her? She knew in her soul that hadn't been the case.

Her mom's expression crumbled. "Because we bound it. We took it from you."

CHAPTER FIVE

Jack stayed silent as Meredith and her cousins volleyed questions at Elise. Each one landed harder than the last, their anger rising. He couldn't blame them. He'd be angry too. Hell, he had been furious for years at what the Williams sisters had done. If they hadn't bound their kids, he wouldn't have had to walk away from Meredith. They'd lost years because of what Elise and her sisters had done.

He didn't know what he would have done if he had been in their shoes, but from the outside looking in, what they did felt wrong. It always had.

"Quiet! Let Elise continue."

Ben's authoritative command sliced through the room, silencing everyone. Jack took a drink to keep from smiling. This wasn't funny—far from it—but it was amusing to hear his friend and mentor getting flustered and even rarer to hear his tone crack like a whip.

"Ben, you were there, weren't you?" Meredith's question snapped with tension. "You've been friends with my mom for as long as I can remember. You must have known my dad and uncles."

She hurled the words like an accusation. Jack couldn't grasp the depth of her feelings, but his own had driven an ache inside him for years. Every instinct in him urged him to reach for her, to comfort and soothe. But he hadn't earned that right yet. He'd lied to her too. Walked away.

"I can understand why you're all angry. And probably confused. But you don't know what your mother and aunts went through. Please let Elise finish," Ben said, his tone calmer as he looked each of the W's in the eye, holding their attention for a moment before sitting down.

Jack noticed what Meredith might have missed—Ben, always the tactful leader, hadn't answered her question.

"Thanks, Ben." Elise turned her attention to her daughter. "I know you're angry. You may never agree with what we did, but we can't change the past. So let me explain. Thomas was part of the North American magic council—one of seven councils across the world, created to govern magic people. While his brothers weren't council members, they often advised ours. The councils make sure magics—magic people—stay on the right side of the law. We follow the same laws as everyone else, and the councils ensure that magics don't abuse their power. They even work with agencies like the FBI when necessary, to ensure justice, and keep things balanced. If a magic uses power to harm or manipulate a non-magic, the council intervenes."

Elise paused for a sip of her drink, then looked directly at Jack. He knew where this was going, but after him walking away from Meredith, what was about to be revealed seemed small in comparison. He could only hope that eventually Meredith would forgive him for all his transgressions. He nodded at Elise to continue.

"Not everyone in the magic community agrees with staying hidden. Even though non-magics vastly outnumber us, we still have power that would allow us to overtake them if we wanted. Fortunately, most of us don't want that. We just want to live our lives. Thomas served on the council alongside Curtis—Damon's dad—as well as some other friends. At that time, the council consisted of seven men. Many, including Thomas, Curtis, and Ben's brother Frank, who was an advisor at the time, wanted change. They pushed to expand the council, to include women and become more progressive. But the council's leader wanted the opposite: fewer members and more control. Even worse… he wanted dominance over non-magics. And he wasn't alone. He had followers."

Jack scanned the W's' expressions. This much information at once, and its implications, would be enough to overwhelm anyone.

Rowena raised her hand like they were in a classroom. The others chuckled, and she blushed, lowering her hand. "Auntie, I think I'm following with the council stuff… but what does that have to do with you, Mom, and Auntie Beatrice taking our magic?"

Elise nodded and her tone softened, as if she was reliving her pain. "I need you to understand that you were all in danger, even as children. The council leader and his supporters were searching for a magical artifact, a box believed to grant whoever opened it special powers. The leader wanted this power to rule over non-magics."

"Like Pandora's box?" Jo asked.

"Yes, exactly. But stories passed down over generations say the box contained evil magic beyond our comprehension. And when released, the evil would take over the person or persons who opened the box. It would give them untold powers. Evil powers."

Meredith frowned. "How does that connect to the fire? And to you taking our magic?"

Jack wanted to put his arm around Meredith to prevent her from pulling even further away from him emotionally. This was it—one more nail in his coffin.

"Your father and the others were trying to stop the council leader. That's why we were all at the cabin that weekend twenty years ago. Frank, Curtis, Ben, and a few others, planned to meet us there. Our three families arrived first to keep suspicion low, make it seem like a normal vacation."

Elise's voice faltered for a moment. "As soon as my sisters and I saw the fire, we used our magic to try and put it out, but it spread too fast. By the time others arrived, it was already out of control. Eventually, with all of us using our magic, we managed to contain it. But we were too late. Our husbands and children… they were gone."

Stella reached out from where she sat and squeezed Elise's hand. The two women shared a look before Elise continued. "The fire marshal blamed faulty wiring. But we knew it was set by magic. Someone must have cast a spell in the cabin, putting everyone to sleep. It was the middle of the day. They should have been able to escape. But it didn't look as if they'd even tried. That just didn't seem right to any of us. We think the council leader was responsible."

"What I don't get is, where were we?" Jo asked. "I don't remember any of this."

"You four were with us—your mothers and me—down at the dock, while the others were in the cabin. Your siblings were playing a game inside while your dads brainstormed."

"Aunt Elise, that still doesn't explain why we don't have our magic," Reece said as he poured himself another drink from the bottle on the table.

Reece had the right idea. Jack lifted his hand and, with a

flick of power, filled a mug. No reason to hide anymore. He stuck with coffee, needing a clear head for this conversation.

"Reece," Elise replied, "remember, between your mother, Beatrice, and me, we lost four children that day. We'd heard rumors that other magic children in the community had gone missing as well, but nothing was proven. We feared that the council leader, or someone working for him, would come after the four of you. To kidnap you. Or maybe siphon your magic. And without your powers fully developed, that might have killed you. You hadn't fully come into your magic yet as that happens around puberty. So we had to do something. You were defenseless. So… we bound your magic. We took it to protect you."

"But you took the rest too," Meredith said, her voice low.

Jack winced at Meredith's words laced with betrayal.

"Yes," Elise admitted. "We took all the power you had built up as children. And any memories you had of magic."

Meredith lifted her chin, a tightness in her expression. "Were the men who attacked me tonight part of the council?"

Elise's eyes became glassy. She waved her hand in front of her face and they appeared clear once more. "Jack? Ben? Can you answer that?"

Jack nodded at Ben to take it, deferring to his mentor.

Ben stood, scanning the faces in the room. "I don't know who they were, but they weren't council members. Frank and I believe only a few council members are still alive and we haven't seen them in almost twenty years. The rest were killed. After the fire, every council in the world fell into chaos. Ours was never re-formed."

Meredith turned her head toward Jack, her face unreadable but her eyes stormy, before looking at her mother. Jack had years of practice reading Meredith and knew two things for certain. She had figured out what he was most ashamed of, and her anger was only just starting to simmer. But what she still wouldn't know was why he'd had to leave her.

"Mom," she asked, her tone as hard as stone, "who was the council leader?"

Elise's eyes met Jack's. "Daniel Knight. Jack's father."

MEREDITH'S HEAD throbbed like it might explode. She closed her eyes and drew a calming breath, letting the conversation go on around her while she steadied her emotions.

"Are you alright?" Jack whispered into her ear.

Startled, she opened her eyes and turned to him, not knowing when he moved in beside her. She gave him a look she hoped said, *are you insane?*

"Right. Stupid question," he muttered. "How are you handling all this?"

"This? You mean you coming back after eight years and acting like everything is fine?" Jack winced, but she felt a perverse sense of pleasure making him uncomfortable. She held up one hand and started counting off on her fingers. "Let's see. Long day at work. Bad date. Awkward dinner where my ex shows up out of the blue after crushing me years ago. Got attacked by strange men. Found out magic people exist and I'm one of them. How do you *think* I'm doing, Jack?"

Panic pressed in on her chest, but anger now wound through it, hot and steady.

She lifted her other hand and kept going. "Oh, and let's not forget—my life is a lie. For twenty years I've been denied my innate right to a gift I was born with. I found out my dad, my sister, my uncles, and three of my cousins were not just killed, but murdered. Anything else?" She let the sarcasm pour out with the question. "Nope, that about covers it."

Jack winced again. "I can only imagine what you're going through, but I'm here for you."

Meredith choked on a humorless laugh. "Really, Jack? Really? You're here for me now? And where the hell were you the last eight years?"

"I can explain—"

"Don't." Meredith raised her hand, palm in Jack's face. "Don't. I can't handle any more tonight. Please move, I want to leave."

Jack hesitated before moving off the bench and offered her a hand. She ignored it and heaved herself up. She'd hit her limit. At least she thought she had when something else occurred to her.

She spun around. "Do you remember the very last words you said to me?" she hissed at him. Then put her hand up, palm in his face again. "Don't bother answering. I'll tell you, because I will never forget. Never! You told me, 'I hope you find someone who will give you everything you've ever wanted and deserved, Bubbles.' Well, Jack… how the hell was I supposed to do that because magics are only attracted to magics? How, Jack? How? I didn't even know I was magic!"

Meredith glared at him, her breaths coming fast.

"I'm so sorry. I didn't know," he said, his tone low as if attempting to soothe a frightened animal. She wasn't afraid, she was infuriated.

"You didn't know? Yeah, right. You stood there"—she waved her hand toward the middle of the room where he'd done his little demo earlier because maybe he needed a reminder—"and told us magics are only attracted to magics. You're a liar."

"Yes, I knew about that, but your magic was bound. I thought that meant you were like a non-magic."

"Bullshit," she hissed under her breath and walked around him, heading for the front door.

"I'll walk you to your apartment."

She kept her focus on the front door, escape only a few feet away. "No. I don't need you."

"Bubbles, please, let me. We don't know who those guys were yet and if one of them is out there waiting for you."

Meredith pulled open the door, not even bothering to say goodnight to anyone, and walked out into the warm late-summer air. If Jack wanted to follow her, she couldn't stop him.

He matched her stride. "I scanned the street before you opened the door."

As angry with him as she was, she still wanted to learn about magic and what she was capable of. "What does that mean?"

"I used magic to sense if anyone was out here. You'll learn to do it eventually."

She would have to find someone to teach her. Sure, her mom could, or Ben and Stella, or Damon and his mom or sister. But at the moment she wasn't feeling particularly hospitable to any of them. They'd all lied to her.

She didn't like it, but she'd eventually forgive them. Jack was a different matter. He'd claimed to love her and then left. When you love someone, you stick it out, no matter what.

The three Williams's buildings sat in a row with the middle one housing The Magic Plate. The one with the apartments was next. At her building, she put in the code, walked in, and hit the button for the elevator. When the buildings were all completed, her plans included having door attendants, but that was still a ways off.

Her parents, aunts, and uncles had bought all three buildings years ago with grandiose plans to house living spaces and businesses for people to gather and build a community. They'd started with the restaurant, but after the fire her mom and aunts were too busy dealing with grief and raising young kids to do anything else. Meredith had picked up the mantle.

"I haven't been in this building in a long time; it looks fantastic."

Meredith wanted to ignore him, but she'd been rude enough already tonight. When she'd been dating Jack, she and her mom had been living in a house with her aunts and cousins, one they'd bought after the fire to be close together. She looked around the lobby, trying to see it through Jack's eyes.

"Thanks. We all moved in two years ago. It's not complete, but it's coming along." The apartment entrance was flanked by spaces that would be stores. She had an ambitious ten-year plan for all three buildings.

When the elevator doors opened, Meredith stepped inside and turned back to Jack. "You don't have to—" Jack was already in the elevator with her.

"Yes, I do. What floor?"

She was too tired to fight with him. "Ten."

They rode in silence. By the time they walked the short distance from the elevator to her apartment door, Meredith's head felt like it had already exploded. She squeezed her eyes shut and put her hands to her temples and rubbed.

"One of your regular migraines or maybe it's leftover from the concussion?"

He used to rub her shoulders, easing her tension when she had a headache. She'd already melted a couple of times tonight when he put his hands on her. Not again. "I'm fine."

"Here, let me."

Before she could look up, Jack had gently knocked her hands away and cradled her face with his hands. His touch was warm and became warmer. She sucked in her breath.

"Wha… Oh shit." Her headache was gone. She looked up at him. "How did you do that?"

"I've scanned your apartment and it's safe. I'll explain once we're inside."

"I've just got to get my key out…" She gasped and looked at the opened door. "How?"

He gestured for her to enter the apartment and took her bag from her, putting it on the kitchen island. She was exhausted. Physically tired from the long day and mentally overwhelmed from the sheer amount of information she'd learned in just one night. Before she could even finish a sentence, she had another question.

At the moment, her bed called to her. All she wanted was to crawl into it and block out the world for a while.

"Here, have a glass of water." Jack handed her a full glass of water she knew he hadn't gone to the sink to get.

"Jack, stop!"

"Stop what?"

"Stop doing magic shit! I can't handle this right now. I don't know what you can do or when you're going to do it. And forget about explaining the headache relief for now. I need time to process everything."

She put her hands to her temples to rub them. She'd gone for her automatic headache response when stress became too much for her, even though she no longer had a headache. "I don't want you here."

"Bubbles, I know it's a lot."

"Actually, you have no idea. You don't know me anymore."

"I want to again. Now that you know about magic and I don't have to hide, we can be together."

She stumbled back a step. "What?"

He looked nervous, but she didn't know why. The Jack she remembered was confident to the point of cocky. "Eight years ago, I… I had to leave because you were talking about having kids."

"That wasn't the first time." She didn't know where he was going with this.

"I know, but before it had always been more hypothetical. Then it wasn't. I refuse to raise my kids to compromise who they are."

"Why would they have to?"

"Because they'd have to hide their magic from their own mother."

"That's why you left?" Her voice came out on a screech, but she didn't care. "Did you ever think of just telling me the truth?"

"I couldn't. My magic wouldn't allow it."

She looked him in the eye, not knowing what she wanted to see reflected back at her. "When we want something badly enough, there's always a way."

"Even if there was, I would have made your mom the bad guy. You would have resented me for it."

"Or not. I may not agree with what my mom did, but I understand she'd lost my dad and sister, her brothers-in-law, and nieces and nephews. She was afraid for me. If I was a mom I might have done the same thing."

She studied his face, a face she used to know by heart. He looked older, but the years had been good to him. Once more, she wanted to see something specific in his features, but she wasn't sure what. Remorse, maybe? She shook her head. It wouldn't be enough. "I always thought you had more balls than that. Whatever your reasons, they're not enough. Please leave."

"I'll give you some time to process what you've learned so far. Make your lists of questions and plans that I know you will, and then we'll talk."

"Or not," she repeated. "Everything is always on your agenda, Jack. Have you noticed that?"

He winced. A new thing he'd done a lot tonight. "It's not like that, Bubbles."

"Ugh! That proves my point!" If Meredith wasn't so tired, she would have stomped her foot. "You've called me Bubbles for years and never told me why. When I hounded you one year, you told me it was because I'm bubbly, but we both know I'm not. Maybe you'll explain or maybe you won't. It seems that you hold all the cards, Jack. Nothing's changed. I don't trust you. And I won't forgive you. Just go."

She watched him walk to the door. With one hand on the doorknob, he turned back. "I will earn your forgiveness. I'll prove it. Goodnight, Bubbles."

Jack was wrong. She would never forgive him.

CHAPTER SIX

The tension eased from Meredith's shoulders as her body settled into a steady pace. Each stride carried her forward, her running shoes quietly eating up the distance ahead. She didn't bother with music, choosing instead to listen to the early morning sounds—leaves rustling, a few birds calling—while most of the city still slept. For now, it was just her, the road, and peace, before real life crept in.

No matter what she had done over the last week, her mind kept going back to what she'd learned about magics. Not much, but she was armed with questions. She was excited to learn magic, but cautious as well. Before embracing any new endeavor, she needed the facts.

Yesterday, she'd found herself thinking about a moment with her sister and dad. The memory had surfaced out of nowhere, like they did sometimes, but something about it felt off. A chunk seemed missing, like someone had cut it out. She wondered how many of her memories were like that— just slightly wrong—and why she'd never questioned them before.

The sound of a runner coming up on her at a fast clip

interrupted her thoughts. She moved to the right of the path, leaving enough room for them to pass. It wasn't often that she came across others when she ran this early.

The runner came up beside her but didn't move ahead. She kept her pace steady, hoping the person would eventually move forward. After about a minute, she glanced out of the corner of her eye and almost stumbled, righting herself as his arm shot out to steady her. "Jack, what are you doing here?"

"Morning, Bubbles. You've had a week to process and avoid me. Now, we talk."

"How did you know I'd be out here?"

"I know everything about you."

"No, you don't. Not anymore."

When Jack didn't respond, she wanted to push him. To make him admit that he didn't know her. Only she worried that he still did. She may have hardened her heart a little, but had she really changed?

They ran for another mile before Meredith slowed her pace to a walk. Jack matched her stride. She wanted to tell him to go away. Running was her time, and he'd intruded again. On the other hand, it was so nice to have someone to run with. Several years back, she'd tried to convince Rowena and Jo to come with her. She snorted softly as she remembered how that had turned out. Her cousins had talked her into going to a coffee shop instead. She'd run solo ever since.

"What's funny?"

"Nothing." He didn't deserve to know her memories.

"Talk to me, Bubbles."

She stopped and faced him. "You're not part of my life anymore, Jack."

"I want to be again. I didn't have a choice."

"No, Jack, we always have choices."

"Mer, not with magic. It won't allow us to tell a non-magic or a person whose family is losing their magic. It's like our magic prevents the words."

"I'm not non-magic."

"No, but you were like one. Remember the other night? We said that when someone stops using magic, the magic will fade? Generation after generation, it will fade until eventually their descendants are non-magics? Well, that's why we can't say anything. When a person's magic aura isn't clear, it could be because they're losing it, and they don't even know magic exists."

"That's a cop-out, Jack! You knew what happened to my magic. You said you weren't even sure if you could tell me, but the truth is you didn't even try."

She turned and walked to a bench up ahead on the path to stretch, needing some space.

"I know." He stretched beside her and didn't say anything for a while. "You may be right that I don't know everything about you now. But the way your mind works can't have changed. You've been making lists of questions."

It was a statement, not a question, but she didn't confirm. Maybe he still did know her.

"You've lumped them into categories. Give me one."

She didn't bother to deny it. As much as she didn't trust him, he knew about magic and she did have questions. "Magic and how it works, how we break the spell, and memories."

"What about memories?"

Sitting on the bench, she rested her head against the slats. Suddenly drained, she sagged against it. There were just too many things to think about. Turning only her head, she looked at Jack. "Yesterday, I felt like I was missing something. Missing a memory of my dad and Molly." Her voice hitched and she rubbed her eyes with her fists, trying to hold back the tears.

The bench bounced as Jack sat down. "Come here, Bubbles."

Before she could figure out what he meant, Jack gently took hold of her arms and lifted her. He shifted her over his lap until she ended up straddling him.

"No, Jack." She pressed both hands against his chest, trying to push away.

"Please, just humor me." He held her cheeks in his hands. When she met his gaze, something in his expression gave her pause. "Close your eyes, Bubbles."

"Don't kiss me," she whispered.

"No kissing." He kept his hands where they were and she let her eyelids fall shut.

Images flickered behind her closed eyes, fuzzy at first, then sharper. She drew in a breath as a scene unfolded. She saw herself, maybe five years old, with Molly. But it wasn't a memory. She wasn't watching through her own eyes. She was seeing it from someone else's.

They stood in a field with a large cabin in the background. She heard laughter nearby, but didn't see anyone else. Hands rose up in front of her, but they weren't her own. Then she heard Jack's voice, only younger. If she and Molly were five, he must have been around ten.

"Jack, can you make bubbles?" her younger self asked.

"What kind of bubbles?"

"Animals!" she giggled, clapping her hands.

"Yeah, animals! An elephant!" Molly's voice rang with joy as she laughed and threw her arms in the air.

"Okay, here goes."

A large bubble formed between his hands. A shapeless, shimmering mass at first, then slowly it twisted before settling into a shape.

"An elephant!" Molly's excitement bubbled over. "More, Jack! Please!"

More bubbles spun to life in his hands. He tossed them into the air, each one shifting into an animal as it floated up. One elephant after another.

"Meredith, what kind do you want?"

"A bear... and a giraffe... and a dog... and a—"

Jack laughed and held up his hands in the universal sign for hold on. "Let me get started and then I'll add more."

Meredith—her five-year-old self—stood with her hands clasped in front of her, bouncing on her toes with excitement. Her eyes widened as the next bubble stretched and twisted, its neck growing longer and longer before the rest of the animal took shape.

"A giraffe!" Her small voice sounded reverent. "Thank you, Jack. Thank you, I love it." She paused, quieter now. "It's my giraffe."

The memory faded and Meredith opened her eyes. She felt a tear touch her lips and realized she was crying, but this time, they were happy tears. She looked into his eyes. "Thank you."

"Here, let me." His voice was gruff but soft. She didn't know what he meant until her tears were gone, her face dry. He dropped his hands and rested them on her hips. "That was my memory. I replay it in my mind now and then."

"Bubbles."

His lips hitched up in a small smile. "Yes, Bubbles."

"What did you call Molly? Bubbles, too?"

"No, I called her Elephant and shortened it to El. She liked it."

They sat there smiling, the sky slowly lightening as the sun started to emerge.

"Meredith..." Jack cupped her face in his hands and leaned in. His lips brushed hers. Soft at first, with just a whisper of contact.

Her hands found his shoulders, muscle memory guiding her actions. When her lips parted, he deepened the kiss, his tongue sliding against hers. He tasted like coffee and comfort and felt like home. The rest of the world fell away. Only Jack existed as she soaked up every bit of their kiss.

His hands slid from her face to her back, drawing her closer.

She kissed him with years of pent-up longing, pouring everything she'd held for years into the one kiss. Her breasts pressed against his chest, tingling at the contact, and she couldn't ignore his hard length beneath her as she straddled his lap.

The friction of their running clothes rubbing together snapped her out of the moment.

She broke the kiss and scrambled off his lap. Silently, she cursed herself for falling for him. Again. She should have known better than to let her guard down. To give him her precious control.

Without a word, she broke into a light jog. Stretching could wait.

Jack followed her into the building and up to her apartment, mirroring the event from a few nights ago. Awkwardness descended. The déjà vu made the silence heavier. Her open-concept apartment felt crowded, like there wasn't enough room to breathe.

She walked to the fridge and grabbed two bottles of water. Since he wouldn't leave, she forced herself to be civil and turned to offer him one. "Would you—"

Jack stood by the table with a half-empty bottle of water in his hands.

"How?"

"I conjured it."

She put one back in the fridge, unscrewed the cap on the other, and downed half in one go. "How many times did you have to stop yourself from doing something like that when we were together?"

Jack set his bottle on the kitchen table and walked to her. "I know you're still angry—"

He cut off mid-step and stumbled forward, grasping her arms as a strange wave surged through her body.

Her knees buckled. "Jack!"

Jack's grip on her loosened as they both fell to the floor. "Oh fuck!"

JACK HIT the ground hard and reached for Meredith, who had landed beside him. "Meredith, are you hurt?"

"Uh, no, I don't think so. What happened?"

He scrambled to his feet and helped her up. "I think we've been taken in a soul jump."

"Like when you flash?"

"Not exactly." His gaze swept the field they were standing in, taking in the meadow stretching at least a hundred yards in all directions. Wild grass and flowers grew in bunches all around them, catching the early light. In the distance, peaks that looked like the Rocky Mountains rose in the sky. He hoped they were still in Colorado. But for all he knew, they could be in Montana, or even Canada.

He pushed his magic outward, scanning the area for immediate threats. Nothing registered. A good sign. But telling Meredith wouldn't be fun as she hated the loss of control. And how they got there was a huge one.

Before he could stop himself, he leaned in and pressed a kiss to her forehead, grounding himself in the moment. She didn't protest, probably too shaken to react. "A soul jump means we've left our bodies. Right now, we're lying on the floor in your apartment."

"What?" She patted her chest, then her arms and legs. "No, that can't be true. I can still feel myself."

He took her hands and held them still. "What you're feeling is a copy of your body. It's real and can be injured, or even killed, and whatever is done to you here will also affect your real body left behind. Usually, a person fully in control of their power—like me—can't be taken. I expect this is the work of the grand council. They're the only ones with enough power to pull it off."

"What's the grand council? Why would they do this?"

"It's a group made up of the leaders from the world's seven councils. As to why they did this? I have no clue, but I doubt we'll have to wait long to find out."

"No, I meant why would anyone want to soul jump? You can flash to a place, right?"

"Yes, but flashing long distances burns a lot of energy. Depending on how far you want to go, you might need to stop partway to rest or even eat. A soul jump lets you go further without those needs, but only for a short time. You've got about twenty-four hours, give or take a few."

"Is that the only reason to soul jump?"

"No, it's also useful to hide your actions. Excellent for teenagers who want to sneak out of bed at night. Or execs who don't want someone to know they've left the office." He winked and she let out a small chuckle, exactly the reaction he'd hoped for to help her panic recede.

Every hair on the back of Jack's neck rose. His magic and cop senses snapped to hyper-alert. "We'll be getting company soon. I feel something."

The words were barely out of Jack's mouth when he felt a presence. "Someone's here." He turned fast, pushing Meredith behind him.

Seconds later, a lone person appeared at the tree line, walking their way. Female, probably around his age. She stopped several feet away and looked up to meet his eyes. Her makeup was flawless, her outfit impeccable, her gaze direct and unwavering. Definitely not a random hiker.

"Thank you for coming," she said, her voice strong and low, laced with an accent—Eastern European or maybe Hungarian.

Jack didn't bother hiding his irritation. "We didn't have a choice. Who are you, why are we here, and how did you manage it?"

"Hello, Meredith." The woman smiled at her, before turning back to Jack. "You can call me Emissary. I represent the grand council. And yes, Jack, I know what you are thinking."

A figure of speech or something else? He stayed still, his expression neutral and his mind blank.

"We did not use any tricks, only extremely powerful magic. Normally, adults cannot be taken in a soul jump," she said, nodding at Meredith before focusing on him. "But together, we are more powerful than you have ever faced. What you're experiencing is a gift."

"A gift?" Meredith's voice was almost a squeak.

Jack squeezed her hand in reassurance, but didn't let it go afterward. "We could have done without your *gift*. Tell us why we're here."

"Now, now, Jack," the Emissary said with a sigh. "You need to learn to be more cooperative, as we will be working together. We're glad you've returned to Blue Mountain."

Meredith addressed the Emissary. "Do you know who those men were the other night?"

The Emissary shook her head. "No, but they will not be the last. They want you and your cousins, Meredith. They will not stop until they have you."

"Why us?"

"Once your magic is restored you will all be incredibly powerful. There are people who want to prevent you from standing in their way."

"But our magic isn't restored. We're still bound."

"For now. After Beatrice's death, we suspected your mother might decide to confess the truth. The unbinding had been foretold years ago—the attack only sped up that timeline."

Jack narrowed his eyes. "Why bring us here?"

Once again, the Emissary paused and smiled at Meredith before looking at Jack. The Emissary may have been trying to decide how to continue or perhaps she liked to build suspense. He'd had it with the dramatic shit. He wanted to know what the hell was going on.

"We needed your full attention. As you know, the North American council collapsed twenty years ago. The other councils in the world stood back and did nothing—too afraid of retaliation from those remaining members. Not anymore."

"Why now?"

"The other six councils also had some bad apples in the mix, but that has been rectified. The previous six council leaders have finally seen the light and retired. The councils are now run by new leaders, leading pairs actually. Jack, you and Meredith will be the seventh pair and will lead the North American council."

He wasn't thrilled with the timing. "Why us?"

"Meredith and her cousins are extraordinarily powerful. Three sisters marrying three brothers, all from strong bloodlines. You know what that means. As for you, Jack, you already know why. We believe your powers are unprecedented and you have the ability to wield magic that no one has seen in decades."

"Since my father, you mean?"

"You are not like your father," she said, her voice sharp, her gaze unflinching.

Jack should have seen this coming. He'd had a vision years ago that helping lead a council would be inevitable, but that still didn't make the timing any better. Not until Meredith forgave him. He especially didn't appreciate the Emissary's tone or manipulation. And he wouldn't tolerate anything or anyone that could put Meredith in danger. A simple request would have done the job.

"Nice to meet you, Emissary, but I'm not impressed by these theatrics." Grasping Meredith's hand tighter, he turned to send them both back to their bodies.

His feet didn't budge. Magic bound him in place like boots stuck in cement. This was a simple spell, one he could break without much effort. But first, the Emissary needed to know he wasn't someone to be messed with.

He turned back, barely leashing his temper. "Enough."

"Jack, we need you to lead this new council." Her stare hit hard, but he didn't flinch. She was a worthy opponent, he'd give her that, but he wasn't ready to play this game.

"We chose you," she continued. "But it's still your choice. You are the right person to lead and to guide Meredith. She is not ready now, but with time and your help, she will be. Since you and Meredith will be the new leaders of the new council, it makes sense for the two of you to arrange the unbinding ceremony. It will allow you to work together and give Meredith insight into our world. I'll provide all the information I can."

Jack's feet released from the spell. He used his magic to send himself and Meredith back to her apartment.

Lying on the kitchen floor, he reached for Meredith and pulled her into his arms. "Are you okay? Do you hurt anywhere?"

She tilted her head to look at him, her eyes shining with what he assumed was relief. "I'm not hurt," she whispered.

He wanted to hold her longer, kiss her until the world fell away, but she was already pulling out of his grasp.

They stood and Meredith straightened her already straight clothes and fiddled with her ponytail. Her face had gone pale and her lips trembled. "She said we could co-lead a council. How does that work?"

"I don't know all the details, but there's a ceremony and we're given extra power. We, along with the other council members, would help magics and determine punishments when warranted."

"You sound angry. You don't want to lead?"

Jack hesitated. "It's not the leading I have a problem with."

"Then what?"

"I don't like being manipulated and not having control."

"It sucks, doesn't it?"

Jack cracked a smile. "Touché."

At least one good thing would come out of this... Meredith would have to spend time with him.

CHAPTER SEVEN

A knock on the open office door yanked Meredith's attention from her computer screen. She closed the document and looked up. "Come in."

Jack stepped inside, handed her a take-out cup, and dropped into the chair across from her desk as if he belonged there.

She read the printed label. He'd remembered her favorite. She sipped, let her eyes drift shut to savor the taste, and wished that when she opened them he'd be gone.

No such luck. "I appreciate the coffee, but I'm busy right now, Jack."

"Your assistant said you don't have any meetings today."

"Doesn't mean I'm not busy."

"True." He hauled the chair closer, bracing his forearms on her desk. "We still need to talk."

"About?" Even she startled at the bite in her own voice. Rudeness had been creeping in lately, thanks to Jack. He dragged it out of her. He used to draw out love, hope, excitement. Now he drew out irritation and rudeness. No—

not rudeness. Efficiency. Straightforwardness. Much better descriptions.

"We need to work together."

"No, we don't."

"Damn it, Mer." He scrubbed a hand through his hair. "Can't you cooperate a little?"

She was a team player, just not when the roster included Jack Knight. Not anymore. "I don't want to work with you, Jack."

"You don't want to break the binding?"

"I do. But I'm sure there are others who can help me." She took another sip, buying herself a second to think.

"You hate me that much?"

If only she could. Hating him might be easier. Instead, she feared she still loved him, and always would. But she didn't trust him. "I don't hate you, Jack. You're just a part of my past and I want to keep you there."

"What if I want more?"

"You should've thought of that before you walked out on me."

"Mer, I told you why I left. I know I hurt you and I need to earn your forgiveness, but I can't do that if you won't talk to me. Besides, I really want to help. If you work with me, we can break the binding. You'll have your magic back."

She wanted that desperately. With her power back, she could date other magics. And, hopefully, spot them on sight. She met his gaze. "When my magic returns, will I be able to sense someone else's?"

"Yes." His eyes narrowed. "Is there a reason that came to mind?"

"When I'm dating, I want to be able to recognize magics."

"Why do you want to date?"

She rolled her eyes. "Are you purposely being obtuse, Jack? You've always known I wanted to find *the* one, settle down, and have a family. That's why you left, isn't it? Because I wanted a family."

"You're twisting my words, Mer. I left because your magic was bound and I didn't want my future children to have to hide who they are."

"So you've said." She still wanted those future children, but not with someone she couldn't trust. Someone who made all the decisions instead of talking to her. That meant finding someone else. But until she could recognize magics for herself... she'd need help.

That sparked an idea. "I'll work with you."

He narrowed his eyes again. This time he looked like the distrustful one. "Why the sudden change of heart?"

"My heart hasn't changed. But until I'm unbound, I'm going to need help identifying magics I can date. That's where you come in."

His eyes widened. "You want me to find you magics to date?"

"Yes." The more she considered it, the more it appealed to her. She'd help Jack prepare for the unbinding. In return, he'd set her up on dates. Not just random guys either. Actual prospects. "But there are ground rules."

He leaned back and crossed his arms. "And what would those be?"

Meredith grabbed a pen and pulled her notepad across her desk. She mentally ran through the criteria she'd typed into dating apps more times than she cared to admit, such as age, career, distance, and jotted them down.

Setting the pen aside, she looked at him. "Whoever you set me up with must be a serious contender."

He grimaced. "Okay. Give me the criteria."

"The prospect must have a career and be between twenty-five and thirty-five."

"No homeless eighty-year-olds. Got it. What else?"

She exhaled slowly. "If you're not going to take this seriously, the deal's off."

"Bubbles, you know this is ridiculous. I want to be with you and you expect me to set you up on dates?"

"It's not ridiculous. I've been dating the wrong men for years. I've never felt chemistry with any of them, something you probably knew since you know *everything* about me," she said, using air quotes. "Now, you need my help, so you have to help me with this."

Jack's jaw ticked. "Fine."

"Maybe we should—" She shut her mouth before she lost her nerve and told him to forget it. She and Jack had always clicked. They'd moved in sync, like they were built for each other. They'd both wanted to please the other. But that time was over. Pleasing Jack was no longer her job. If he wanted her help, he could do this for her.

She flicked her eyes to the list then back to Jack. "He must live in the city; be intelligent, kind, ambitious; be educated enough that we can talk about anything. Hmm… he must also love to run, be a morning person, punctual, and keep his promises."

Satisfaction curled in Meredith's chest. A solid list.

Jack's grin spread, slow and smug.

She replayed her words. *Shit.* She'd just described Jack. She racked her brain for another add-on that wouldn't rule out too many prospects. "And he must love cats and want at least two."

"You know I'm allergic to cats."

She widened her eyes, feigning innocence. "Really? Oh, right. I guess I forgot. It's been so long." She wasn't up on the latest allergy meds; just in case they'd improved, she needed another filter. She flipped through memories of their whirlwind months together: laughing in The Magic Plate, binge-watching movies, double-dating with Damon, or with her cousins. So many were bittersweet. "And he must like pineapple on pizza and be willing to try karaoke. That's it." If she tacked on too much she might rule out everyone Jack knew.

He scoffed. "Really? Cats, pineapple pizza, and karaoke?"

"Yes. But karaoke isn't mandatory—he just has to be willing to try."

She didn't care what Jack thought of her list. He just needed to quit looking at her like *he* still qualified.

She'd weaponized logic and coffee and somehow convinced him to help her find someone else. Brilliant. And completely insane.

Jack stayed stone still—even his blink reflex froze.

Damn. She was serious.

But he hadn't accepted the deal. Yet. Because he was staging a quiet meltdown while keeping his expression neutral.

Meredith stared him down, daring him to refuse. Any second, he expected her to crank out a contract. Maybe have him sign it in blood. If he refused, she'd never trust him again. Never forgive him. He just needed more time to remind her how good they were together. No problem. He was an expert in strategy and tactics.

"Alright, Bubbles. I accept."

Her mouth fell open for a split second before she recovered. "That's great. When—"

He leaned in and laid a finger across her lips. They'd always been so soft. He wanted to rub his fingers along them, then pull her across the desk and kiss her until she forgot all about her stupid plan. He lingered, then drew back. "I have a few terms of my own."

She blew out a loud breath. "Of course you do. What?"

"We work together for a week. Non-negotiable."

"Sure. It might take you that long to find suitable candidates anyway. Anything else?"

"We need to break the unbinding before you go on your first date."

She chewed on her lip. "Are you trying to delay my meeting someone?"

Absolutely. "No. If you want me to match you with magics… fine. But you need to be able to recognize them first."

"But I don't know how long it will take to get ready for the unbinding."

"Then you better work with me to make sure we get it done fast." Guilt pricked him, but Meredith's heart was on the line. No one else could ever love her the way he would and he wouldn't give anyone else a chance.

"Fine. That it?"

"No. I won't start matchmaking until you've practiced your magic and can detect other magics."

"Hold on a second. You had years to practice your magic."

"If I am to accept your stipulations, you need to accept mine."

She hesitated—not long, but enough for him to notice—before she said, "Twice."

"Twice what?"

"I'll practice my magic twice. Have two lessons. Then you start matchmaking, and within two days of the second practice, I need to be on my first date."

"Two weeks."

"No. One week. Take it or leave it."

He didn't remember her being such a good negotiator

before. But they'd been young, in love, and in sync. "Fine. One week."

"Okay. I'm on the first date within one week of my second time practicing magic. And…" She slapped her hand on the desk lightly. "I can practice my magic with anyone."

"No." The word was out of his mouth before he could even think about it. If he allowed that, he'd lose two more chances to be with her. At the rate she was gunning for these dates, he would need every opportunity he could get to convince her to give him another shot. "I'll arrange training for you and your cousins."

Jack stood to shut the negotiations down. Not that he wanted to fix her up on dates, but it was better than her recruiting someone else and shutting him out completely.

He offered his hand when he really wanted to seal the deal with their lips. But a kiss wasn't the best tactic here and if he pushed her now, she might never trust him again.

She gripped his hand. "Deal."

Jack could only hope he hadn't made a mistake.

Hours later, he still second-guessed himself.

Had there been another way to spend time with Meredith? One where she might've trusted him again?

He shifted on the couch where he'd been planted for hours, the beer in his hand warm. He took a sip, grimaced, and disappeared it. He let the cushions swallow him and shut his eyes.

Sixteen years ago—half of his life—he'd made a promise to himself: no child of his would ever have to compromise who they were. No shame, no lies, no hiding. No worry about not being enough just as they were. After years of abuse at the hands of his father, he'd finally done what he had to for survival, and he wouldn't let the horror that still haunted him be in vain.

At the time of his vow, love hadn't even been on the

horizon. It wasn't until after college, back in Blue Mountain, that Meredith had become his everything.

He'd been naïve, thinking they could make it work long-term. Elise had warned him. Told him that she was never going to tell Meredith and her cousins the truth. But he hadn't listened. Hadn't wanted to accept it. Not until he and Meredith started talking about their future and having kids.

That was when he knew he had to leave.

He couldn't bring a child into the world knowing they'd have to hide who they were. Either that, or he would have had to tell Meredith the truth. It would have exposed the lies her mom had built her life around, turning the only parent she had left into the villain.

Even if his magic had let him reveal the truth, he couldn't have done that to her. Couldn't make Meredith choose between him and her mom.

And if they couldn't break the binding? What then? What would that have meant for their kids? For Meredith? Either their kids would be forced to lie, hiding their magic from their aunts and uncle who were still bound, or Meredith would've been heartbroken, unable to teach her children to be all they could be.

He raked a hand through his hair and yanked the ends. And now that everything he wanted with her was finally in sight, he needed to help her find someone else to love her.

All because of the day he'd made his vow. The day that had changed his life forever.

Jack lost track of everything except survival. The training session was his third for the day, but only the first for his teacher. His instructors switched out regularly to stay fresh.

Louis Copeland led this session and the man was especially brutal to Jack. Copeland always favored Charlie, Jack's twin. His brother had been one to bend the rules when it suited him, something Copeland appreciated. Charlie hadn't seen things as either right or wrong the way Jack did. Since Charlie's death in a car accident with their mother four years earlier, Jack's life had become a continuous torture session ruled by his father and appointed instructors.

Jack forced the pain away, flooding himself with soul-deep cold. He'd learned long ago to project cold through his system. It temporarily stopped all feelings of pain. The cold also had another benefit. It blocked his emotions from overtaking him, which could render him useless in a fight.

Tomorrow he'd be black and blue again, old cuts ripped wide. He'd need healing, but survival came first. It had become harder and harder to be thankful he was alive. He often wondered what Charlie would think. If their roles had been reversed, would there be times his twin would have wanted to lay down and die?

The thought of Charlie made him take in a deep breath and focus on his opponent. Charlie was no longer here to make decisions, good or bad, so Jack was determined to live for him.

Jack refocused and sidestepped, a bolt of magic grazing his chest. Before he could aim, another shot came at him and then another, both hitting him in the ribs. The pain lanced straight up, sharp enough to steal his breath. Using his magic, Jack directed a shot of cold right to his ribs, attempting to dull the pain.

Running on fumes, he fired another blast at Copeland.

Too slow, Jack caught a third shot to his ribs, this time on the other side. The blow caused him to fall forward, his hands outstretched to catch himself. He pushed off the floor, struggling to get to his feet. Again, he wasn't fast enough.

Copeland took advantage of Jack's downed position and flashed the few feet to Jack's side, stomping on his spine. Just as the boot hit, Jack sent a protection spell coursing through his body. It barely softened the blow. Pain detonated through Jack in a burst of white-hot sparks, but the deflection kept him alive.

"You're weak and distracted." Copeland towered over him, sneering down, and lifted his foot again. This time the kick landed

on Jack's ribs, the impact driving him sideways. He sucked in shallow breaths as he rolled to the side.

"You are pathetic, Jack. A disgrace to all magics. We have taught you what so many would beg to learn, and yet you continue to shun wanting more power. Your father should be ashamed of you."

Copeland struck again, then lazily flicked away the sweat beading on his brow. He looked clean and fresh as he turned, giving Jack his back in dismissal.

Jack pulled himself to his feet, the pain almost crippling him. Even the cold trick failed to numb him now. Every one of his nerves felt like they were on fire, his body one big blazing inferno.

He wanted to lie down and curl up and let the world fall away, except he couldn't. The torture would never end if he didn't do something to stop it. No one was going to come and save him. It was up to him to stand up for himself and for Charlie.

Jack dug for his last scraps of energy and lashed out at his teacher. But in that moment, he was aiming at more than just a man. He was directing his anger at all the unfairness he'd been dealt in his sixteen years. The unfairness of the endless teachings, the loss of his twin, losing his mother, and the brutal torture from his father. It all melded together in one gigantic ball of pissed-off-teenager and Jack let it go.

The blast hit true, a lethal strike that Copeland never saw coming. The massive assault of energy hit his side and spread upwards. It engulfed the entire left side of his face, scorching through the flesh and bone. The man opened his mouth to scream, but no sound came out as he fell to the ground.

"Noooooooooo!" The high-pitched scream from behind Jack was deafening in the small room.

Jack turned as his father ran toward his fallen teacher, then lovingly caressed the unburned side of Louis Copeland's face.

Flopping down on the bench against the wall, Jack gripped the edge to keep from falling over. He kept his gaze locked on his father.

The man had never caressed Jack that way, never shown him the kind of love a father should give a son.

His father bowed his head and then slowly stood and faced Jack. "You are weak and lack control." His voice was low as he spit the words out, his brows furrowed in anger as he glared at Jack. "You should have died in that car accident, not Charlie."

Jack had heard the speech dozens of times in the last four years, and each time he had braced himself for the punishment that was to follow.

But not this time.

Using the bench as leverage, Jack pushed himself to his feet and faced his father. Sucking in a large breath, he ignored the pain in his ribs and culled as much energy from his surroundings as his weakening power would allow.

Today Jack would put an end to his suffering one way or another. Either he would kill his father or his father would kill him. He refused to live like this any longer, enduring the agony day in and day out.

His magic tingled at his fingertips as he waited for his father to make the first move. Jack might be weakened from participating in three fights, but his father was arrogant. Jack hadn't seen his father fight in years. He'd grown soft, while Jack was young and fighting for his life.

The first strike came at Jack as a flame to his left and he dodged, dropping into a crouch. He shot out a strike of electricity from his fingers, hitting his dad in the shins and knocking him to the ground.

Jack lurched forward, his knees threatening to fold. His energy was almost depleted. If he didn't rest and get something to eat soon to refuel his body, he'd be done.

Drawing in what power he could, Jack pictured his brother in his mind. A calm came over him as he aimed his hands toward his father.

Jack hurled every remaining spark through his fingertips. The recoil slammed Jack onto his ass. His head hit the floor with a soft thud and he closed his eyes.

He sipped shallow breaths to stay conscious and waited for his father to berate him.

The cruelty and criticism never came. After a couple minutes, Jack lifted his head and looked across the room. His father lay beside Copeland, unmoving.

Jack rolled to his side, groaning, and clawed up to his knees. Using the bench, he pulled himself up but couldn't straighten. His ribs screamed in pain and his whole body trembled with exhaustion, every muscle spent.

Jack shuffled across the room and looked down at his father. His eyes were closed, but his jaw hung slack. Charred, black fabric clung to his father's body. Dropping to his knees, Jack ignored his pain as he reached for his father's shirt and ripped it open. His dad's flesh had blackened and bubbled, swelling like tar in the sunlight. It lay around open wounds, bone and flesh visible through the gaps in his skin.

Jack sagged back on his ass, his breathing ragged.

He was free.

CHAPTER EIGHT

Meredith collapsed onto the sofa in Jo's apartment, the cushions sagging beneath her weight as if they sympathized with her exhaustion. The familiar smells of vanilla and freshly ground espresso permeated the air. At any other time they might have calmed her, but tonight she felt like she'd been through the washing machine's spin cycle and got stuck. For two days she'd second-guessed her deal with Jack, resulting in a massive headache.

"Wine or coffee?" Jo called from the kitchen, just as her apartment door opened.

"Wine," Rowena said as she walked in.

Meredith smiled at her cousin and called out to Jo, "Same."

"Don't get up, sweetie. I've got it." Rowena picked up two glasses Jo had already poured and walked into the living room, handing one to Meredith.

"Thanks."

Reece walked in next, a large tray balanced on one hand as he kicked the door shut behind him. "I brought dessert." He walked into the living room and set it on the coffee table, before going back to the kitchen and pouring himself a scotch.

Jo brought her wine into the living room and sat on one end of the couch, pulling her legs under her. "We're all set, Mer. Ever since your call yesterday, I've been dying to know about the deal you so cryptically mentioned. Teasing isn't nice. Start from the beginning and don't leave anything out."

Meredith sipped her wine, hoping it would dull the throbbing in her temples as Reece got settled.

"I thought this was just a general let's-talk-about-magic chat," Reece said. "Something's happened since the soul jump?"

"I made a deal with Jack," Meredith blurted out. "I'm going to help him set up the binding ceremony and he'll set me up on dates with magic men."

All three of her cousins stared at her as if waiting for the punch line.

"I don't get it. You've never had any problem getting dates in the past," Jo said.

"That's just it. I've had hundreds of dates and there's never any chemistry."

Rowena's expression softened. "So you think Jack—the guy you once were madly in love with and planned to marry —is the answer to finding the right date?"

Put like that, it didn't sound like such a good idea, but she wasn't going to back out. "I haven't been attracted to any of my dates because they weren't magic. Jack is going to correct that. And I gave him criteria."

Jo chuckled. "This should be interesting. I can't wait—"

"Hello? Is this just for the young, or can an old lady join you?"

Meredith looked up to see her mom walk into the apartment.

"Come on in." Jo got up and gave her aunt a quick hug before grabbing the wine bottle and another glass.

Smiling at her mom, Meredith knew how lucky she was. When she was young, like most kids, she probably took her mother for granted. For the longest time she never really stopped to think about what her mother had been going through—too wrapped up in her own childhood grief. It wasn't until she'd lost Jack and was wallowing in sorrow once more that the reality of everything her mother had suffered finally sunk in.

Now, they'd lost Aunt Beatrice as well. Meredith could see the true toll all the losses over the years had taken on her mother. Although still a beautiful woman with long, brown, wavy hair, a statuesque figure, and all the right curves, Meredith could see evidence of her grief. Her mom wasn't standing quite as tall as she always had and there were more lines etched on her face. Even her hair didn't look quite as luxurious as usual, though her outfit was as put together as always. She wore a fashionable sweater and slacks with a beautiful silk scarf around her neck.

As her mom took the wine glass from Jo and sat down in one of the big, comfy arm chairs near Rowena, something about her appearance changed. Her mother's skin was now radiant, her hair looked shinier and healthier than it had a moment ago, and the gray was gone. "Something changed. Mom, what did you just do?"

Her mom shrugged. "You were looking at me like something was wrong, so I thought I must have looked a little worse for wear. I did a glamour spell, nothing big."

"It's a bit scary that you can change your appearance, but on the other hand it's also kind of cool. Can you teach us that, Auntie?" Rowena sat forward. "That could really come in handy."

"Sure, it's a simple spell." Her mom looked at the others. "What were you all chatting about?"

Reece grinned. "Oh, not much, just how your daughter is having the love of her life set her up on dates."

Her mom whipped her gaze to face her. "Explain that one."

Meredith shrugged and gave her mom the Cliff Notes version.

"Hmmm, we'll see how that goes."

"See?" Jo rubbed her hands together as if in anticipation. "That's what I said. I can't wait."

Her mom looked at each of them in turn. "I didn't know if this day would ever come, but I both looked forward to it and dreaded it at the same time. Your moms did as well."

Meredith looked at her mom and saw that the statement belied the shine of her skin and face. She looked all fluffed and fresh on the outside, but her quiet resolve suggested something was still weighing heavily on her. Guilt? Grief?

She reached out and placed her hand on her mom's leg. "Mom, what's wrong? Do you not want us to go through with the unbinding?"

Her mom shook her head. "No, you need to do it. I was just thinking back to when we bound you. I was lost and hurting. We all were, me and my sisters." She looked at her nieces and nephew. "No one expects to lose their spouse, especially so young, but to lose a child, it…" Her mom's words trailed off as if the pain was too much to speak about aloud.

Meredith watched as her mother conjured a tissue and wiped her eyes. She couldn't imagine what her mother and aunts had gone through. What Meredith felt at the loss of her sister and father was almost like it had happened to another person. The memories were distant and a bit faded. But her mother had the added burden of having taken her daughter's magic away as well, and then she watched both her sisters die.

Her mom disappeared the tissue and Meredith got up to give her a hug. "I love you, mom."

"Love you too, sweetie."

Releasing her mom, she pulled back and straightened, the move shifting her mom's scarf. Meredith gasped. Several thin, black lines, starting high up on her mom's neck snaked downward, disappearing under her shirt. Although faint, the lines were unmistakable.

She met her mom's gaze. "When did they start?"

"What start?" Rowena asked as she came to kneel in front of her aunt.

"The lines." Meredith closed her eyes for a quick moment and took in a deep breath. Once the lines had started on her aunt, there'd been no stopping them.

Her mom had been wearing a lot of scarves the last couple of weeks, but that wasn't unusual since the weather had started to get colder. Her internal temperature had always run a bit on the cold side, and she joked that her thermostat broke when she had kids. Meredith hadn't even thought to question the new wardrobe addition.

"Auntie Elise, when did they start?" Rowena repeated Meredith's question, her voice verging on hysterics, not a common occurrence for her usually calm cousin.

Reece leaned his forearms on his knees. "Like what killed our mom."

"Yes." Lowering her eyes to the table as if to fortify herself, her mom blew out a breath before she looked up. "Glamour spells won't work on this."

"Why not?" Jo asked.

Meredith glanced at Jo before facing her mom. "It doesn't matter why the spell won't work, just the fact she has them is the problem. But I'm missing something, aren't I? So, why won't it work?"

"The lines are magic."

Still confused, Meredith waited for her mom to explain.

Elise twisted the tissue in her hands. "The lines came from a build-up of magic, so they're magic. Magic cannot always cover magic."

When she looked at Meredith and then her nieces and nephew, her eyes were clear and bright. "Taking on extra magic with no outlet builds up over time. The magic is trapped in me because of the spell. Even if I use my magic and expend energy, the excess power from taking it from the four of you is still eating me alive. That's what happened to your moms."

Meredith felt a lump swell in her throat and swallowed it down. "That's why you and Aunt Beatrice said there was nothing that could be done when she was dying."

Meredith had stated a fact, but her mom answered it like a question anyway. "Yes. It was the same thing that happened to Lillian."

"If it was the same thing, why did my mother die so many years before Auntie Beatrice, and you're only getting the lines now?" Rowena gasped, then looked at her aunt again. "I didn't mean it like that, Auntie. I don't want you to die, I just wondered why it affected my mother more quickly."

"Oh child, I understand." Her mom placed her hand on top of Rowena's and gave it a quick squeeze. "I can only speculate, but my sisters and I believed it was because Lillian was the one who spoke the spell and had the most control over it. She may have taken in more magic than Beatrice and I did. Or it could have been because of the spell itself. We'll never really know."

Rowena sat back in her chair and Meredith addressed her mom. "Will the unbinding reverse the effects on you?"

"I don't know. As soon as we cast the spell, the book disappeared. Since we never planned on reversing the unbinding, we didn't think much of it. A decade later your mom got the lines and then Beatrice started getting them a couple of months before she died."

"A couple of months? We only saw them for a few weeks before they killed her." Jo's voice was an explosion in the shocked silence of the room. "She hid it for that long?"

"Jo, I know you're upset, but there was nothing we could do. Your mother didn't want to worry you and Reece. She also didn't want to unbind you. Eventually the lines just got too bad to hide."

"Then we'll do the unbinding." Reece turned to Meredith. "How soon can you and Jack set it up?"

"We're meeting tomorrow to talk about it, so I'll let you know." Her deal with Jack now seemed childish. Date or no, she'd help Jack with the unbinding to save her mom.

JACK LEANED back in the chair across from Ben's desk.

Ben steepled his fingers. "I wanted us to get up to speed, both on the Williams family and what's happening at work. Elise said you and Meredith had a little adventure last week."

Jack scoffed. "That's one way to describe it." He conjured himself a coffee and took a long drink. He needed the caffeine. "I didn't think it was possible. Naïve maybe, but still... I never thought anyone could take me against my will."

"Don't beat yourself up. I wouldn't have expected it either." Ben reached for his mug, looked inside, and shrugged before conjuring coffee into it.

"I still don't think any one individual has the power to

soul jump another. I just wish I knew what to be prepared for next." He didn't trust the Emissary or the grand council.

Ben studied his coffee like it held an answer, then looked up. "I've met the new Emissary a few times. She seems to have the council leaders' respect."

"She doesn't have mine yet. Soul-jumping us was dramatic and complete bullshit."

Ben chuckled. "Maybe she's heard about your stubborn streak and figured she had to go big to get your attention."

"Still not okay."

"Agreed. But it worked. Did she give you any details about you and Meredith leading a council?"

"Not at the soul jump, but she's emailed me since with what needs to be done." Jack snorted. "She could have emailed to begin with, instead of taking us like she did. Meredith and I are going to meet to set things up."

"If you need any assistance, check with Viktor Szabo at the library. He should be able to help you out."

"Will do. How's the twenty-seventh for the unbinding? Will you and Frank be available?"

Ben looked at his computer and then back at Jack. "Both my calendar and Frank's are clear. Any particular reason for that day?"

"It's far enough out to get things ready without pushing it off for too long." Jack had another reason for that exact date, but Ben didn't need to know.

A voice cut in from the doorway. "Ready for me?"

Jack glanced over his shoulder to see Frank standing there. Looking back at Ben, Jack raised an eyebrow.

"I asked Frank to join us," Ben said. "He was involved with the council back when everything went down over twenty years ago. We need his recollection of past events."

Jack nodded at Frank. "Good to see you, sir."

Besides heading the FBI's Blue Mountain division, Frank

had known Jack his entire life. Their families had been close. Frank's son Connor, along with Damon, had once been Jack's best friends, until things fell apart when they were in their late teens. After that, Connor disappeared, choosing to live off the grid.

Frank conjured himself a coffee, the drink of choice among agents, and settled in beside Jack. "Do you know what happened with the council a few years before the Williams fire? You'd have been, what? Ten?"

"About that. I know my dad was looking for the magic box but never found it."

"That's right. At the time, we believed your dad and Parker, Stella's brother, were hunting for the box. We just don't know if they were working together. There might have been others involved."

"By *we*, you mean you and Meredith's dad, Thomas?"

Frank nodded. "Thomas, as well as his brothers, Damon's dad Curtis, and Ben."

Jack looked between his two bosses. "And now, except for you two, they're all dead."

Frank glanced at Ben. They exchanged a silent look, likely speaking telepathically, but Jack couldn't sense it. Even with his immense power, some connections were too strong and deep to detect.

Jack had the utmost respect for Ben and Frank, but if they were talking about him, he wanted to know. "Something you want to tell me?" he asked, looking directly at Frank.

His superior didn't flinch. He didn't deny the silent conversation either. "I asked Ben if you knew what was foretold twenty-two years ago. He said no."

Jack raised his brow again. "And?"

Frank set his coffee mug on the desk and walked over to the whiteboard that took up one entire wall. He picked up a whiteboard marker and twirled it between his fingers.

"There was a woman, an older seer, well-known amongst local magics. Incredibly gifted, but like all seers, her visions were hit or miss with some details."

"She still around?"

"No, she died not long after the Williams fire."

"Did the seer's death have anything to do with the magic box or the council?"

Frank shook his head. "I don't think so. Her husband had died years earlier."

"What did she see?"

"That the magic box would resurface when the children of the old council were adults. Your generation. She said opening it would release evil, and that it would take a new, stronger council of fourteen members to seal it again."

"During our soul jump, the Emissary mentioned seven pairs instead of seven individuals. Did the seer's vision prompt the change?"

Ben moved to the chair beside Jack, turned it around, and straddled it. "Maybe. More people, more oversight. It would also bring some diversity to the councils. But your conversation with her was the first I've heard of a new council in North America. We haven't had one here in over sixteen years."

"The year my dad died."

Ben nodded. "After so many council member deaths, no one wanted to have anything to do with a new one. The other councils were struggling too. For so long, the councils had been ruled by a type of old boys' club and allowed to do as they pleased. The new format might fix that."

"Did the seer say anything else?"

Frank and Ben exchanged another look before Ben turned to Jack. "Yes, she warned that more children would be taken, and there would be more deaths."

Jack leaned forward. "Has that happened?"

Frank sighed. "Yes, one child was recently taken. Luckily she was found unharmed, but her captor got away. Three families have also reported attempted abductions. Again, they were lucky. All three were able to protect their children. They were also too young to have much magic to siphon, although of the four families, some of the parents had strong specialties—two are healers, one could echo old spells, and one had compulsion. He could force a single command into someone's mind—that's how he was able to use it to stop an abduction."

"You think they're taking children now to gain access to specialties when they come into them fully?"

Frank sighed. "I have no idea. But it's a possibility. And those are only the abductions we know about. People go missing all the time and, as you know, without a council for magics to report to, we don't always hear about them."

"True," Jack agreed. "But why these abductions now?" Jack asked. "I thought my dad was the last of the power-hungry maniacs. You think the magic box is back in play? That one of the council members is trying to find it?"

Jack didn't wait for answers as thoughts entered his mind in rapid-fire sequence, one after the other. "Thomas Williams, Edward Hughes, Curtis Stone, and Louis Copeland are all dead. My dad made five. That leaves only two council members unaccounted for."

The two brothers paused as if communicating again.

Frank took the cap off the whiteboard marker. "That's what we're hoping you'll help us brainstorm." He wrote three names: Louis Copeland, Andrew Skalbeck, and Forest Sharpe.

"Copeland's dead," Jack said flatly. He hated talking, or even thinking, about the man. Jack still vividly remembered calling Ben after walking out of his house and leaving the dead bodies on the floor.

Ben's expression turned grim. "I'm not so sure."

Jack narrowed his brows. "Not possible. I burned half his face off. His body was right beside my dad's when I walked out."

"I know. But when Frank and I went to your house right after your call, your dad's body was there—just like you said it would be—but Copeland's wasn't."

Jack's world tilted around him. "What? Why didn't you ever tell me?"

"At first, I didn't want to burden you. You were already dealing with enough. Then you moved in with the Stones, and I meant to tell you, but I think that was around the time Curtis went missing. Everything snowballed. By the time I was ready, you'd graduated early and left for college. When you came back I figured it no longer mattered."

Ben turned to his brother. "Frank, let's draw a timeline to bring Jack up to speed. Start with twenty-two years ago when Stella and I met, and Parker died."

Frank picked up a marker and wrote *Ben*, *Stella*, and *Parker* on the whiteboard beside the number twenty-two, marking twenty-two years in the past. He dragged a horizontal line forward and added *twenty* to mark two years later. Next to that he wrote *Thomas Williams* and *Edward Hughes*.

Jack had known Thomas and his brothers but only vaguely remembered Edward Hughes. "When did Curtis Stone die?"

Frank extended the line again and wrote *sixteen*, to show another time jump, four years later. He added *Daniel Knight* and *Curtis Stone* to the list. "No one ever found Curtis's body," he said. "But everyone, including his wife, believes he's dead. And with Fiona's visions, if she thinks he's dead, he must be. I think it happened around the time your father died. Maybe just before."

"That sounds about right," Ben said, rising from his seat. He crossed to the whiteboard and added *Davis* in the same timeframe marked as the Williams's fire.

Jack frowned. "Why did you write your own last name?"

Ben sighed, his shoulders sinking under an invisible weight. "Shortly after the Williams's fire, a bunch of us gathered to figure out what to do. Frank, Joel, and Stella were with me. That's when we spoke with the seer. While we were meeting, a fire broke out. Connor and his best friend, Drew, were—"

"Wait," Jack cut in. "Drew, our FBI agent?"

Ben nodded. "Same Drew. Connor and Drew were watching two of our kids when it happened. The fire started in the room they were in. It spread fast." Ben's voice dropped. "One child made it out with minor injuries. The other died. My daughter."

Jack had always known Ben lost a child in what everyone called a tragic accident, but he'd never known how. Jack turned to Frank. "That's why Connor left."

Jack hadn't phrased it as a question, but Frank answered anyway. "Yeah. He'd been sixteen and never forgave himself for his cousin's death. He moved to our lake house right after high school and became a hermit. He barely comes back."

Jack nodded. There were no words that would console Ben and Frank. "What does that second fire have to do with the council?"

Frank's voice came out hollow, stripped of emotion. "We were meeting to figure out what to do about the council. The seer told us what she saw just before the fire broke out."

"You think that fire was connected to the Williams's fire? You think my dad had something to do with it?"

Ben sighed again. "Yes, but not in a way we can explain. That's the strange part. The fire was ruled an accident, but Connor's version of what happened never made sense. And magic confirmed he wasn't lying. Still, we couldn't tie it to your dad."

Jack clenched his jaw. Whether they could prove it or not, his dad being responsible for more deaths didn't surprise him. The man had killed the daughter of the only man Jack now looked to as a father. Irony didn't get darker than that.

Jack exhaled slowly. "So Copeland might be alive. But with the damage I inflicted—magical burns that severe—it would be nearly impossible to hide the scars."

His gaze alternated between the brothers. "What about Andrew Skalbeck and Forest Sharpe? They didn't have kids, so I didn't get to know them like I did the other council members. You think they were involved?"

Frank circled three names on the board—*Louis Copeland, Andrew Skalbeck,* and *Forest Sharpe.* "Andrew and Forest disappeared too. We don't know if they were involved in any of the attacks, but we can't rule them out."

"But you're thinking Louis Copeland was since he was so close to my dad?"

Frank nodded. "That's our assumption. Which gives us three likely suspects for the new child abductions and the attack on Meredith."

Jack looked down at his empty coffee mug and disappeared it with a flick of his hand. "But again, why now? It's been years since the fires and my dad's death."

Frank grabbed the whiteboard eraser. "That's the million-dollar question. We never found the magic box. Just whispers and warnings. Supposedly, it holds so much power—all of it evil—that it takes a tremendous amount of power to even locate it, let alone open it." Frank snorted and erased the whiteboard. "If it even exists at all."

Jack stood and stretched his neck. "So, let me get this straight. Three men may still be alive. They may want this magic box. And they may be trying to gather the power they need to find and open it."

He turned to Ben. "Did you get anything out of the guys who attacked Meredith?"

"Nothing useful. We booked them, but it won't stick. Without a council to dole out punishments, they'll slip through the system. Magic makes it too easy—bribery, conjuring, flashing out—it doesn't matter what they pick. We won't be able to prove anything. Not without revealing magic to non-magics."

Frank glanced at his watch and set the eraser down. "I've got a meeting. But Jack?"

Jack met his superior's gaze.

"You left Meredith because she was spellbound, so I'm sure I don't need to tell you how crucial it is to unbind the Williams as soon as possible."

"No, sir."

"Good. They need to be able to protect themselves."

Jack nodded. If only their safety was the *only* thing on his plate. He still had to set Meredith up on a date.

CHAPTER NINE

*M*eredith had always loved the quiet hush that settled over The Magic Plate after closing, but tonight the shadows felt too intimate, like they were conspiring to shove her and Jack closer together until she gave in.

Giving herself an internal shake, she eased into the corner booth anyway. She opened her laptop, prepared to keep track of what needed to be done. Order in her spreadsheets meant order in her head. At least, that's what she'd been telling herself since Jack walked back into her life and blew her carefully organized life to pieces.

"Breathe," she whispered in the quiet room before giving herself a mental pep talk. *Focus on variables you can control: the location, any props we will need, the people who need to be there. Everything else—like the way your pulse jumps whenever Jack is near—file under ignore.*

His footsteps sounded behind her. He must have flashed into the restaurant. She didn't have to look up to know it was him; her body recognized the cadence of his stride long before her brain wanted to admit it. Still, she kept her gaze on the screen, adding a totally unnecessary note about confirming the location with her mom. If he sat across from her, maybe he wouldn't notice the tremor in her fingers.

"Hey, Bubb—Meredith." He stopped himself—something he was doing more often—and it shouldn't have mattered, but the absence of the old nickname stripped away the veneer of casual ease between them. She kept typing.

"The place is locked up?" he asked.

"Staff's gone and alarms set. We're good." She looked up at him, pleased with herself that her voice came out steadier than she felt.

Jack slid into the opposite bench, just like she wanted. So why did she wish he was closer? He smelled like clean mountain air and roasted coffee—dangerously comforting.

He leaned forward, forearms braced. "I spoke with Ben and he agreed to hold the unbinding week after next on the twenty-seventh."

She sucked in her breath. A coincidence? Probably. Jack didn't remember dates the way she did. She had two weeks to prepare. The date was soon enough she wouldn't have to wait long and far enough away for her to come up with a thousand things to worry about. "Why the twenty-seventh?"

"The moon is in Jupiter that night. Extra boost for positive transformations."

That sounded complicated. "Really?"

His mouth quirked. "No. Just kidding… our magic doesn't work that way. Ben and Frank will be available. Logistics, not destiny."

Right. Logistics. She opened the spreadsheet and typed the date.

"We'll need clearance to block the cemetery road."

She lifted her head to meet his gaze. "Cemetery? Are you joking again?"

"Unfortunately, no. I checked with the guy who runs the

magic archives and he said we have to be close to your aunts' bodies because they were involved with binding you."

"Can we just take over a cemetery?"

"I'll get a city permit. Officially it's an FBI training exercise." He offered a half-smile, like they shared a private joke. Once, that smile had melted her. Now it reminded her what they missed out on when Jack walked away.

She glanced down at her spreadsheet to avoid him seeing the disappointment she was sure was clear in her eyes.

"I was expecting more questions from you. Anything you want to know, ask away."

Why didn't you fight harder for me? She cleared her throat and clicked on another tab. She needed a distraction, but she hadn't written down any questions yet. So unlike her, but Jack had thrown her world into chaos. "How does magic work?"

"I don't know exactly, it's just a part of who we are. We're all born with our essence inside of us. The essence allows us to absorb energy from our environment and use it to conduct magic. As we grow, so does our essence, and it becomes stronger, more powerful. That allows a person to wield more magic or do more things with it."

"I guess that makes sense, but it still doesn't tell me how it works. I mean... how do you make something happen or appear?"

"The most common way is for you to use the magic essence inside of you to take energy in from your surroundings. You then think of what you want and your essence will conjure it." He waved his hand and a glass of water appeared on the table in front of her.

"You can also physically direct the energy to do something, like when your mom directed her magic to heal you. Or like this..." The glass floated over to him. He plucked it out of the air and took a drink. "Depending on what you're doing and your level of competence and power, you may or may not need to direct the magic. Your thoughts alone may be enough."

"You said that's the most common way—what's another way?"

"People can use spells. You're still pulling energy and using the magic essence within you, but instead of something simple, such as conjuring, healing, or flashing, you might be doing something that needs some assistance. Like your mom and aunts did when they bound you."

"Is that what happened during our soul jump? The grand council members used a spell to transport us?"

"I expect so. From what the Emissary said, it took several or all of the council leaders working together to have enough combined energy for the spell. It's possible for magics to assist each other too, by sharing or directing energy."

Meredith didn't know what else to ask and when the silence settled around them, she became acutely aware of Jack's gaze on her face. Heat unfurled low in her belly and she hated herself for it. She couldn't let herself forget how easily Jack had walked away. "Anything else?" she asked, keeping her tone brisk and businesslike.

"Yeah." Jack's voice dropped, intimate as his hand on her bare skin. "You."

She blinked. "Excuse me?"

"You're part of the ceremony, Meredith. Not just helping me organize it. Copeland's people already targeted you once. If you go into this wrung out, you'll be vulnerable. You need sleep. Real meals. Maybe," his eyes warmed, "some company for distraction because I know you'll come up with a thousand things to worry about."

Heat bloomed in her neck and cheeks—embarrassment that Jack knew her so well. And anger too. "Drop the innuendos, Jack. You keep acting like you can waltz right back into my life and pick up where we left off. You can't. You're the one that walked out, remember?"

Jack's shoulders dropped. "You're right. I'm sorry."

His easy apology chipped her defenses. Meredith hated that. She needed to keep her walls up around Jack. She picked up her laptop and stood. "I've got lots to keep me busy and *distracted.*"

Jack nodded, looking contrite. "Right." He stood as well. "The Emissary has already confirmed that she'll lead the ceremony. And once I know we'll be able to block off the cemetery, you and I need to check it out. Just so we know how much space we're dealing with and how open the area will be."

She hesitated. Being alone with him in the restaurant was one thing, but among her family's graves felt too raw. Too intense. But if she refused he could renege on their deal. And that wasn't something she could afford to happen, especially if Jack was here to stay. She needed to find someone else she could love. "Fine. Let me know when and where."

"Will do," he said, but didn't move. He continued to look at her.

"Anything else?" she asked.

"Actually…yes." He lifted his hand and lightly ran the back of his knuckles across her cheek. The action transported her back eight years and she wanted to melt into him the same as she would have then.

"Mer, I know you don't trust me, but I'm going to prove to you that I'm here to stay. It's why I set the unbinding for the twenty-seventh."

"You said it was because of logistics."

"No. Well… yes, logistically, the date works, but…" He visibly swallowed and something like vulnerability flickered across his features. "I also chose it because it's the anniversary of the night I left you."

She sucked in a breath; he did remember.

He raised his hand again as if to touch her, then shoved it in the front pocket of his jeans. "I want that night to stop meaning loss."

If only it could. "We can't erase those years and we *did* lose something that day."

"We can start over," he said quietly.

Meredith looked away, his gaze too intense. The saltshaker on the table caught her eye. She imagined flipping it, white grains scattering everywhere, impossible to gather every piece back. Wasn't that what forgiveness felt like? Spilling parts of yourself you might never reclaim?

"I can't forget the past, Jack."

His jaw flexed and for a second she saw the determined younger man she'd fallen in love with. "I'm not going to give up, Bubbles."

A part of her hoped he wouldn't. It was the optimistic part of herself that thought he wouldn't walk out on her again. But the realistic part knew better—she couldn't trust him. And couldn't forgive him because if he'd really loved her, he never would have left.

"I better get going." She gripped her laptop tighter and moved around the booth.

Jack didn't budge, their bodies nearly touching. If she took a single step forward, she'd be in his arms. Meredith inhaled sharply, her senses betraying her with a rush of memories: his lips, the taste of coffee, the earth-shaking kiss on the bench—

Stop. She angled away, but Jack mirrored her movement, blocking her exit with his broad shoulders. "Jack, please. Let me by."

"Say you'll let me walk you upstairs first."

"Don't be an ass."

His hand lifted—just a hover near her cheek, not a touch. Still, heat licked across her skin. "Please," he pleaded.

It was the please that did it. She nodded once.

They turned all the lights off and slipped into the hallway that linked to the residential elevator. The ride to the tenth floor flew by in silence thick with all the words they weren't saying. At her door Meredith pulled out her key.

She turned to thank him. Or dismiss him, she wasn't sure. Jack stood with his arm braced on the doorframe, crowding her space without moving in.

"Good night," she said as a clear dismissal. He had to leave soon, because she was only so strong.

He didn't answer. Instead, he studied her face as if cataloguing her features, like he had before. Heat coiled in her core and—

"Meredith…"

She heard the plea inside her name, and something in her cracked. She rose on tiptoe, intending to kiss his cheek. Instead, her mouth had a different idea and found his.

He responded instantly, one large hand sliding into her hair, the other gripping her hip as though she were the only solid thing in existence. The kiss was deep, lush, edged with eight years of what-ifs. Meredith opened to him despite every line she'd drawn.

For three scorching heartbeats she pushed anger, spreadsheets, and loss from her mind. She was nineteen again, greedy for him.

He tightened his grip in her hair, a reminder of what she used to love, and reality slammed back. Giving in equaled forgiveness, which equaled believing what he did was okay. She wrenched away.

"God—no," she whispered. Her fingers pressed to her lips as though she could erase the warmth. "I can't do this."

Jack's eyes were storm-dark, his breathing heavy. He lifted both palms. "I crossed a line."

"I initiated it." Self-loathing churned in her gut. "Just a momentary lapse of judgment."

"Will you ever—"

"Please stop." She stepped over the threshold and faced him, the doorframe between them like a shield. "Thank you for confirming what needs to be done. Please text me if there's anything else. Good night, Jack."

She shut the door and leaned against it. Still breathing hard, her lips tingled from the kiss. But her heart hurt. She hated that she already wanted to replay the touch, cataloguing every moment and feel.

No. She pushed off the door and laid her laptop, almost forgotten in her arms, on the kitchen island. She opened her phone and added the date of the unbinding to her calendar app. In the notes, she typed: *He left once.*

She stared at the words for a moment, then bolded them. There wasn't anything to say he wouldn't leave again. This time she'd be sure to move on.

THE FAN from the air conditioning was the only noise in the cocoon of the car's interior. Jack loosened his hands on the steering wheel, his fingers having tightened with the tension in the vehicle.

In the four days since she'd closed her apartment door in his face, they hadn't mentioned the kiss or if she'd ever forgive him. Each day he'd shown up to run with her, but they hadn't made idle chit chat.

He stole a glance at Meredith. Mid-August sunlight poured through the windshield, painting her auburn waves with copper sparks where they draped her shoulders. Even with a scowl on her face, she was the most beautiful woman in the world.

She'd spent the entire thirty-minute drive watching the scenery whip by, silent except for the occasional polite nod when he offered water or asked about the air-conditioning. Now, as the sign for Brookvale Cemetery came into view, she sat even straighter, her palms braced on her thighs, as if preparing for an impact no seatbelt could soften.

Jack slowed and guided the car through the open iron gates. The cemetery spread out in front of them: buildings on the left, white and gray slashes of stone in row after row on the right.

He pulled into a spot in front of the first building and turned off the engine, making the silence between them deafening. Jack opened his door and heat slammed into him like a solid wall.

Meredith emerged a moment later, her gaze shielded by dark sunglasses.

"It's beautiful now, but a storm is forecast for later. We should miss it," he said in the hopes of starting a conversation.

She nodded but didn't answer.

They walked side by side through the parking lot. Meredith hesitated at the edge of the path that wound through the grave stones they were heading to. He waited, giving her that moment.

"It's so bright," she murmured at last.

He put his hand at the small of her back, offering his support, and let out a soft breath when she didn't pull away. "It's not going to stay that way, so we should continue moving."

Their shoes crunched on the pea-gravel path as they moved further into the cemetery. He hadn't gone to

Beatrice's funeral but he still remembered where all the Williams were buried. He'd accompanied Meredith and her cousins to the family plots more times than he could count.

The trees around the Williams's graves were tall, providing some shade. Elise and her sisters had arranged for them to be planted shortly after the funeral. Now their trunks were several times the size of Jack's forearms. The lowest branches, once easy to reach, even when Meredith was only seven, hung well overhead, blocking out the morning sun. Jack reflected on the passing years by the width of those trunks and the spread of those limbs. Two decades of missed birthdays, holidays, and empty dinner table chairs.

Meredith passed the graves of her aunts, uncles, and cousins, stopping at the last two stones: Thomas E. Williams, and to its right, Molly J. Williams. A sunflower engraved in Molly's stone caught the light.

Meredith drew a breath that sounded almost like a sob, but when Jack stepped closer, he saw her jaw locked tight. She crouched, brushing stray pieces of grass from the bases. Her fingertips grazed the letters as though committing them to memory.

"Except for Aunt Beatrice's funeral, it's been almost two years since I've been here," she whispered.

Jack said nothing, giving her space. He used the time to look around and refamiliarize himself with the area.

"As the years went on, I got on with life and avoided coming," she continued after a while, quietly, as if speaking to herself. "Staying away meant I could bury the guilt I felt about surviving." She traced the sunflower's petals with her finger. "I never actually forget, just push thoughts of them aside."

He wanted to tell her that guilt was a sign of love, not

failure. But platitudes were useless here. He crouched beside her and waited.

"I've been so caught up thinking about coming here for the unbinding that I didn't even remember to bring flowers."

Jack pulled on his magic, creating a bubble around the area to blur them from sight. Once safe from being seen, he conjured a large bouquet of sunflowers.

"Oh, they're so cheerful, just like Molly. She would have —" she choked on the last word as she took the flowers from him. She placed them in front of Molly's gravestone. "Thank you."

It was on the tip of his tongue to say he'd give her anything he could, but he didn't think she was ready to believe him. "You're welcome."

After a long moment, Meredith straightened. Her eyes were glassy, but no tears fell. "What do we need to do?"

"For the unbinding? Nothing. I just needed to reacquaint myself with the area. I'm good." He fell into step with her as she started back along the path. "How about I take you to lunch?"

"You don't have to do that."

Jack put his hand on her, getting her to look at him. "I know, but I *want* to. I want to spend time with you, Bubbles." She hesitated, so he tacked on, "Just friends having a meal together."

"Okay."

They were almost at his car when she spoke again, kicking a pebble, sending it skittering. "I shouldn't have gotten so caught up in my own life. I should've come sooner. And brought Mom."

"Guilt means you care. That's the part that matters. Your dad and Molly... you think they're tallying visits on some scoreboard?"

"They're gone, Jack. They're not tallying anything." She raked a hand through her hair. "But I am."

Her torment hit him like a blow to his chest. "Then start fresh. Come next week, or next month. Bring sunflowers, bring nothing. Talk, stand in silence. Just…show up. You already did the hard part today."

She nodded once, decisive. At the car she looked back once more to where they'd been. "All right."

Jack pulled onto the main road, the cemetery receding in the rear-view mirror. In just over a week they'd be back, then Meredith would be learning how to use her magic. After that Jack would have to fulfill his end of their deal, setting Meredith up on a date. He dreaded the task, but in the meantime, he'd use every moment he had to get to know Meredith again and show her that he was there to stay.

At a red light, he looked over at Meredith. She looked back, giving him a small smile, and for the first time since he'd come back into her life, he felt a fragile thrum of possibility.

CHAPTER TEN

eredith's hand trembled, visible to Jack even from a distance. The pan she held clanged against its companions as she pulled it from the cupboard to start dinner. It took everything in Jack to stay where he was on the stool at the kitchen island after Meredith had firmly told him she had things under control.

She'd tossed him some vegetables and told him to make a salad. Yes, tossed. Across the kitchen. She'd never been so casual before that she'd toss food around. That one action alone told Jack that Meredith was anxious. Or perhaps, this was one more way she'd changed over the years, and he'd missed it.

They'd met with the rest of the group at The Magic Plate earlier. The Emissary had arrived and been introduced to everyone, and plans were all set for the unbinding ceremony tomorrow. But instead of staying with the others for dinner, they'd come up to Meredith's apartment to eat. Meredith excusing herself from the family dinner had surprised everyone, even him.

Jack couldn't remember the last time he'd seen Meredith

this anxious, and she hadn't been exactly calm recently. It had been just over a week since they went to the cemetery, but her guilt wasn't the only thing they had to contend with. Elise's health was a main concern, and there was still the threat of whoever had attacked Meredith.

Jack ran with her every morning, and if she had to go out and he couldn't be with her, Damon was, or Ben assigned someone from the FBI to watch over her. Since Ben's FBI task force was made up of magics, he had the jurisdiction to assign people wherever he wanted. Rowena, Jo, and Reece all had protection as well.

Hopefully after tomorrow the spell would be broken and the W's could start using their magic.

"Shit!"

Meredith's curse pulled Jack from his thoughts. He was at her side in an instant. "What happened? Let me see." He reached for Meredith's hand but she pulled away.

"No, Jack, I'm fine, it's just a cut. I'll run some water over it."

Jack took a deep breath and forced his voice to remain low and calm. "Bubbles, please let me see. Your hand is dripping blood. I don't think water is going to be enough." He conjured a towel and carefully wrapped it around both of Meredith's hands as she clasped them together. Gently coaxing her over to the kitchen island, he nudged out a stool and helped her onto it. "Okay, let me see."

Meredith sucked in her breath when Jack unfolded the towel and peeled it away. The cut looked deep, but nothing was gushing so it didn't look like she'd hit an artery.

"The knife slipped."

"It's okay, I can fix this."

"You're a doctor now, Jack?"

"No, but all magics have some healing powers and I have a bit more than average. I've also studied and practiced healing." Jack used his magic to force cooling air over Meredith's hand to slow the flow of blood and clean around the injury. He met her gaze. "This might hurt a bit."

She bit her lip and nodded.

Jack used his magic to look into the wound. He could heal it, but healing was always painful, and he didn't want to hurt Meredith.

She sucked in her breath when he started to close one end of the laceration. He decided a distraction was in order. "The first time I woke from a nightmare was right after my mom and Charlie died. My father had never been the warm and fuzzy type." He scoffed out a harsh laugh at his own understatement and continued to seal Meredith's wound as he spoke. "But I wanted someone to talk to and figured my dad was grieving too so he'd understand. I reached for my bedroom's doorknob and felt an extreme pain, unlike anything I'd ever felt before."

He remembered the shock of it, so intense it felt like it was engulfing his entire body. The doorknob had seared into his palm, the fierce heat blistering his skin and jarring his senses. "The doorknob burned my hand."

"The scar on your palm? You told me it was grabbing the poker out of the fire when camping. Another lie." She tried to pull her hand away, but he didn't let her.

"I know." Yes, another lie. So many. All because he hadn't been able—or willing—to tell her about magic. Nothing he could do about it now. "It was a lesson from my father. He had spelled the doorknob to make sure I didn't leave my room at night. I was still too young to flash out of there."

"What did you do?"

"I healed my hand." The memory of him pulling his hand away from the doorknob was as seared into his brain as his flesh had been onto the knob. Cradling his hand with tears streaming down his cheeks, he'd made his way to the bed. "I managed to turn on my bedside lamp with my uninjured hand and even in the low light I could already see the blisters forming around pieces of missing skin. My hand had already started to swell."

Jack was almost finished with healing Meredith's hand; the distraction had worked.

"What did you do next? Could you call for anyone?"

"No, there was no one to call. I was twelve and didn't have my full powers yet, but I had enough." The pain had intensified and he'd feared he would pass out. He'd taken a deep breath and closed his eyes to focus on the wound from the inside to get a sense of the damage. It was the first time he'd ever looked at the inside of his hand. But even to his untrained eye, the scorched layers of skin didn't look right. Pushing his magic into his hand to cool the area, he repaired the skin by instinct, layer upon layer.

"I made two promises to myself that night. The first was that I would learn more about the human body so I could become a better healer." He cleaned her hand, careful not to disturb the newly healed flesh.

"What was the second promise?"

"That I would leave my father one day." He vowed he would never allow himself to be vulnerable and trapped by someone again. The first promise had been easy to keep. Even though healing wasn't his specialty like it was with some magics, he already had more ability than most. Then he studied basic anatomy and physiology to enhance even that.

As for the second promise, it came when he'd been sixteen. He didn't mention the third promise he'd made to himself—never to compromise who he was—because it didn't matter now. The damage had been done.

"Okay, Bubbles, that's it."

Meredith jumped as she looked at her hand. "Holy cow, you healed me. I didn't even notice and it's like brand new."

Jack held up his right hand and smiled. "I've learned a lot in the last couple of decades."

Meredith rubbed the rough skin on Jack's palm before she clasped Jack's hand in both of hers and brought it to her lips. She placed a small kiss over the jagged scar tissue.

Jack's cock hardened at her touch. He'd always reacted to her that way, and being around her but not being able to make love to her was killing him. He gently pulled his hand back. "Let's clean up and finish dinner."

They worked quietly side by side until dinner was ready and they opted to eat at the kitchen island.

"Jack, you mentioned that all magics have some healing power. I mean, my mom healed my concussion. But you said you had more than average. Does that mean some people have more healing ability than you?"

"Yes, some people are truly gifted in healing, just like others have different specialties."

"Like what?"

"Well, both magics and non-magics can have special talents. Just like someone excelling at music or sports, magics can have magical talents as well. They could be gifted at healing or have powers of persuasion or be able to see some of the future."

"Is that what the Emissary meant when she said you have unprecedented power? I think she said you have the ability to wield magic that no one has seen in decades."

Jack nodded and looked down at his empty plate. If only life was that easy. Have unprecedented powers, lead a council, and all would be fine. Sure, fine. But empty and lonely too without Meredith. He met her gaze. "Like I said, some people have special abilities, but every now and then someone has a bit of each specialty, like me."

"What can you do?"

"A lot of what others can do, like heal and flash, but sometimes faster. I can flash faster and farther than others."

Meredith furrowed her brows, what he thought of as her thinking face. "But that's not all, is it, Jack?"

"No, I get flashes of the future, but not usually when they concern myself. I am exceptionally strong, I can cast powerful spells, and I can persuade people to do things they might not want to do."

"That's it?"

He laughed at her innocence. "That's enough for now."

They had to get through the ceremony the next day. Then Jack had to set Meredith up on a date and hope she didn't fall in love with someone else because no amount of power could undo true love.

STANDING IN FRONT OF HER AUNTS' gravestones, Meredith wondered about the implications of what they were about to do. She knew they were there to save her mother, but the thought of disturbing the dead to pull something from them made her shiver.

"It's creepy, isn't it?"

Meredith turned her head and gave Jo a small smile. "Yes, but I think your mother would be okay with this."

"Me too. Ro, you doing okay?"

Rowena had come up on Meredith's other side and all three of them stared down at Lillian's and Beatrice's gravestones. "I'm a bit weirded out, but we need to do whatever we can to save Auntie Elise."

"And not just that, we'll get our magic back and be able to protect ourselves," Reece said, standing beside Jo. "Am I the only one who thinks having magic will be cool?" Reece bumped his sister's arm. "Huh?"

Jo chuckled. "Hmmm. I may have thought about it a time or two."

Meredith loved watching Jo and Reece interact, but sometimes jealousy popped up and picked at the healed wounds over her heart. She used to have a sibling too, but not just a sibling, a twin. Once you got past their almost identical looks, she and Molly were as different as night and day, but they had been close. Their father said they were the yin and the yang to balance each other out. Meredith was used to looking at the differences in her cousins, Reece so massive next to his petite sister. They had their own sibling yin and yang and made her yearn for what she'd lost.

Her cousins talked about all the things they'd be able to do once they had their magic back, but she only half-listened. She didn't look at them, instead keeping her gaze straight ahead. Her dad's and sister's graves were just to the right, but she couldn't think about them today. Her focus needed to remain on her mom.

A minute later a figure appeared on the other side of the gravestones. "Good morning." The Emissary nodded at each of them. "Ready?"

Meredith didn't think she'd ever be ready for this.

Reece chuckled. "As much as anyone can be to take magic out of their dead mother and aunt."

Another shiver coursed down Meredith's spine at the thought of what they were about to do—release magic from her aunts' bodies. If someone had told her a month ago what she'd be doing today, she would have referred them to Rowena for counseling.

Looking out over the cemetery, leaves flitted and floated above the ground in the light breeze. So beautiful and innocent, almost picture-perfect. But they weren't. They were green now, but already halfway to the colors that represented death, eventually to be welcomed back into the earth.

Nature was a cycle, and her mother and aunts had messed with it. They had taken a gamble and they'd lost. No one would ever know what would have happened if they hadn't spellbound their children. Just as they wouldn't know what would happen when they all got their magic back. They could only hope to save her mom's life.

How ironic. The past was supposed to provide insight and it was the future that was to bring the unknown. That was the way life worked. They'd all die eventually anyway, and no one ever knew when. Another gamble, the proverbial toss of the dice that was life.

As the Emissary gathered everyone together, Meredith pushed her morbid thoughts aside, and focused on the woman. After that, things moved quickly. The Emissary directed people to their required places for the ceremony.

Meredith's mom stood between the graves of her two sisters and the rest of them formed a circle around the three. Meredith and her cousins each had someone near them to guide the magic and to guard them in case something went wrong. Jack stood just behind Meredith and even without them touching, he gave her a sense of safety.

Bouncing on her feet while waiting for everything to start, all she wanted was for it to be over. She faced forward, watching her mother twist her hands together in front of her. It didn't bode well if her mom was nervous.

Jack wasn't in Meredith's line of sight, but she swore she could feel his calming presence. She'd have to remember to ask him later if that was her imagination. Could he really project his calmness onto her? Or maybe it wasn't magic at all. Maybe it was just Jack.

That thought had barely registered when the Emissary's

voice broke through the whispered chatter, bringing all conversation to a stop.

"I have placed a ward around the cemetery. No one will hear or see us." She raised her hands skyward. "Let's begin," she said, her voice loud and commanding. Her hands remained in the air, palms pointed toward where Meredith's mom stood in the center of the circle.

Jack, Damon, Ben, Frank, and Fiona, Damon's mom, followed suit.

Fiona's participation had surprised Meredith, but the Emissary said that Fiona was very powerful and somewhat of a seer.

The word *surreal* kept bouncing through Meredith's head. She didn't know what to expect. They were performing a ritual in the middle of a cemetery like they were characters in a movie.

She heard a noise from her left and turned her head to see the Emissary as she seemed to be pulling energy from the air. She was going to use it to suck the magic from her mom and aunts. At least that's what Meredith had gotten from the Emissary's explanation.

What started out as a low hum grew into a crackling bombardment of sound. The noises threatened to engulf all thought. It sounded like a battle between static electricity and crickets, each trying to drown out the other.

Too terrified to move, Meredith didn't cover her ears. The deafening noise reached a fevered pitch and the sky darkened like someone had suddenly turned off the sun. It was then she could see the energy stretched between the six pairs of hands.

It formed an enormous dome over everyone, stretching down to the ground and encompassing them all in a bubble of electricity. Suspended above their heads, the energy jumped between their hands, bouncing from one to the other in a frenzy of movement and light.

Struggling to focus against the barrage of sound, Meredith whipped her head back around and focused on her mother. That was when she saw the blackness. It wasn't smoke, she knew that instinctively, even though she didn't know how. It was thin at first, but within seconds it had thickened, engulfing the ground around them.

The smoke-like substance stretched up from her aunts' graves and poured out from her mother. The thunderous clatter and the blackness seemed to pulse along with the sounds, picking up speed and swirling amongst the graves. It snaked around Elise, starting to envelop her like a shroud.

"No!" The word ripped from Meredith as she reached for her mother, but the wind was too strong, and it pushed Meredith back. As the wind continued to increase in strength, she fought to stay upright. Currents of air came out of the graves, pushing the blackness outward and upward.

Meredith's long hair whipped around her, the ends stinging her face like little needles as they hit. The wind was crushing, pushing back against her as she tried to reach her mother. The blackness lashed at her face, obscuring her line of sight.

"Mom! Mom!" She struggled against the force of the wind, through the blackness and the wall of sound. There wasn't any evidence her mother could even hear her. The crashing turbulence and strange crackling sounds reverberated in the air, blocking out all other sound. She called to her mom anyway as she fought to move forward. The feeling of uselessness ate at her as she continued to fight, only to get nowhere.

The others around her weren't visible anymore. They were obscured in the darkness. Only glimpses of those closest to her were revealed when gaps opened in the swirling mass of blackness as it moved throughout the circle. The wind moved in waves as it tried to penetrate the dome of energy suspended above them.

They're coming! She heard Fiona, her words blasting inside Meredith's head.

Hold your positions! The Emissary's voice sounded in her head too.

Meredith still couldn't see anyone as the wind and blackness pushed against her with a pressure that threatened to take her breath away.

Then it did. She opened her mouth to scream as a ripping sensation tore through her body. It robbed her of the ability to speak or even call out.

She bent over, arms wrapped around her waist, and squeezed her eyes shut against the torment. A kaleidoscope of color played behind her lids as searing pain punched through her gut. Gasping for breath, she struggled to fill her lungs with air.

As she battled to breathe, pressure took over her chest. Sharpness lanced through her upper body and she fell to her knees. The torturous pain in her stomach became nothing in comparison to the excruciating agony threatening to rip her heart out of her chest. She hunched over, unable to move.

A thunderous crack pierced the air, followed by shouts.

Hold. He's fine, the Emissary said, her voice calm now inside Meredith's head. She didn't have the energy to care about what was happening around her, as the torment consumed her.

As fast as the pain came, it left.

She blinked. A tingling sensation coursed through her from her head down to the tips of her toes. It was unlike anything she'd ever experienced. Almost like a cooling breeze flowing within her, but not quite.

Then all conscious thought left her as she was tackled from behind and pushed to the ground. Jack lay on top of her, shielding her from above. His head tucked in close to hers, his arms circling around both their heads to protect them as best he could.

"Don't move!" he shouted in her ear, barely audible above the noises.

She lay still for what felt like forever—but was probably only moments—when everything changed.

The wind and the pulse of energy stopped.

No gradual end like the final strains of a song.

Just nothing. Like someone turning off the radio in the middle of a tune.

Jack rolled off her and popped up to his feet, bringing her up with him. Cupping his hand around the back of her neck, he gently tugged her into a fast embrace.

"My magic says you're fine—no bruises, no breaks. True?"

"I'm good." She rolled her shoulders, just to check. "Wait… Did it work? Why were the Emissary and Fiona in my head? What did they mean?" Her hands gripped the front of his shirt. He put his hands over hers, and she felt a calmness seep into her, as if Jack had given her his.

"We were attacked."

"By who? Are they gone?"

"I didn't think I'd get to you in time when the shield cracked. The minute I sensed the protective dome break—" He hugged her again.

She sank into his embrace just as a strange, undulating sensation rippled through her. Looking up at Jack, she saw the corners of his lips tick up.

"You feel that?"

"It's my magic, isn't it?"

His smile widened. "Yes, and it feels like it's reaching for mine."

"That's so coo—"

Her words were cut off as her cousin's scream pierced the air.

CHAPTER ELEVEN

*J*ack took her hand and hurried them over to where Jo crouched beside Reece, several others standing around him.

"Oh my god! Reece! What happened?" Meredith kneeled beside her cousins and took Reece's hand in hers.

The earth around Reece was charred black. Large dark patches covered the space, smoke still rising from the ground like a fire had ripped through the area, leaving only devastation in its path. The scorched surroundings made a stark contrast to the bright green grass on the fringes of the circle.

"Do something. Jack, please help him," Jo urged from beside her brother.

Jack, already kneeling beside Reece, had magically scanned his body. "Jo, he's alive. I can feel him breathing."

"Help! Damon's hurt!" Jack looked up when Rowena yelled. She was on the other side of what had been the circle.

"Fiona, go to Damon, I'll stay with Reece. He's fine for now." Fiona flashed to her son before Elise even finished her sentence.

"Jack, you go too. We'll stay with Reece. He's safe."

Jack nodded at the Emissary and flashed to Damon.

The ground by Damon looked the same as did it surrounding Reece. Large black burn marks ravaged the area, where only minutes ago lush grass had enveloped the ground.

Damon was lying down, but unlike Reece, he was conscious. Fiona was already tending to her son, and except for some gashes on his arms, he didn't look badly hurt.

"What happened?" Jack asked Damon, breaking the silence while keeping his voice low.

"I heard my mom warn us, then the dome cracked. I pushed to get to Rowena, but got hit by some of the energy from the collapse."

"He got hurt protecting me." Rowena's anguished cry cut through the stillness in the air. "If he hadn't—" Her voice broke on the last few words.

"Rowena, this isn't your fault," Fiona said as she finished healing Damon and sat back. "Until I got the vision moments before it happened, no one saw this coming."

Jack turned to Damon. "Did you get a look at who it was?"

Damon shook his head. "No. They came at us from the sides. When the Emissary told us to hold, I did, then rushed to Rowena."

"They're gone."

Jack turned to face Ben. He had almost forgotten that Ben and Frank were there. "Did you see them?"

Frank shook his head. "No. They cracked the dome, I'm guessing to stop the ceremony, and then hightailed it out of here. I don't know how they could have even seen us."

"They couldn't."

All heads swiveled toward the Emissary. "I think that's why they did so little damage. They somehow knew we were here, but couldn't see through the spell I cast. I think they aimed where they thought it would do the most damage." She gave a small smile. "It worked. Everyone is unbound and the lines on Elise have disappeared. But now we have a new problem—there's a spell on Reece."

The attack on Reece had overshadowed Jack's joy of a successful ceremony. "How is that even possible?" he asked the Emissary.

"I'm not sure. It would have taken someone very powerful." She looked down at Damon. "Are you alright?"

"Yes, I'll be fine."

The Emissary nodded at Damon and turned to Ben and Frank. "Let's get everyone out of here. Then we can assess the damage."

They had arrived at the cemetery in several SUVs since the W's couldn't flash. The rest of them drove to conserve energy for the ceremony.

Jack turned toward the vehicles when Ben held up his hand to hold him back. Frank and the others had gone ahead, but Fiona stood beside Ben. When the others were out of hearing range, Fiona said, "I saw something but it was hazy. I think there will be another attack."

Jack wasn't surprised to hear about her vision, or that it could get worse. "We'll protect them."

"They won't be alone," Ben agreed, "but like Fiona said, I'm worried about what more is to come. When the dome cracked, everyone tried to hold the protection, even though the spell was still pulling the magic from Elise and her sisters. I'm just glad it was enough."

Jack nodded. Partway to the vehicles, he tripped and had to catch himself as a premonition suddenly flooded him.

Fiona stopped him with her hand on his arm. "You had a vision." It wasn't a question. Jack looked at her and nodded.

"I don't get them often, so something may have triggered

it." Jack didn't enlighten them as they continued walking. He wondered if he had the same vision Fiona had, only clearer.

He would keep it to himself until he knew more.

In the vision Elise lay on a bed, but she didn't look asleep. She looked dead.

CHAPTER TWELVE

Meredith hovered around the door to Jo's bedroom while Jack made sure Reece was taken care of. When Jack held his hand out to her, she hesitated for only a moment. She put her hand in his and he wordlessly led them upstairs to her apartment.

He physically locked the door before waving his hand at it and telling her, "I've placed a no-disturbance spell on the door."

They stood in awkward silence for several moments. Meredith shivered as a chill overtook her. She wiped the back of her hand across her eyes as they welled with tears.

"Come on," Jack said quietly as he picked her up and carried her over to the couch, settling her in his arms.

Warmth surrounded her, like hot blankets straight from the dryer. Probably Jack's doing and she was thankful. They sat wrapped in each other's arms for several minutes, her tears wetting his neck.

He didn't talk, only hugged her tighter as grief swamped her. When her tears finally stopped, she took the tissues he held out to her and wiped her face. "That actually happened, didn't it? We were attacked… Damon… Reece…" She choked out the words as her tears started anew.

Jack didn't offer any platitudes, didn't say everything would be okay. He'd always been pragmatic. Didn't tell her everything would work out. Didn't promise her sunshine and rainbows. The Emissary hadn't been able to identify the spell on Reece or say what the long-term effects would be.

He ran his hand along her hair and back and continued to hold her until her tears subsided.

When she tilted her head back to look up at him, he could have easily leaned down and kissed her. Being with her and holding her was what he'd wanted for so long, but not like this. Not when she'd been crying and was worried about those she loved. And not when she might regret it later because she hadn't forgiven him.

He lifted her off his lap, and when she was steady, stood and took her hand, pulling her with him. "Let's get showers —they'll help us relax. I'll use the spare bathroom." He reached for the hall closet. "Are the extra towels in here?"

"No, don't open that," she said as her hand shot out, covering his as he grabbed the closet doorknob.

"What's in here, Bubbles?" he asked slowly, trying to stop the smile pushing at his lips. She did that to him—made him want to smile. But right now might not be the best time. He had a feeling he knew what was behind the door.

"Nothing," she said, biting one corner of her bottom lip.

"I'm not buying it. I'm going to open this door."

"No, don't. Please don't," she pleaded with him. "It's not bad, it's just messy, and I don't want you to see it."

She tried so hard to be perfect and he wished he could show her how perfect she already was. Guilt ate him, knowing he hadn't helped her insecurities by leaving her without a real explanation. "Really? A mess? That's what you're worried about?"

"You don't get it. I don't *do* mess. I'm neat and organized." She continued to worry her lip between her teeth.

He brushed her lip with his thumb, releasing her poor flesh from its teeth prison, and then bent forward, brushing his lips lightly against hers to soothe the tender flesh. "It doesn't matter if you're neat or messy. But you've got me curious and I can't *not* see this so-called mess now." This time he couldn't stop the grin that was teasing at his lips.

"I don't want you to think less of me. Uh… even if we're just friends."

He ignored the "friends" comment. It wasn't what he wanted in the end, but it was a start. "Nothing you could do would make me think less of you, Bubbles."

He watched as she rubbed her hands on the front of her jeans, capturing her poor lip between her teeth again. She was so cute when she was nervous, but he didn't think she'd appreciate the sentiment and kept his expression neutral. "I'm certainly not going to think less of you because you have a messy closet."

"Okay, but I warned you."

He pulled the door open, then jumped back. Two massive balls narrowly missed hitting him and several boxes toppled to the floor.

"Ah, wow… um, you weren't kidding."

"I told you."

"What is that? Why do you have such big balls?" He chuckled to himself at how dirty that sounded.

She laughed and swatted his arm with the back of her hand. "They're exercise balls and good for posture. I didn't have anywhere else to put them and they don't match the décor, so I don't like leaving them out."

He flicked on the light switch he'd noticed on the outside wall beside the closet door. Wary of more flying objects, he took a tentative step inside.

The place was packed, except for one narrow strip obviously left for maneuvering through the mess, but it only went in a few feet. Boxes, clothes, small appliances, and odds and ends lay everywhere. It looked big enough to have been a massive walk-in closet at one point, but there was definitely no walking happening now.

He didn't care. It was just a mess, even though it was not characteristic of his Meredith. He turned to her.

Her bottom lip was once again a prisoner and her eyes were swimming with tears she hadn't let fall. "It's just a closet," he said softly.

"No, it's not."

"No?"

"It's a representation of my life." She lost her battle and the tears began to fall.

It was his undoing. He took her into his arms, holding her snug against him and wrapping her in his warmth. After kissing the top of her head, he held her for a few moments longer.

"Meredith, it really is just a closet."

When she looked up into his eyes, her lashes were damp. "Sometimes, when I can't handle things, I shove them away. Anything I didn't know how to deal with, I put in that closet. When I designed this apartment, I made sure it had two enormous walk-in closets. I knew I'd need an extra one, although I had hoped this time would be different."

She took a step back and wiped her eyes with her sleeve. "After you left I was so lost and scattered. It took me a long time to get my shit together and I wanted to be uber organized, but there are just too many things to handle each day. By the time I get home at night, I don't have enough energy to make any more decisions about anything. If I come across something I don't want to deal with, I shove it in the closet. It's been worse over the last month. Now I wish I could shove myself in the closet."

She didn't say the last month had been worse because of him, but they both knew the truth. Her tears almost did him in as she looked up at him, her eyes bright.

"Maybe that's why my mom and aunts could so easily brainwash me. I was willing to shove away the painful thoughts of my dad and sister. And I did it again after you left."

Leaving Meredith had hurt her far more than he realized. He'd believed what he did was for the best. But maybe it was only best for him. He pushed the thought aside for now. There'd be time to deal with it later.

"They didn't brainwash you. It doesn't work like that. Yes, you may not have wanted to deal with the pain of losing those you loved, but no one does. And that wouldn't affect the binding spell. You were just a kid. You didn't stand a chance against your mom and aunts. And even though it seems wrong now, who knows if it really was? Maybe they were right to bind you. Maybe you weren't ready to deal with the losses and your growing power."

"Maybe... But I'm an adult now and I should be able to handle things better." She looked toward the closet at the discarded stacks of clutter and mess. "I'm not supposed to be this way," she said as she turned back to him. He opened his arms and she stepped back into his embrace.

"What way? Messy?" He felt her nod against his chest. "Says who?"

"Uh, me?" She looked up at him, her eyes still bright with unshed tears, and he felt his love for her grow a little more when he didn't think that was possible. His love for her felt like a physical ache in his chest that needed to be let out. With the binding gone now, they could be together, but he still had to earn her forgiveness. Confessing his love now would be too much pressure for her, so he kept the words to himself.

"Watch." Turning her in his arms to face the closet, he directed his magic inside. Boxes and bags floated away from the walls, suspended in the air. Next, shelves appeared, first on one wall, then on the opposite, and finally at the back.

Jack then turned his magic to the bags and boxes. They floated to the various shelves and neatly arranged themselves. "Better?" He looked down at Meredith's wide-eyed expression.

Leaning against the door jamb, he watched as she walked into the closet and ran her hand along the shelves. There must have been hundreds of times in the last eight years he could have made her life easier, but instead he'd thought of only himself.

And here he was doing it again—coming back because *he believed* it was time for them to be together. He would just have to prove to her that they were meant to be.

JACK SCANNED THE CLEARING. They were in the field the Emissary had brought him and Meredith to in the soul jump. Only an hour's drive from Blue Mountain, it was remote enough they shouldn't come across anyone.

Jack expected that the soul jump here all those weeks ago wasn't just a way to get Jack and Meredith alone and undistracted. The Emissary was a sneaky one, planting the seed for him to use this field, without him even knowing.

The clearing was safe. Perfect for what they needed. They erected a barrier with a spell as added protection to ensure the high levels of energy being used didn't alert anyone to their presence. Some magics had the ability to pick up high energy draws from miles away. Their shields were on the edge of the forest and gave them plenty of room to work.

Jack looked around at the women, each one ready to learn how to use their magic. They'd hoped Reece would join them, but after three weeks, he wasn't any better. Jack didn't want to wait any longer. Although, if it wasn't for the safety of the W's, he'd wait a long time. The longer it took for Meredith to practice her magic, the longer it would be before he had to set her up on a date.

Oh, his arrogance. He'd been so sure he'd have won her over by now. But she still didn't trust him. At least he got to spend time with her. He would be the one teaching her, and he also asked Damon and Javier, an FBI agent, to assist with the lesson. Damon said he was fully recovered and would help Jo, while Javier would teach Rowena.

"Let's spread out." After confirmation from everyone, he took Meredith's hand and walked her out into the middle of the field, away from the others. He held her hand as often as possible, needing to touch her. Most times she didn't argue.

"You ready?" Jack turned to Meredith, her eyes wide as saucers.

"Yes," she said, then shook her head no. "I'm nervous, Jack."

"I know. But it'll be fun." He gave her a wink and positioned himself behind her.

"But what if I can't do it? What if I'm terrible or I hurt someone? I want to learn, but I've always been a bit clumsy." Her words tumbled together one after another, barely leaving her time to breathe.

He laid a kiss on the top of her head, something she probably didn't even feel, but he couldn't stop touching her. "We've already been through this. Your magic is in you. You're just learning to control it. After you know how, you decide when to use it, remember?" She nodded. "You need to trust me. And yes, you'll probably be terrible at first."

"Hey." She shifted sideways enough to backhand his arm.

Jack chuckled, the teasing eliminating the heaviness of the moment. "You're just learning. No one is good at something the first time. Learning magic is no different. As for hurting someone… You won't. That's why I'm here."

She took a deep breath, letting it out on a long exhale. "Okay, let's do this."

"Remember, your magic is a part of you. You call it forward to control the energy around you. The more experience you have, the easier it will get. It'll become second nature."

"What if I'm really mad at someone and just wish for them to go up in flames?"

Jack forced himself not to laugh, knowing how scary this must seem to her. As an adult, she'd seen firsthand some of the horrible things magic could do. This scenario wasn't like when a child embraced their magic while they grew, only seeing the joy and possibilities as they experimented and learned. "It doesn't work like that. It's also why we don't come into our full powers until we're in our teens, and sometimes later. You can think things all you like, but it's a conscious effort to use your magic essence to pull energy into yourself then use the magic to project it or conjure something or create a spell. Even when you get to the point you can do it almost instantly."

She nodded but didn't look convinced.

Moving closer to her back—but not touching—he placed his hands on her hips and leaned down to whisper in her ear. "Close your eyes and concentrate." He could feel the warmth of her body, as if it was reaching out to him, but he kept some space between them or he'd be a goner. He had to focus. "Do you feel something inside your chest? Like butterflies?"

He felt Meredith suck in a breath and tilted his head to the side to see her squeezing her eyes shut tight. "Relax. Blow out a breath." She did as he instructed and it wasn't long before she relaxed and was copying his breathing.

After several minutes, he sensed the essence of her magic stirring because of a lack of experienced subtlety on her part. "That's it, now feel the energy around you. Gather it and push it forward, imagine it punching through you."

"Will it hurt?" Her voice came out hushed, as if afraid to disturb her magic.

"No, it will feel more like an adrenaline rush."

He felt her magic stir again. This time stronger. "That's it," he said again, quietly in her ear. "Now push it forward."

A rush of energy burst from her, lighting up momentarily. Barely discernible in the brightness of the early morning sun, it was like the flash from a sparkler before it was quickly snuffed out.

"I did it!" She whipped around and pounced on Jack, wrapping herself around him. She would have taken them to the ground if his reflexes were slower. He stepped back to steady them.

"Yes, you did." Her grin was contagious, and he felt his body start to heat as she rubbed up against him. He pushed some magic through his system, cooling himself to ensure his jeans didn't get too tight in the crotch. It was a trend when he was around her.

"Okay, try again," he said, turning her around before he let himself get carried away. It would probably be easier if he put more physical distance between them, but he didn't want to.

She continued to practice, with Jack providing direction. The more she focused, the stronger she became. Quickly she would surpass the toddler stage, but middle school level was still a ways away.

About forty-five minutes later, Jack called a break and chuckled as he heard calls of relief coming from the group—from both students and their instructors. Watching someone struggle wasn't any easier than being the one doing the struggling. Calling forth magic could be draining, and it would be even more so for the newbies.

Jack conjured a cotton blanket and laid it on the ground. He hadn't spoken yet when Meredith flopped down ungracefully. He couldn't help the smile that stretched across his face as he handed her a mug of cold water.

"Thanks." She took a long pull of water before turning to him. "I've seen you conjure a bottle of water before. Why the mug?"

He shrugged. "I thought having a handle might be easier."

"So…" Her eyes glinted with mischief. "Can you conjure M&M's?"

Jack didn't miss the hint in her voice and held out his hand. A pile of colorful chocolate lay in his palm.

"Thanks," she said, holding her hands in a cup for him to pour the pieces into. "I'm in heaven."

"Well, pleasing you is easy. A blanket, cold water, and chocolate." She'd always been easy to please. He'd just forgotten.

She popped a couple of chocolates into her mouth and closed her eyes, savoring the taste. "Mmm, yum."

Meredith leaned back on her arm and turned toward her cousins. "Jo, Rowena. Ask for chocolate."

"What?"

"Huh?"

Jack heard Damon and Javier chuckle, followed by exclamations of excitement from the women.

He settled on the blanket beside Meredith.

"What was it like when you and Charlie were learning to use your magic?"

The question threw him for a moment. She didn't ask what it had been like for her and Molly, but maybe she wasn't ready yet for the emotions that those memories could bring. He wasn't sure how to answer and took some time to find just the right memory to share.

"Sometimes, it was just like this. Our mom would conjure us a treat and teach us how to do the same. Charlie's favorite was strawberry ice cream." Jack lay down on his side, propping his head up on his hand.

"I remember one time when we were about six or seven. I woke up in the middle of the night and Charlie wasn't in his bed. I found him in the kitchen surrounded by piles of ice cream." He chuckled at the memory. "Charlie hadn't quite mastered conjuring a bowl, and I don't know why he didn't just pull one out of the cupboard and conjure the ice cream into it, but he didn't. There were little piles of ice cream on the counter and the kitchen island, all starting to melt and ooze across the surfaces and drip down onto the floor. And there was Charlie, with a spoon in each hand, trying to eat as fast as he could."

"Why did he have so many piles of ice cream?"

"That's what I asked. He said he was trying to make a new flavor and couldn't get it quite right."

"What did you do?"

"I was a seven-year-old boy. There was only one thing I could do. I grabbed a spoon and started eating. I mean, I couldn't leave that mess, could I?" he said as he looked down at her.

"Of course not. That wouldn't have been a very supportive brother, would it?" Then her eyes darkened and her expression sobered. "I wonder if Molly and I would have been like that. I'd like to think we were. But maybe we weren't since I was the far more serious one."

"Say it isn't so," Jack teased.

"Ha-ha." Meredith playfully swatted his arm. "I have so few memories of my sister. I love that you gave me the bubble memory back."

They lay side by side for several minutes. Neither spoke, both lost in their own thoughts and enjoying the lingering warmth of the fall morning.

"I can practically hear your gears turning. What are you thinking?" Jack asked.

"About the big picture."

"What do you mean?"

"I'm not really sure how to describe it. Being magic, I guess. I don't understand why so many people have had to die and why there is so much evil tied to it."

"It's not a magic thing, and that question is as old as time."

"What do you mean?"

"It's a people thing, whether they're magic or non-magic. There will always be people who want more and are driven to get it. Most of the time it's actually a good thing. If there weren't people who were driven to have more and be more, we likely wouldn't have all the technology and things we have today. Like what you're doing. Making old buildings better and creating a community. Wanting something better and being able to control it is normal. It's only when it's used for evil that it becomes a problem. History is full of people who wanted to control others."

"Yeah, you're right. I guess I'm just really focused on magic people right now so I forgot about human nature in general."

"A new council will eventually ensure that magics are kept in line, like a justice system. It's just been a long time without any magic control in this part of the world. It will take some time to get rules and processes in place."

"I haven't thought much about a new council. Just focused on the unbinding. You think we should start a new council?"

Jack sighed. "I know deep down we need one. I'm just not sure I'm the right person to co-lead it."

Meredith raised a brow in question for him to explain.

"For the longest time I equated the council with evil, but that was the thinking of a young boy, and I held onto it for too long. I also thought the council corrupted my father, but it didn't. It was the other way around."

"Then why aren't you the right one to co-lead it?"

He paused and looked down at her. She was so beautiful, inside and out. "I'm not sure about taking on more power." He stood and offered a hand to pull her up. "Come on, let's practice some more," he said and disappeared the items they'd used.

"Nice change of subject, but I'll let you get away with it for now." She elbowed him, laughing.

He was thankful she was willing to move on. "Let's try something else for a moment." *Meredith.* He threw her name into her head telepathically.

Meredith took a step back, her eyes wide. "Oh wow. You talked inside my head. Like the Emissary and Fiona did at the cemetery?"

Jack couldn't help but grin. "Yes."

"How'd you do that?"

He walked behind Meredith, like he had earlier. This time, he pulled her back to his front. Touching. Loving the feel of her against him. "Close your eyes," he whispered in her ear. "Just like before, pull your energy into you and feel your magic essence. Think about one word and imagine sending it to me." He sent words to her again and again in an effort to let her feel what it was like.

She confirmed each time she heard him, but couldn't talk to him in the same way.

"Ugh!" Meredith threw up her arms ten minutes later. "Why can't I get this?"

"It's okay, Bubbles. You'll get it. I probably shouldn't have asked you to try that yet. It's an advanced technique. Let's try something simpler."

They practiced for another ten minutes before Jack called a halt to it.

"I want to flash," Meredith said.

He hesitated. "That's pretty advanced. Most magics can't flash until they come into their full magic after puberty. By then they've been using magic for years."

"I get it, but if I can flash, I can get out of dangerous situations."

"Let me check with Damon and Javier." Jack walked over to the other couples. Meredith followed.

"Hey. Meredith wants to flash, what do you think? Too soon?"

Rowena bounced on her feet like an excited child. "Yes, let's try that."

Jo shrugged. "I'm game."

"Sure," Javier said and looked at Damon.

"Since we're out in the open and there aren't any walls to worry about, I think they'll be okay," Damon agreed.

Jack still wasn't sure, but maybe he was just being overly protective with Meredith. A part of him wanted her to know how to use her magic, but another part of him wanted to wrap her in thick cotton to keep her safe. Oh, the irony. He'd left her eight years ago because she didn't have her magic. Now, he was worried because she did.

Jack, Damon, and Javier spent the next few minutes explaining how flashing worked, what to expect, and giving some demonstrations.

Looking around the field to see what could possibly trip them up, Jack decided to have them face west. There were no nearby trees in that direction. "Let's try flashing in this direction. You can start with a flash of about twenty yards, just like we showed you. Who wants to go first?"

Rowena put up her hand like she was in school. "I will!"

Everyone chuckled and Damon gave Rowena one last bit of instruction about keeping the distance in her mind, then he stepped back.

"Here goes nothing," Rowena said. She disappeared.

Jack laughed when he spotted her about twenty yards away, jumping up and down. "I did it!" she shouted.

"Flash back," Damon yelled to her.

Rowena came back, a grin splitting her face from ear to ear.

"Me next," Jo said and then she was gone. "I did it, too!" she yelled from her spot in the distance and then flashed back. "That was amazing!" She laughed and turned to Meredith. "Mer, your turn."

"Okay."

Jack took Meredith by the shoulders and gently turned her toward him. She'd been so excited before and now she seemed anxious. "You don't have to do this if you're not ready."

She pulled back and straightened her shoulders. "I'm good."

"Remember to keep the distance in your mind."

Meredith nodded. "I know." Then she disappeared.

Jack waited for her excited yell and looked at the spot where Jo and Rowena had both landed in their flashes. Meredith didn't appear.

CHAPTER THIRTEEN

With a quick look at Damon and Javier, he nodded and flashed. Jack couldn't wait before following Meredith's flash signature or it would be too late. He caught a faint glimpse of it. She'd stopped about a thousand yards away. His feet hit the ground, but she wasn't there.

He flashed again and found a new signature. This time it was headed east. Guessing Meredith tried to course correct, Jack took off after her. He could feel sweat pepper his hairline and break out on his back as the seconds ticked by.

Jack landed too quickly and caught himself, straightening up. Meredith was gone again. Without waiting, he took off after her signature, but there was no sign of it. He stopped and tried again. Then again. His breathing picked up as panic set in. He had no idea where Meredith was.

Flashing back to the others, he looked at them expectantly. "Meredith?"

There was a chorus of no's as everyone shook their heads. "Let's look for her the non-magic way," Javier said. "I'll walk east. Rowena and Jo, the two of you stay together and walk south."

Jack pulled in a deep breath and calmed himself. "Good idea. Damon, you take north and I'll take west."

Damon and Jack set off after the others. Pulling in some energy, Jack sent magic to his eyes, sharpening his vision. He looked toward the tree line ahead, continually scanning from left to right as he jogged forward. "Meredith!" He called her name every couple of minutes and paused to listen.

After being greeted by silence for twenty minutes, Jack thought about heading back to the others to get more help. He could flash back but thought it best to stay on his feet to scan his surroundings as he went, worried he could miss her if he flashed.

Jack turned to head back when something to his right caught the sunlight as it poured through an opening in the trees. He moved closer. Light reflected off the high-visibility strip of a person's running shoes.

"Meredith." He flashed to her, kneeling beside her prone form. Saying her name again, he scanned her magically for any injuries. He found nothing except a small goose-egg sized lump on her forehead. After he healed the lump, he pulled Meredith into his lap. Supporting her head and neck with one arm, he brushed her hair off her face. "Meredith. Wake up, Bubbles. Please wake up. You're safe." He continued to caress her face and mutter reassurance.

"Jack? What happened?"

He let out a huge breath as if emptying his lungs of all the worry and panic from the last half hour. It all flowed out of him as he looked into her beautiful hazel eyes.

"That's what I was going to ask you." Jack stood with her in his arms and walked toward the clearing.

"I got lost."

"Okay. Let's get back to the others."

She struggled to get out of his grip. "I can walk."

"I know you can, but I just need to hold you for a minute. You scared the fuck out of me."

Once they were clear of the forest, Jack pulled in as much energy as he could control at one time and flashed them two hundred yards. Even with his immense power, he couldn't flash with another person for more than a short distance. Another fifty yards and he was spent. The others became visible in the distance and he walked the rest of the way. "The others aren't much farther now."

"Jack, put me down, I'm okay."

He lowered Meredith to the ground and wrapped his arms around her, burying his face in her hair and breathing in her scent. His hands trembled when he held her. Sucking in a deep breath, he pulled back and looked into her eyes, but he didn't have the right words to convey what he felt without scaring her.

He'd watched her from afar for so many years, always worried about her. Now that he was close, he could have lost her. She could have flashed over the side of a cliff. Not that he'd seen any cliffs in the area, but his mind imagined all types of illogical danger. He kissed her forehead, then took her hand and started back toward the others.

They walked in silence for a minute until they could see Rowena and Jo up ahead. All three women hugged when they reached each other.

Jack looked around. "Where are Damon and Javier?"

"Here," Damon said, coming up behind Jack. Damon pointed to the trees to the west. "Javier is just coming out of the tree line." Javier joined them a second later after he flashed the rest of the way.

"Mer, what happened?" Jo asked.

"I got lost." Meredith let go of Jack's hand and crossed her arms over her chest. He wanted to take her hand back and reassure her that everything would be okay, but he expected it wasn't going to be that easy.

Rowena put her arm around Meredith, giving her a squeeze. "You always were a bit of an overachiever, sweetie. Did you just go too far?"

Jack kept his eyes on Meredith as Rowena's teasing fell flat and Meredith looked down.

"I'm not sure. I pictured twenty yards in my head like I was supposed to but I ended up in the forest. Then I turned around to go back, but because I didn't know how far I went the first time, I didn't know how far to go back."

"Meredith, when I came out of the forest, I saw Jack carrying you. Were you hurt?" Damon asked.

"Not really." Meredith shuffled her feet and looked down again. "When I tried to get back, I flashed against a tree. I must have knocked myself out."

Jo laughed, then covered her mouth with her hands. "Sorry, Mer."

She shrugged and turned to Jack. "Whether I was successful or not, this still counts as a lesson."

Damon frowned. "Counts for what?"

Jack closed his eyes for a brief moment as Meredith explained their deal. Damon and Javier were going to have a heyday teasing him about this.

Damon slapped Jack on the back, forcing him to stutter step to avoid falling on his face. "Should we book another lesson for tomorrow?" Damon asked, not trying to hide the amusement in his voice.

"Yes. That work for everyone else?" Meredith asked.

Jack felt his future slipping away.

CHAPTER FOURTEEN

Meredith put her keys on the table by the door, kicked off her shoes, and paced to the balcony. Then paced to the kitchen. Then across the living room. Her apartment was a good size, but not big enough for her to expend the kind of energy she had buzzing around inside her.

During her back and forth, Jack leaned back against the living room wall and crossed his arms, watching her. She turned toward him now. There were small crinkles at the corners of his eyes like he was trying to hold back his amusement.

"You said it would be like an adrenaline rush… and it was. I thought after my little flashing disaster I wouldn't feel much, but… My god… When I think of what magic can do for me, I feel giddy. I'm super excited for tomorrow."

She clenched her fists and shook them in front of her chest, as if the feeling of euphoria was about to burst free. "If I could bottle this feeling and then use my magic, I could get an entire week's worth of work done before breakfast."

She thought of many of the tools she used on a daily basis

—spreadsheets, charts, tables—to work and make her dreams come true. Now she had something better than a color-coded Gantt chart; she had magic. She could flash to meet someone and never get stuck in traffic. Could she save time and money by not hiring contractors? Just a wave of her hand and the tiling was done? No more long waits for material. Another wave and she'd have it? She'd be able to shave hours off a workday.

"Here."

She stopped and looked over at Jack. He held out a bottle of water. She took the water and drank down half of it. "Thanks, I was parched. Did you read my mind?"

"No, not a specialty of mine." He grinned and held up his hand as if to ward her off. "And even if I could, I think I might get lost."

"Ha. Funny man." Meredith gave him back the bottle and watched it vanish. "Yes! I could do that too." Energy coursed through her as she continued to think of what she'd soon be able to do.

A deep laugh rumbled out of Jack, something she didn't hear from him often. She gave him a side-eye, but kept her tone teasing. "Are you laughing at me?"

"Never. Just enjoying your enthusiasm."

"How about enjoying something else?" She gasped as soon as the words were out of her mouth. Jack's lifted brows said he was as surprised by the question as she was.

Maybe she shouldn't have been. They'd been brewing for a while. They'd fallen back into their old camaraderie that had once been so comfortable, and with it had always come sexual tension. Maybe that was what she was feeling. Not a rush from the magic at all, just plain old lust from being around Jack.

Neither of them made a move as they eyed each other.

She'd had sex with a few guys since Jack, but no one had

sated her the way he had. She studied the man she once thought she would marry. He'd always been the hottest guy she ever knew. That hadn't changed. He might even be hotter now. There was a maturity in his face that hadn't been there before.

She took a step toward him, his gaze never leaving hers. Her fingers itched, like they needed to reach out and run through his hair, with his long strands on top and shorter ones on the sides. Then she would brush along the stubble on his jaw, following them up with her lips.

Her hand lifted as if it had a mind of its own, but stopped midair. Would giving in once really hurt? They could have sex—expend the energy buzzing through her—then get on with their lives. Besides, the sex couldn't really be as good as she remembered. It didn't matter that his kisses were better than her memory recalled. Sex couldn't possibly be better too. Could it?

There was only one way to find out.

She put her hand on his chest. "Jack?"

"Hmm?"

"Wanna fool around?"

His brows lifted again. "You forgive me for leaving?"

She ignored the question. "I want sex. I'm buzzed. Want to put this energy to good use?"

His lips twitched up at the corners. "You want to use me for sex?"

"Yes." She didn't see any point in lying. She wanted to believe that she'd have sex with Jack, it wouldn't be as good as it was before, and she'd finally be able to move on.

Jack leaned down as she went up on her toes. Their lips touched. Almost a brush, like testing the waters.

It didn't last long. The adrenaline from using her magic and the longing for Jack that had built up over the years all coalesced in a tsunami of lust.

Their mouths crashed together as if this would be the last time their lips would meet. The kiss was long and perfect, and was over far too fast.

Jack pulled back first and looked into her eyes, a question in his own.

All the years apart disappeared in a second and she could read him like a book. He wanted to know if she was sure, and to know where this was going. "I'm only promising this. Fuck me, Jack."

For a brief moment, he seemed to hesitate. Then he grasped her hips, lifted her up, and she wrapped her legs around his waist. They continued to kiss as he walked to the bedroom.

He tossed her on the bed so she landed with a bounce, huffing out a laugh. She sat up enough to tug her shirt off and toss it on the floor. While meeting his gaze she reached behind her back and undid her bra. She lifted her chin in his direction as she added the bra to the shirt. "Your turn."

Jack's gaze intensified as he looked at her. "My pleasure."

His clothes disappeared. It took only a second for Meredith to notice them neatly folded on the chair in the corner. She crooked her finger at him. "You'll have to teach me that trick. Later."

He crawled up over her. When her lips met his, she felt a rightness, like coming home. But she didn't live there any longer. She had to remember that.

His kisses trailed along her jaw. "You are so beautiful," he whispered, and her heart started to melt.

No. He couldn't make love to her like he used to. She wouldn't give in and pretend like the eight years apart hadn't happened.

This was sex. Scratching an itch. "Now, Jack. Not slow. I need you. I need to feel you inside me. Now. Fuck me."

He lifted his head as he dropped his hips, rubbing his hard length against her soft folds.

"Yes," she said, the word coming out as a guttural groan.

Jack held out his hand and a condom appeared in his palm. He sheathed himself in seconds and a heartbeat later he pushed into her wet heat.

"Fuck, Bubbles. You feel even better than I remember."

There was a hunger on his face that she knew mirrored her own. "Move, Jack."

And he did. A torturous, slow glide in and out.

She reached forward and gripped his ass cheeks, trying to tug him forward. "Faster. I need more."

"No." He grunted the word as he grasped her wrists in his hands and moved her arms to her sides. She raised her eyebrows in question, but he didn't respond. Grabbing her by the hips, he pulled out and flipped her over on to her stomach, tilting her hips up. Instinctively, she raised herself on to her hands and knees.

"Yes!" she ground out, lowering her torso onto her forearms, her butt in the air.

She didn't want slow and easy. She wanted to feel alive. He gripped her hips and entered her in one smooth stroke. They both let out a groan at the unbelievable sensation. The position stretched her like a tight glove around him.

He started to move, creating a rhythm that was steady and fast, and she pushed back, needing him deep inside her. His balls hit her on each stroke, and she cried out in pleasure.

Jack leaned over her, his chest pressed up against her back. "You feel incredible. I'm not going to last long and I want you to finish with me." She felt him lift off her back, one hand gripping her shoulder for better leverage to drive into her as he snaked his other hand around to her core and found her bundle of nerves. She was soaked. When he rubbed her clit, she let out another guttural groan of pleasure, grinding down into his hand while pushing back onto his cock.

Their scents mixed in the air, wild and animalistic. Only a few seconds later, she felt her legs stiffen, an earth-shattering sensation coursing through her as her core squeezed him tight and she exploded around him.

She continued to tremble. Her orgasm seemed to go on forever as he placed both hands back on her hips and drove into her four more times. He yelled her name as she felt him let go.

He held her hips for a few moments more as they both continued to pant, trying to get their breathing under control. She turned her head and flashed him a grin. "Almost better than magic," she teased.

He blew out a breathless laugh. "Almost? I'll have to up my game." She felt him trail kisses along her lower back before gently pulling out. He disappeared the condom and crawled back up the bed, pulling her back flush against his chest, one arm under her head and shoulders, the other over her waist. She wiggled her butt against his groin, eliciting a moan from him.

He squeezed her waist. "Give me a few minutes to recover first."

She chuckled and he pressed a kiss to the top of her head before snuggling her in tighter. Those little kisses on her head and forehead reminded her of what they'd once had—a love Jack had walked away from.

JACK KNEW the moment the sexual high faded and Meredith came back down to earth. She stiffened for a moment, then sat up, swinging her legs over the side of the bed.

He had no regrets about what they'd done, but he expected Meredith would. She claimed it was just sex, but she wasn't built that way. She was fighting her feelings for him and he feared she'd win the battle.

She pulled on his shirt and left the bedroom. Using his magic, he conjured and donned a pair of sweatpants. He found her in the kitchen staring into the fridge.

Meredith looked over her shoulder at him. "Did you always know?"

Gently moving her to the side, Jack shut the fridge and pulled out two plates from the cupboard. "Let me." He conjured two large sandwiches with chicken, cucumber and avocado. Her favorite.

Her eyes widened. She looked at him, the sandwich, and then back at him. "All those times you had lunch waiting for me, did you conjure it?"

"It depends on what it was. Sandwiches? Sometimes. But anything with spices I cooked so the smells permeated the apartment."

"Thanks. This looks great."

They sat at her kitchen island with their sandwiches and he conjured them glasses of water. After a few bites, he put his sandwich down and conjured some napkins, passing one to her. "Earlier, you asked me if I had always known. Known what?"

"What? Oh… right. Known what we are. Since the unbinding, I've started to have flashes of things. I think they're memories that are returning, but I'm not sure. They feel different than when you gave me the memory of the bubbles."

"It could be because that was my memory. Yours is likely long gone because you were so little when it happened. But, yes, I always knew, and you did too. No one has to tell a lion or a bear what they are, or even a child, and quite frankly they probably wouldn't care. There are some things that are just innate and other things you learn."

"Do you ever wish you weren't magic?" She shivered slightly and he sensed how important his answer was to her. He expected she was still struggling with accepting how different she was from what she'd believed most of her life.

She ran her finger along her water glass, pooling the droplets of condensation. His eyes followed her finger and he didn't respond for a while, wondering how to answer. "Not me, but there have been times when I've wondered if magics shouldn't exist at all."

"Do you wish that now?"

Jack wasn't sure where she was headed with this, but when he returned to Blue Mountain to win her back, he vowed he would always be truthful with her. "No. I get frustrated with abusers, but there are those that will take advantage or do horrible things in all walks of life. It isn't something exclusive to magics. I enjoy what magic can do for me."

"You never talked about your family. I know your mom and your twin died in a car accident, but I don't know much else about them." A sly smile crawled up her lips. "Except that Charlie liked strawberry ice cream. Tell me about them?"

He leaned down again, this time to stall, and gave her a slow, heated kiss, then rested his forehead against hers, taking in her scent and warmth. He waited several heartbeats to see if she'd protest or say it was just sex. When she didn't, his hope that she would eventually forgive him climbed.

"I was twelve when my mother and brother died."

"You told me before, but I don't remember it or them, even though we were friends. I always thought I'd blocked all memories from that time... Do you think my mom took them?"

"Probably. My family died a couple of months before

yours, when you still had your magic. My dad said they died in a car accident, and I've never doubted it, but sometimes I wonder how much of an accident it was."

"Why do you say that?"

He never liked talking about his family, but if he wanted a future with Meredith, he would have to be open. "Let's get comfortable." He waved his hand over the dishes and they disappeared.

She frowned. "I liked those dishes."

Jack grinned. "I washed them and put them away."

"Really?"

She stood, but Jack took her hand. "Trust me, they're there. You can check later," he said, tugging her toward her living room. Whether she wanted to admit it or not, he still knew her.

He lay on the couch, pulling her down beside him. Wrapping one arm under her, and like he had before, snuggled her into his side. Her head found his shoulder and her hand settled on his bare chest, just like it used to.

He picked up several long strands of her hair resting on his chest right below his chin, letting it slide through his fingers. It was easier to get this out without looking her in the eyes. "I was supposed to be with my mom that day, not Charlie. I think my dad intended to kill me instead, and my mom was just collateral damage."

"How could a parent do that?" She sounded incredulous, but she'd never really known his father.

"Being the leader of the North American council wasn't enough for my dad. He wanted more power, wanted to be revered. And he didn't like it, even at twelve, that I would stand up to him. It wasn't just that he wanted the magic box, he was obsessed with it. Believed himself to be superior to everyone around him." Jack paused for a moment, the memories bombarding his consciousness. "People have choices, and like anything, magic can be used for bad. We saw that the day of the unbinding. I think my father believed no price was too high for him to get what he wanted."

"I wish we didn't have that in common. The loss of our twin."

He trailed some kisses along her forehead. They both understood what it was like to lose so much. There were no words to make things better. Even time couldn't heal all wounds.

She traced the intricate soccer tattoo on the left side of his chest. "You told me that this is a memorial tattoo for your mom and Charlie. Is that true? Lately, I… I want to question everything you've ever told me."

Her fingers continued to move along the tattoo, heating his flesh. "I'm not going to lie and say I never omitted anything when talking to you, but I did my best to always tell you the truth."

He looked down at the tattoo, such a part of him now that he usually forgot it was there. Flames and lilies interwoven with each other surrounded the black and white soccer ball. He'd been so proud when he'd gotten the ink.

"Yes, it's a memorial tattoo, but the part I left out was that it's embedded with magic. It's a tradition for many magics to get a tattoo in remembrance of a loved one. It's to serve as a reminder and to keep them close. It's also symbolic in that you bleed for your loved one.

"My father wouldn't allow me to get a tattoo after my mom and brother died, said I was too young. So I got it when I left home at sixteen."

He paused for a moment, his hand lazily running up and down her arm. His voice came out quieter and deeper when he continued, the emotions clawing at him. "It's not a tattoo in the traditional sense. It's still done with a tattoo machine, and still hurts, but magic is woven in with the ink and embedded in the skin. There are only a few magics who can create these types of tattoos. When the tattoo is being created, magic is pushed into it and the design is imbued with a memory or a feeling of your loved one."

He put his hand over hers, flattening her palm on top of the tattoo. "When I lay my hand on it, I can still hear Charlie's laughter."

"I can feel warmth." She sighed, moving her arms to envelop him in a hug.

A look of hope crossed her features. "Is it too late for me to get a tattoo for Molly and have a memory embedded?"

"I'm not sure, but we can check. You deserve to have that."

She lifted up and leaned over him, melding their lips.

Keeping their mouths tangled together, he rolled them over, his body covering hers. His hands roamed her body, caressing her face and moving down over her breasts, kneading them. Lowering his head, he hitched up her shirt at the same time, exposing her bare breasts. He first took one nipple and then the other into his mouth. He sucked and teased, her moans the only sound breaking the silence that hung suspended around them.

Holding out his hand, he retrieved another condom and suited up. She didn't remind him that this was just sex, and he didn't bring it up.

Flipping her over him again, she steadied herself with her hands on his shoulders and straddled his lap. He lifted her and slowly lowered her onto his length. All the urgency from their earlier session had vanished. They both moaned at the glorious sensation.

Rocking up into her, he used his hands to entice her pleasure, setting a slow rhythm and going deep. When he sensed her starting to tighten, he increased his pace. She continued to bathe his cock in her heat as he took her mouth in a kiss to end all kisses. Her muscles squeezed around him as he followed her over the edge, feeling her milk him of everything he had to give.

Later, after they'd thoroughly washed each other in the shower, taking their time, he felt her start to emotionally withdraw once more. He'd pushed her too hard and now he feared he would pay for it by sending her on a date with another man.

CHAPTER FIFTEEN

"Sweetie, what're you doing out here all by yourself? It's a little cool for September," Rowena said as she pulled up a wrought iron chair beside Meredith's, wrapping her arms around herself. "Is it Jack or magic?"

Meredith looked at her cousin and offered her a small smile. "Both."

"A lot to think about."

Meredith heard the back door of the restaurant slam shut. Yup, Jo was right on time.

"Hey, ladies. What's up?" Jo swept the seat of a chair clean with her sleeve before sitting down.

Meredith dropped her head, her chin touching her chest. She took a deep breath then looked at her cousins. "I've been going down memory lane."

"How far back?" Jo asked.

"All the way."

"Oh, shit. This needs wine." Jo shoved out of her chair and headed back to the restaurant.

Wine was Jo's answer to most situations women had.

Shopping? Wine. Heartache? Wine. Bitchiness? Wine. Not that she was complaining.

"Come on, let's take this inside where it's warmer," Jo called over her shoulder as she opened the restaurant's back door.

In the three days since she and Jack's adrenaline-inspired sex, she'd done nothing but think. She'd been trying to avoid Jack as much as possible for fear she'd want to jump his bones. As much as she wanted to be with him, she still couldn't trust him. Sure, she knew about magic now, but she still felt he should have found a way to stay with her back then. True love doesn't leave. Jack left.

Now, she wished he would again. Avoiding him had become a full-time job. He showed up to run with her every morning. She enjoyed their time together and then wanted to kick herself for it.

Lucky for her they didn't talk about much except running and some of their favorite things. She felt like a hypocrite, telling him to leave while craving his presence. Jack also texted her during the day, sending her random comments and memes, and in the almost two months since he came back, he'd become a permanent invitee to the family dinners her mom continued to host.

"It smells so good in here," Rowena said as they walked in the kitchen, pulling Meredith out of her thoughts.

The kitchen staff were preparing for the dinner rush as Meredith moved around them to wash up at the sink. She stood back as Rowena took her turn. Her cousin had a peacefulness about her. There was something so good about Rowena that being around her made Meredith want to be a better person. The way she treated people, how she looked at different situations, how she listened. Just being in her presence calmed Meredith and let her push some of her confusing thoughts to the back of her mind.

By the time they were cleaned up, Jo had a bottle of wine open and was pouring three glasses.

"Why is your shirt wet?" Meredith raised her eyebrows at her cousin.

Jo looked down at her shirt as if she was remembering how it happened, then grinned up at Meredith. "I tried conjuring the wine first."

"Without a glass?" Rowena asked and Meredith bit down on the corner of her lip, trying not to laugh.

"Very funny." Jo rolled her eyes. "I used glasses, but I guess my aim was off."

Each with a glass in their hand, the three of them crossed to a back room off the kitchen and locked the door. They settled at an old, small prep table with four wooden chairs that had been shoved in the corner of the room.

Leaning forward, Rowena took a fortifying sip of her wine, then blurted out, "I don't want to go back to my job in Denver, I want to stay in Blue Mountain." Letting out a big breath as if the declaration had taken everything she had, she sank back into her chair. A defeated look passed over her features before she took a huge gulp of wine.

"That's fantastic! What's the problem?" Meredith asked.

"That's great, isn't it?" Jo asked at the same time.

Rowena sighed again and took another drink from her glass. She would answer in her own time, thinking through her answers before she spoke.

Jo leaned forward and topped off the still nearly full glasses before settling back in her chair. Meredith hoped the restaurant was stocked with wine because they were going to need more.

Resting her glass on the table, Rowena met her gaze and then Jo's. "I worked so hard to build my clientele list and make a life for myself in Denver, but being back home has made me realize how much I've missed it."

"You can build a practice here," Jo said.

"I get that, but it will be hard walking away from my practice there. It's just that… I miss you guys. I want to stay here with you and learn more about my magic. I was even thinking of changing the direction of my practice. I don't know if there are many psychologists who specialize in working with magics, but I could. This way I could help them with problems in all aspects of their life, not just the non-magic ones that a non-magic practitioner could." Rowena sounded out of breath as the last words spilled out in a rush.

Sudden guilt weighed down on Meredith when she realized she'd been so caught up in her thoughts about Jack, she'd forgotten her cousins were going through their own changes as well. "I'm happy you figured that out, Ro. And I'm happier you're staying."

Meredith snugged her chair in tight to Rowena's side and pulled her cousin into a fierce hug. Rowena's shoulders heaved as she gave in to her tears. That was all it took for Meredith's own dam to break.

She swallowed past the lump in her throat as Rowena's quiet sobs continued to pull at her heart. The last two months had been hard on all of them, especially so soon after Beatrice's death. And now with Reece injured.

Meredith didn't know how much one family was expected to endure. "I'm glad you're finding your way," she whispered into Rowena's hair.

Jo pulled her chair over to theirs, burrowing in close so they were all touching knee to knee. They sat wrapped in each other's arms, holding tight and forming a triangle. The three of them stayed like that for a while.

For so long everyone had been holding strong, supporting each other year after year, through death after death. They had lost mothers, fathers, sisters, brothers, aunts, uncles, cousins, and friends. So much death. The list was endless. It was no wonder her mother and aunts had bound the remaining children, trying to keep them safe. Meredith pulled back and tugged a tissue out of the box on the table. "I get it now."

"Get what?" Rowena used her sleeve to wipe the tears from her cheeks.

"I finally get why our mothers bound us. I thought I got it before, but I didn't... not really. Grief overshadows everything. Now multiply that many times. That's what our mothers faced. No wonder they tried to prevent any more loss." Meredith couldn't say that she would have done any different if she had been in their shoes.

Meredith looked at her cousins as she tried to figure out how to phrase what she wanted to say next. "I'm embracing my magic, but I'm not so sure about co-leading a council."

Jo leaned forward, her forearms on the table. "Because you have to do it with Jack?"

"Exactly. I don't trust him. I'll eventually find someone else to love, but just being around him is hard. And how will I be able to love someone else when I'll be working with Jack and constantly reminded of what we once had?" Meredith hated herself for focusing on Jack and not how lucky she was. She had a great business, fabulous cousins, and she still had a parent. She couldn't imagine what Jo must be feeling with the loss of her mother still so new and Reece suffering, maybe even dying, from an unknown spell. Rowena had lost both her parents and siblings. Meredith silently reprimanded herself for being a miserable bitch.

"Watch this." Rowena held out her hand, palm up, in front of the others. "I love learning about magic. This is small, but totally cool—I can make tissues. Javier taught me."

Three tissues appeared before their eyes, one on top of the other. With her other hand and a slightly self-deprecating smile, Rowena plucked one up at a time and handed it to each of her cousins before taking the last one for herself.

Rowena wiped her eyes and nose and then looked at her cousins. Meredith expected her hazel gaze was as puffy as Rowena's and Jo's, but it didn't matter. This was her family.

Jo playfully elbowed her cousin. "What else has Javier taught you?"

Rowena bumped Jo back. "Nothing, we're just friends." Rowena focused on the crumpled tissue in her hand and it disappeared. Turning her gaze on the other two tissues, they disappeared as well, snapped right out of Meredith's and Jo's hands.

"Another good thing. Now, no more ewwy, snotty tissues laying around," Rowena said with a laugh.

"Okay, that was cool, but watch this." Jo looked at the table and an enormous jug of wine appeared on the edge. "Oh shit!"

Three pairs of hands reached for the jug, catching it before its weight toppled the table. Their laughter followed, lightening the heavy mood in the small room.

Jo didn't miss a beat. Her brows drew down in concentration as she tried again. This time the cup of wine was no bigger than a thimble. "Shit, I can't get this right!"

Meredith still didn't have flashing right, but how hard could conjuring liquid be? "Let me try!" She concentrated on the table and three ceramic cups the size of shot glasses appeared, each one filled with dark amber liquid. "Woot woot! Drink up, ladies! To making booze!" she toasted as they each downed a shot. "Oh wow," she said through a cough. "Way too strong."

"Uh, yeah a little strong, but still good," Jo said, shaking her head after swallowing the shot. "My turn again." Jo stared at the table in concentration. This time the cup was larger, but still a far cry from the size of a wine glass. Her eyes sparkled as she stood up and grabbed her first attempt at making wine in the enormous jug with both hands and took a big swig. "Oh, that wasn't bad. I will not be defeated!" she declared, putting the jug back on the table. Jo concentrated again and this time a vase full of wine appeared. "Shit!"

Meredith covered her mouth with her hand, trying to contain her laughter, but lost the fight. Rowena joined in and soon the two of them had their arms around their middles. Meredith's ribs hurt from all the laughing.

Cups and glasses were soon crowding the table. One after the other appeared as Jo tried again and again to perfect her wine conjuring. Meredith got up and began moving some of the cups to the counter on the back wall, fearing the small table would soon collapse under the weight.

Rowena chuckled as she helped move more. "Jo, I think we've got enough."

"Start drinking," Meredith said through her laughter. They each grabbed a cup, touched the beverages in a toast, and downed the contents in one go.

As they drank, Meredith picked up the earlier thread of their conversation. "Rowena, if you want to talk about anything, please come to me. I'm sorry I've been so inside my own head. We've learned the hard way that we don't know what's going to happen tomorrow. You have to grab onto life." Meredith wondered if she was being a hypocrite. Jack was back, but she wasn't grabbing onto him with both hands. Well… she certainly had three days ago. She snorted at her own joke, then let the thought dissolve in her alcohol-induced haze.

"I know you're right. It's just that everything has been so overwhelming lately."

"Okay, Mer, that's what has Rowena's panties in a knot. Why were you stewing? Jack?" Jo asked.

Meredith looked at Jo and then Rowena. "Yes. I can't trust him."

"Could you again?" Jo pushed another wine glass toward Meredith. "Mer, you pretty much just told Ro to grab life by the balls. You need to do the same. Life has no guarantees."

"Jo's right." Rowena leaned over and squeezed Meredith's leg. "Why aren't you taking your own advice? I think if you look deep inside yourself, you'll figure out how you truly feel about Jack."

And there laid the problem. "I know how I feel about Jack. I don't trust him. But we have a deal. I had to have two magic practice sessions and then Jack would set me up on a date with a magic guy. I've had my lessons. The ball's in Jack's court."

"I'd always been so sure you and Jack were going to be married some day. Even after he left." Jo snorted out a laugh. "You were the one who made everyone play prince and princess when we were little. Are you sure you want to look for a new Prince Charming?"

At one time, Jack had been her knight in shining armor—ha. Jack Knight, her knight. He'd been her everything. Then he'd crushed her. Moving on hadn't worked, but now she knew why.

Did she want to look for a new prince? No. "Yes. The reason I was never attracted to any of my dates was because they weren't magic. Now, I'll find *the* one."

"If you say so." Jo wiggled her eyebrows at Meredith. Chances were Jo would continue to push because she'd always liked Jack, but at least she was willing to give her a reprieve for now.

"Okay, back to the drinks. Let me try, but first drink more so we've got some room." Rowena passed a cup to each of her cousins and took one for herself. Another salute and they downed three more glasses of wine. Too bad they hadn't figured out how to disappear the glasses yet.

All eyes were on the table as Rowena tried her hand at conjuring. After a few seconds, a huge brick of chocolate landed on the table with a thunk, sending cups of wine crashing to the floor.

Three pairs of eyes looked at the broken cups and their spilled contents on the floor and then at each other. They burst into laughter.

"I'll get a knife to cut the chocolate," Rowena said, rummaging through the drawers below the counter. "I'm not ready to try my hand at conjuring sharp objects yet."

"Good idea." Meredith grinned as she conjured three more shot-sized cups. "Scotch! Come on, drink up!" She reached for her own cup.

"Ugh! I think you need to practice that one, Mer. It tasted like rot gut," Jo said.

Before long there were flakes of chocolate and empty cups littering the table, counter, and floor. They conjured every kind of liquor they could think of.

"Oh, practicing is good. That last one had a kick to it." Meredith stood up and then sat right back down. "Shit. I think I'm a bit tipsy."

"Me too!"

"Me three!" Rowena said and then her eyes became as big as saucers. "Uh oh!" She hiccupped, which started another round of laughter as all eyes swiveled to the men standing in the open doorway.

Jack stood off to the side of the door frame, Damon and Javier beside him. All three men looked amused. "Having fun?" Without waiting for an answer, Jack turned to the other two men. "Should we help them out so they won't feel the effects of this in the morning?"

"Sure, why not?" Damon said and lifted his hand as Javier and Jack did the same.

Meredith felt a cool sensation rush through her body and the fuzziness in her head disappeared like a cloud being blown away on a windy day, leaving a clear blue sky. She stood and looked at Jack. "What did you do?"

"We flushed your systems so you won't have a hangover in the morning."

Jo stood and stared at the men, ignoring her chair that clattered to the floor behind her. "Holy shit! You mean I can drink wine and not worry about hangovers?"

Jack shrugged. "To an extent."

Jo clapped like a little kid being told she could have as much ice cream as she wanted. "Yay! Another reason to love magic."

The men crowded into the small room and shut the door behind them. Damon reached for one of the closest cups on the table. "What have you got?" He took a drink and made a grimace. "Well, it's not the worst. Jack, remember that time…"

Meredith listened as Damon and Jack went down memory lane. Memories she could have been a part of if Jack had told her the truth. And never walked away.

Now that Jack was back, he'd slotted himself right back into her family. If she fell in love with someone else, could she finally relegate Jack to the friend-zone and still be around him?

Yes. Because she didn't see any other choice. She couldn't be with someone who could casually walk away from her. Then believe he could just waltz back in.

CHAPTER SIXTEEN

When their little party in the prep room broke up, Damon and Javier both flashed away. Jo strolled out right after them, going to check on Reece, marveling at her newly wine-proof metabolism.

Jack ushered Meredith out, saying he'd help Rowena clean up the mess. Meredith swept past him with an airy "Saturday, Jack. Don't forget," before she left through the back door of the restaurant.

Only he and Rowena remained and he shut the door, giving them privacy.

A faint smell of chocolate floated in the air, competing with the scent of wine as Rowena emptied the glasses and cups into the small stainless-steel sink.

"Rowena," he said, getting her attention. "I've got this."

Jack directed his magic over the sink, table, and floor, vanishing all evidence of the debauchery that had taken place.

Rowena flopped into a chair. "Handy… Wait, if you could do that, why didn't you just say so? Why did you tell the others you'd help me?" She straightened, hazel eyes narrowing with suspicion. "Jack Knight. You wanted to get me alone because you've got something up your sleeve, don't you? And I don't mean a magic trick." She snorted at her own joke, then sobered. "What are you up to?"

Jack pulled out a chair, turned it around and straddled it, resting his arms on the top. "I need a favor."

"I have a feeling I'm not going to like this."

"It's about Meredith."

Her expression softened, but only a fraction. "I wouldn't have guessed anything different. So?"

Jack dragged a hand through his hair. "You know about the deal Meredith and I made?"

"Yes. The one I can't believe you agreed to."

There were moments Jack couldn't believe he'd agreed to it either. "I didn't have a choice if I wanted to be around her and earn her trust back."

"And how's that working for you?" she asked. She sounded just like he expected she would in her psychology practice when checking in with a client she thought had made the worst decision ever.

"I guess that depends on how you look at it. I've got her a date. A colleague of mine. He's magic and everything she asked for."

Rowena let out a small snort. "And now you're worried."

"Terrified. He's an FBI agent and is a stand-up guy. If I didn't find someone who met Meredith's criteria she'd think I wasn't serious about our deal. Then she'd *never* trust me."

"I sympathize, but… Jack… you got yourself into this."

"I know. But, I'm determined to earn her forgiveness."

Rowena snorted again. "By having her fall in love with someone else?"

"No, of course not. But I couldn't back out." He exhaled. "So I'm making it a double-date."

Rowena's brows shot up. "With whom?"

"With me." He held her gaze. "And you."

Silence stretched. The sounds of the kitchen staff preparing the evening meal could be heard through the door. Then Rowena laughed, almost like a giggle erupting from her. "You're crazy—and not in the clinical sense—in the this-is-a-harebrained-idea sense. You want me to play chaperone while you torture yourself watching her flirt with another man?"

"I hadn't exactly looked at it like that. Years ago I would have told you that I wanted her to be happy, and would have loved to see her find someone…"

"And now?"

"I don't want her to love anyone but me. I can't break my word, Ro. But I also can't stand aside and let her fall in love with someone else. Mike's a good man, and he really does meet her criteria, so I need to be there."

"Why me? Why not have a real double date?"

"Because I don't want to date anyone else. Plus, it would send the wrong message to Meredith."

"Good point."

Rowena sighed. "And you figure I'm neutral enough not to be threatening."

"You're her cousin and my friend. She trusts you. I trust you." He grinned. "And I'm not a horrible date. I swear. You'll have a good time and get a good meal out of it."

"We own a restaurant."

Jack knew he'd won her over, but continued to play the game. "Consider this a change of pace."

"Fine." Rowena studied him, the way he expected she would do to the stupid-decision-making client. "Jack, you realize this could backfire. Meredith could think you're trying to control the situation… again."

"I'll tell her tomorrow morning. When I sing Mike's praises." He managed a faint grin. "Besides, you can always help mellow her out with wine if she's angry, since you're both expert at conjuring the stuff now."

"So true." Rowena leaned her forearms on the table and gave him a piercing stare. "Some conditions."

"I should have known. You are Meredith's cousin after all. Okay, I'm listening."

"One: full honesty. She knows exactly why you asked me —no secret manipulations. Two: no pouting if Mike gets dessert privileges."

Jack couldn't hold back a wince, but nodded.

"And three—" Rowena poked a finger into his chest, sparks crackling. "If Meredith ends the night upset because you couldn't handle your jealousy, I will make sure Javier or Damon teach me a spell to sour every cup of coffee you drink. Forever."

He swallowed a laugh. "Deal."

For a heartbeat, relief coursed through him. Maybe the double-date was reckless, but he couldn't stand by and do nothing.

They both stood and Rowena reached for the light switch. "Jack?"

"Yeah?"

"She still loves you." Compassion glimmered in her eyes. "But love isn't the big issue anymore. Trust is. Earn that back, and the rest will follow."

She flicked off the light and moved past him, waving to the kitchen staff as she left. For a moment, Jack stood in the doorway in the dark. Hope and dread waged a war in his chest, both equally strong opponents.

Saturday would be here far too soon. One evening, one promise, one more test of how much pain his heart could take. He thought of his apartment and flashed, ready to plan a double-date.

MEREDITH TOLD herself she wasn't making a mistake. The nervous flutter in her stomach was just a normal reaction to anticipating something new. Meeting someone new.

She'd been on dozens of dates and this one shouldn't feel any different. Yet it did. All day she'd tried to convince herself that it was the anticipation of meeting someone who she might actually click with. And that it had nothing to do with Jack coming along on the date with Rowena.

When Jack first mentioned the double-date, she'd run through the gamut of emotions. Anger at Jack's audacity to intrude. Pride for not letting Jack back out of the deal. Excitement for meeting a potential partner. Dread at sitting through an intimate dinner with a man while having Jack by her side. Thankful she'd have an ally in Rowena, and lastly, sadness because the only person she'd ever wanted was Jack and now she couldn't trust him.

She also wondered if her mistrust had become a comforting blanket. But if someone broke trust in the way Jack had, should they ever be trusted again? The answer should be no, but lately it didn't feel quite as cut and dried as it had for years.

Jack had arranged for a car to pick up her and Rowena, saying he and Mike would meet them at the upscale Bistro where he'd made reservations. Since she didn't know Mike and Jack said he didn't want to pressure her, meeting them would be best. Meredith wondered if he had something up his metaphorical sleeve. Strategy and tactics were his strong suit, but she let it go. She was trying not to question everything Jack did. It wasn't easy. Once burned and all that.

The bistro was one Meredith had heard people raving about and she'd been meaning to try it. So, no matter what happened during the evening, she would at least get to experience a new restaurant.

It sat halfway down a quiet street, its brick façade softened by string lights that glowed against the early evening dusk. A charming hand-painted sign swung above the door. Inside, low lighting and exposed beams gave the space a cozy, but still elegant, feel. A hum of jazz in the background and the scent of multiple spices blended into a fragrant bouquet greeted them, reminding her of The Magic Plate.

The entire atmosphere seemed romantic—perfect for a first date. Perfect for a double-date with your ex? Maybe not.

Rowena leaned into her side. "It's going to be fine," she whispered.

Before Meredith could respond, a hostess stepped forward to greet them. "Welcome to the Brick Row Bistro. Do you have a reservation?"

Meredith smiled. "It's under Jack Knight."

"Right this way, please."

She followed the hostess, with Rowena right behind her, to a table in the back, next to a large stone fireplace. Meredith noticed Jack first, dressed casually in slacks and a button-down shirt that might seem ordinary on anyone else, but he wore it with a presence. Like everything else he did.

Her date, Mike Hendrix, stood beside Jack, but the moment he saw them approach, he came around the table to greet her. Like Jack, he was tall, and judging by how he filled out his dress shirt and dark jeans, muscular. His hair was cropped close to his head, his nose straight and his jaw chiseled, showing a dimple. Overall, he was a good-looking man.

"Meredith." Mike held out his hand to her. "I'm Mike Hendrix. So glad to meet you. Jack has spoken highly of you over the years."

His hand was warm in hers, with just the right amount of pressure in his grip. She resisted looking over at Jack to ask what he'd said about her. "It's nice to meet you too."

SHE INTRODUCED ROWENA. Mike held out a chair for Meredith and took the one across from her. Jack did the same for Rowena, putting the two cousins beside each other. A server arrived and they ordered drinks.

Meredith picked up the leather folder containing the menu, as the others did the same. The selection wasn't vast, but everything looked delicious.

Mike looked over the top of his menu. "Have you been here before?"

She smiled at him. "No, but I've heard great things about this place."

"Same. It all looks good, but I'm just not one to pass up a good steak, so I'm going to have the bison."

Meredith grinned. "I expect you won't be alone in that choice. Right, Jack?"

"You know me so well." Jack's gaze practically smoldered, making Meredith's blood hum with lust.

Shit. She'd brought attention to Jack and not her date—she almost face-palmed herself. Turning back to Mike, she focused all her attention on him. "How long have you been in the FBI?"

He didn't seem bothered that she and Jack were so familiar with each other. "Five years. I joined a year after I finished my degree in criminology."

"Your parents must be so proud of you."

A shadow passed across Mike's face. "I think they would have been. My dad died when I was ten and my mom a few years later."

"I'm sorry. I lost my dad young too, but I still have my mom."

Mike looked at both her and Rowena. "From Ben, I know a bit about what happened in your family. Something horrible we all have in common." Mike waved his hand, as if shooing a fly, but she expected it was magic. His next words confirmed it. "Some protection, so we can talk freely. So… tell me, how're you enjoying practicing your magic?"

Rowena nudged Meredith's shoulder, a teasing note in her voice. "You want to tell him about the tree or the wine and chocolate fest?"

Meredith felt heat slide up her neck and groaned. "I'm never going to live that down, am I?"

"Nope, not the tree incident. It will go down in Williams family infamy, but since I was part of the fest, maybe."

Mike looked between them, then turned to Jack. "This sounds like something I've got to hear. You know what they're talking about?"

Laugh lines appeared at the corners of Jack's eyes, and he seemed to loosen up for the first time since they'd arrived. "I do. Let's start with the tree. It was their first—"

Their server arrived to deliver their meals. Once everyone had taken a few bites and exclaimed how perfect everything was, the waiter left and Mike told them he would keep the barrier reinforced.

Right after that Jack grinned at Meredith and looked at her date. "Mike, thinking way back to when you first started to experiment, did you ever flash into anything?"

Looking amused, Mike glanced at Meredith. "The tree incident?"

If the flashing-tree incident was one of those stories that was going to be brought up for years to come, there wasn't any point in being embarrassed. She smiled and shrugged.

"As a matter of fact," Mike continued. "When I was about nine, I thought I could flash out of my tree fort." He held up his arm, showing a six-inch scar running down the back of his forearm, and winked at Meredith. "We've all been there. I think the wine and chocolate fest sounds much more interesting."

Rowena flicked her blond curls out of her face. "Oh, it was. It started with Jo—our youngest cousin—trying to conjure wine. The chocolate came later after we were already three sheets to the wind." Rowena gave a small snort-laugh and continued the story.

At times, Meredith and Jack chimed in to offer their opinions, and Mike asked questions. During one part of the retelling, Rowena embellished with dramatic hand-flails and laughter spilled around the table.

Through the entire meal, Jack listened, joined in the conversation, and added gentle jabs that made Mike chuckle rather than bristle. Jack never once showed jealousy or looked threatened by Mike's presence.

As they were finishing their main course, Meredith remembered she was supposed to be on a date with Mike. Instead, it felt like four friends just having a really good evening out. She enjoyed Mike's company, and even found him attractive, but like all her other dates, she didn't feel the same as she did with Jack.

Her eyes kept sliding over to the man who had once been her everything, and she had to tell herself to focus on the conversation.

Halfway through dessert, Meredith's gaze snagged on a stranger standing near the bar—an older gentleman with thick hair and a still-sharp jaw in an expensive suit. Something wasn't right about him, although she couldn't pinpoint what that was. His features wavered for a moment like the buffering of a video.

With Mike and Jack talking about running, Meredith nudged Rowena with her elbow. "Do you know him?"

Rowena followed her line of sight. "No, but he seems kind of smarmy."

The man noticed their scrutiny, smiled—a polite, all-teeth smile—and lifted his crystal tumbler in a silent toast.

Ice slithered down Meredith's spine. She turned to Mike and Jack, who were still chatting, and waited for them to finish. It was probably nothing, but her gut was telling her otherwise.

Both men stopped talking and turned to her, Jack's features in a scowl. "What's wrong?"

"I… do men ever glamour themselves when they go out?"

Mike chuckled. "Sure. Anyone feeling like they need a little extra might use one. Why?"

"There was an older man across the restaurant, and something didn't seem right." She looked across the restaurant to where the man had been standing, to see the space empty. "He'd been standing by the bar."

"Did Ben mention the attack?" Jack asked Mike. When he nodded, Jack stood, dropping his napkin on the table. "We still don't know who ordered it. I'll just take a look around."

Rowena stood as well. "I'll go with you. We can pretend to be using the restrooms."

Mike rested his forearms on the table, leaning toward Meredith. "You okay?"

She flicked her gaze to his. "Yes, just spooked for a moment. I don't know why."

"You've just gone through something big—it's not every day someone learns they're magic and how to use it. And after the attack, it's understandable that you're cautious."

"I guess." Meredith liked Mike—truly. He was interesting, kind, respected her opinion and was a good conversationalist.

If Jack wasn't by her side as a constant reminder of what they'd once had, the chemistry between her and Mike might grow and she'd fall for him. But in reality, every comparison between Mike and Jack sharpened Jack's appeal.

He left you, her heart protested. *He didn't fight for you. But then you didn't fight for him,* the devil on her shoulder said. She thought of last week's adrenaline-inspired sex and everything she used to love about Jack. His ability to know what she needed, like her closet organization. How he protected her, like at the cemetery. How he made love to her. And every little thing he did that said he was thinking about her. If only she could convince her heart that he wouldn't make life-altering decisions for her in the future, or leave her again.

As Jack and Rowena made their way back from the restrooms, the server cleared their dessert plates.

Mike smiled. "Do you like Karaoke? I'll admit I suck at it, but it's fun now and then. There's a pub down the street that has it tonight. Would you like to go?"

"I'd love to." To avoid waffling about Jack, she had to truly give Mike a chance.

CHAPTER SEVENTEEN

Jack feared he wasn't making any headway with Meredith. And not because of Mike. Meredith had dropped Mike's name a couple of times, but it was all a ruse to keep him on his toes.

Mike had cornered Jack after a meeting a few days ago and told him to up his game. He said he and Meredith had met for coffee a couple of times and while they liked each other, there wasn't any real chemistry between them. *"She's an amazing woman,"* Mike had said. *"Get your head out of your ass and convince her to forgive you before she falls for someone else."*

In the ten days since their double date, Jack had managed only snatches of time with Meredith. If it weren't for their morning runs, he would have gone days without seeing her. Even then, she kept the conversation surface-level, like they were casual friends who happened to work out together—not like two people who had once shared every secret and dreamt of a future together.

It was killing him.

He'd known winning her back wouldn't be easy, but he'd

underestimated how monumental the task would really be. Her every smile felt guarded, every glance measured, like she was keeping a tally in her head of how close she could let him get before she had to pull away. He'd spent his life learning to read people, and Meredith was the one person he'd never been able to fake it with—or fool himself about.

Jack swirled the water in his glass as he listened to the conversations going on around him. Technically, he had no family left, but each week since he'd moved back, he found himself at a family dinner in The Magic Plate. Tonight, the usual crowd had gathered. The older generation—Elise, Ben, Stella, Frank, and Fiona—along with the W's, Damon, his sister Kate, and Jack. For two hours he'd been surrounded by the familiar smell of spices in the air, the low hum of overlapping voices, and the occasional bursts of laughter.

When Jack walked away from Meredith all those years ago, he'd also walked away from the people who had accepted him as family.

Reece had been the first to leave. He'd felt well enough to come down and eat, but he hadn't stayed long, the visit draining him. Then the older generation departed, and a few minutes ago Damon and Kate headed home, leaving only Jack, Meredith, Rowena, and Jo.

"Jack, I've got a question about memories," Rowena said.

"What about them?"

"Over the last week, I think I've gotten some memories back, but I'm not sure if that's what they are. It almost feels like they're from my imagination."

"Can you describe some of them?"

"One that came to me was when all eight of us kids were together." Rowena closed her eyes for a moment and drew in a large breath.

Jack didn't push her to continue. Her two siblings and

two of her cousins from that memory were dead; he could only imagine how bittersweet the memory must be.

"Sorry, I needed a moment. Anyway… I think we were all at the cabin playing in the lake, in a roped-off section close to the shore. We were racing canoes—boys against girls, which was totally unfair since the boys were bigger and had an easier time with the oars." She chuckled. "We were racing to the shore and the boys were winning. I was in the same canoe as Jo and she swung our canoe so the tip of it hit the canoe in front of us. My brothers screamed as their canoe rolled and they both fell into the lake."

Jo slapped the table. "Oh my god. I remember that, it just came to me. I used a bit of magic to make our canoe crash into theirs."

Jack smiled. "Well, that answers your question. It was an actual memory. It could have been erased because your mothers erased all your memories associated with magic."

Meredith laughed. "Yes, and it had magic because Jo used it to cheat."

"Hey!"

Jack watched as the cousins went back and forth sharing their new memories, teasing each other. They needed this lightness after all they'd been through. He hoped the seer and his own vision were wrong, and that more death wasn't in their future. This was what he wanted for them—many more happy moments.

"Oh god!" Meredith turned to Jack with horror in her eyes.

He scooted closer to her. "What's wrong?"

"I just got a memory of the fire."

Jack heard Rowena and Jo gasp, but he kept his gaze focused on Meredith. "What did you see?"

"It was right after the fire, when the firemen had arrived as well as Frank, Ben, and Curtis, I think. There was another man there too, but he kept to the shadows. I think I only saw him for a moment before he disappeared. I don't know if I told my mom at the time. But why wouldn't I?"

Meredith's voice had risen and Jack could see the panic in her eyes. He purposely kept his voice low. "It was chaos after the fire. You were all in shock and just a kid. It could have slipped your mind. Maybe you didn't even know there was a problem with someone else being there. Did you recognize the man?"

She nodded slowly. "He was the man at the restaurant."

Jack frowned. "The one you thought might be glamoured?"

"I think so, but it's been twenty years."

"Don't doubt yourself, Bubbles." Jack didn't believe in coincidences. "Can you describe the man?"

"About five foot ten, short gray hair, clean shaven, maybe in his sixties."

"Any distinguishing features?"

"No." Meredith's shoulders dropped and she huffed out a breath. "That's not much help, is it?"

It wasn't, but it was better than nothing, and he didn't want her to feel discouraged. He gave her leg a squeeze. "We'll figure it out."

"Oh, there was one more thing. His face buffered."

"What do you mean, *buffered*?"

Meredith bit her lip, a frown marring her beautiful face. "Like a video. But maybe buffering isn't the right word. More like wavered or shimmered. Coming in and out of focus."

Jack had a sense of foreboding that he wasn't going to like it when they figured out who this man was. "I could try to see your memory, but let's try this first." Holding out his hand, Jack grasped a picture he magically retrieved from his office. Turning the picture around, he watched Meredith's face for a reaction. "Do you recognize the man here?"

Meredith took the picture slowly, as if afraid it would bite her. He knew the picture well. Jack had been only ten when he took it of his dad and several council members. During the years since his father's death, he'd thought about destroying the picture, along with many others, but something had made him keep it in his files at the office. He hadn't wanted it in his home.

"This is your dad, isn't it?" Meredith asked, pointing at Daniel Knight in the picture.

"Yes. Do you recognize anyone else?"

"Not these two men, but yes, this man on your father's right is the one from the fire. But…"

"What?"

"When the memory of the fire came to me I was sure it was the same man from the restaurant, but now I'm not so sure."

"This picture was taken over twenty years ago. Not only has the man—Louis Copeland—aged, but so have you, so your perceptions will have changed."

Jack closed his eyes as realization dawned. Frank and Ben had been right. Louis Copeland wasn't dead.

Meredith passed the photo across the table.

"I don't remember seeing him at the fire, but he looks like the guy at the restaurant," Rowena said as she handed the picture to Jo.

Jo studied the photo a moment before handing it back to Jack. "I've never seen him before."

"Copeland was my father's right-hand man. He also became a council member when Stella's brother, Parker Finnegan, died. And he was one of my teachers."

Meredith drew in a sharp breath as she looked at Jack, her eyes wide. "You mean the teacher you told me about? I thought he died."

"So did I." Jack stood and walked up to the window,

looking out. He'd already relived the memory of killing Copeland once in the last couple of months, he didn't need to relive it again.

He snorted to himself. He thought he'd killed Copeland, but obviously he hadn't. Maybe his father was right and he wasn't cut out to lead; he couldn't even kill someone properly. Jack gave himself an internal shake. That was his father talking, not him. Jack turned and faced the women. "Until recently, I truly thought I had killed Copeland when my father died, but Ben and Frank told me that Copeland's body was never found."

"So where has this man been all this time?"

"No one knows. He was badly injured sixteen years ago when I fought with him. That's why I thought he was dead. He may have been lying low because he was injured. I expect he was complicit with what happened to your fathers, and he no longer had my father around to protect him."

"Jack, what kind of injuries did Copeland sustain?" Rowena asked.

"Yeah, Ro, good question." Jo nodded at her cousin and turned to Jack. "Could his injury have anything to do with why Meredith thought his face shimmered?"

"And why you thought he had glamoured himself?" Rowena added.

"It could. Half of Copeland's face was burned almost to the bone. That's why I thought he was dead. You already know that it's really tough for magic to cover magic, and since he was burned by magic, maybe he couldn't do a normal glamour spell to cover the burns."

Meredith turned to Jack, resting her hand on his thigh. "Couldn't he have had plastic surgery?"

"I doubt it. It's really tricky territory when you're dealing with magic wounds, especially ones as severe as his. Perhaps surgery could have helped somewhat, but if it didn't work out as expected, it could have raised questions."

Rowena leaned forward, resting her arms on the table. "Then it's possible that he still has burn scars and had some kind of spell covering them when Meredith saw him?"

"Yes, it's possible." But Jack's biggest concern wasn't Copeland's injury, it was why he was hanging around the restaurant.

CHAPTER EIGHTEEN

A couple of days after the new memories and revelations about Copeland surfaced, Meredith needed to be alone. To not think about Jack or Mike or how her life had turned upside down. She also needed to eat and didn't feel like cooking.

She arrived in The Magic Plate just as the chef finished shutting everything down. "Hey Jennifer." Meredith tried to hide her disappointment that everything was already turned off and cleaned up.

"Oh, hi Meredith. Did you need something?"

"I was hoping to snag something to eat… but that's okay." Meredith didn't want anyone to stay late on account of her. She looked around, as if a solution to her hunger would suddenly materialize. Even Jennifer's sous chef, her husband, wasn't around. "Clinton already gone?"

"Yeah, he flashed home to relieve the babysitter who's got an early exam in the morning."

"Flashed? Oh, I didn't know." She'd been surrounded by magics her entire life and didn't know. She really needed to hurry up and figure out how to identify them so she didn't feel like such an idiot. "Really, don't worry about it, Jennifer. I'll just raid the fridge for something."

"You don't have to do that. If you'd wanted to cook, you would have stayed home." Jennifer looked at her watch. "This will only take seconds and soon you won't need me to even do this. You'll be able to conjure dinner yourself."

The chef took three large and three small plates off a stack of clean ones, setting them in a line on the counter. "Extra for leftovers, or if someone else shows up." Jennifer waved her hands over the three plates. Seconds later a beautiful aroma wafted up. "Oven roasted chicken with basil lemon pan jus, wild rice pilaf, and grilled asparagus. Plus, white chocolate raspberry cheesecake for dessert. How's that?"

Meredith's mouth watered. "Amazing. Thank you."

"My pleasure. You'll clean up?"

"You bet. I'll clean up and lock up."

"Then I'm off," Jennifer said, and disappeared with a flash.

Meredith wasn't ready to try flashing again, but some day. In the meantime she had a delicious meal to eat.

She carried her plate to a back table in the restaurant, away from the front windows. The music had been turned off so the only noise was the muted sound of traffic outside. She'd forgotten how peaceful the restaurant could be after hours. Peaceful, but lonely.

She took a bite of the chicken. It was incredible, of course, but her appetite had diminished somewhere between the smell of lemon and the realization that she might have a lot of lonely meals in her future. As a teenager, she'd envisioned life in her late twenties so different from her current reality. She'd had dreams of a husband and children, maybe a dog, and a house full of love and laughter.

A knock on the front window pulled her from her thoughts.

With her fork paused mid-air, she turned to see Jack. A second later he was standing in front of her table.

Her stomach twisted. Excitement or nerves? She didn't know, but then she hadn't expected to see him tonight.

She didn't get up, but met his gaze. "The restaurant is closed," she told him, then groaned silently. *Duh, Ms. Obvious.*

"I checked your office and apartment. Thought you might be here. Are you hiding or would you like some company?"

"What if I said the former?" The smart thing to do would be to say goodnight and not offer him one of the extra plates Jennifer made up. It would also be smart to keep her walls up and heart safe.

But she wasn't feeling particularly smart. He looked tired. Not physically as he always looked good, but in the way he stood, like a large weight rested on his shoulders.

Meredith waved her fork in the direction of the kitchen. "Jennifer made up some extra plates and I haven't put them in the fridge yet. Help yourself."

"Thanks." A few moments later, Jack sat across from her with his meal. She wasn't sure what she was doing by letting him get close, but the idea of a future of eating alone felt heavier than the risk of letting him stay.

After a few minutes and a few bites, conversation flowed between them as easily as it always had. They talked about innocuous things such as likes and dislikes.

"You can't be serious." Meredith laughed at Jack.

"Yes, I'm serious. Broccoli is an evil, man-made creation. I won't eat it."

"How could I not have known that?" She shook her head. "But you'll eat other man-made things, like chocolate."

"Of course. That's supposed to be man-made. Broccoli is a vegetable and vegetables shouldn't be man-made. I don't trust it."

"But broccoli is planted and grows like other vegetables."

She wasn't going to give up; she was enjoying herself too much. Their lives had been so serious since he'd been back. At least when she wasn't trying to avoid him. But he'd always been able to make her laugh.

"Maybe so, but broccoli was engineered by the Italians from cabbage. And I don't like cabbage. It's like a sneaky parent trying to get you to eat something you hate. When broccoli was first introduced into England in the mid-eighteenth century, they called it Italian asparagus."

She gestured to his empty plate, not a single piece of asparagus remained. "You like asparagus."

"Yes, because it's not disguised cabbage."

Meredith gave an inelegant snort, and covered her face with her hand, careful not to spill her wine. Jack's eyes crinkled at the corners and she saw him struggle to keep a straight face.

They'd finished their dinner a while ago and were enjoying a bottle of wine and each other's company. Their conversation had been varied, but neither of them mentioned their past. Or what they'd once been to each other. Or her dating someone else. Meredith knew the reprieve wouldn't last. Her palms sweat at the thought of such a discussion. She wiped her free hand on her pants and took another sip of wine.

It was as if Jack read her mind because his face sobered. "Bubbles, we need to talk about us."

Meredith cupped the wine glass, needing to still her fingers. "We're friends."

"Yes, but I want more."

"You had your chance."

Jack reached across the table, taking her hand in his. "I know. But I want another one."

She wanted one too but fear held her back. She let out a slow breath and looked Jack in the eyes. "You've been gone for years. Why now?" she asked, keeping her voice calm. "And don't say it was because I didn't know I was magic. I'm done with that answer. It's a cop-out, Jack."

"No, it's not. Your mom said she would never tell you about magic."

Fed up with him not realizing he had other choices, she pushed back her chair and stood. "So, what you're really saying is that you didn't love me enough to find a way to stay?"

"My hands were tied, Bubbles. I couldn't compromise who I was or who our kids would be."

They'd reached an impasse. She couldn't get over her hurt to trust him again and he would never see that he'd had choices.

She picked up the wineglasses and walked to the kitchen.

She heard him follow her, but didn't turn around to look. Busying herself cleaning up, she told him, "It's late. I'm going to finish this, lock up, and head home."

"This isn't over, Mer. I'll somehow make you realize that we're meant to be together." Jack placed a soft kiss on her temple before she could respond. Then he vanished with a flash.

Once she perfected flashing, she could be the one to make the dramatic exit.

MEREDITH PRESSED her heel to the building's wall, stretching her calf, and smothered a yawn. Sleep had been a lost cause. Jack's dramatic exit still pissed her off and not because he'd left. She'd told him to. No, it was because he'd had the last word.

Her alarm had ripped her out of a dead sleep—one she'd

only recently sunk into—and for a tempting moment, she'd almost burrowed back under the covers. But then she'd miss her morning run. It had always been a time just for herself, before the world intruded. A time to prepare for the day.

Jack's insistence on showing up to run with her had changed that. But when she'd thought about going back to sleep, her first thought had been she wouldn't get to see Jack if he showed up.

The few times he hadn't, Damon had. The first time he'd tried to make it sound like a coincidence.

Ha. Fat chance. He didn't live in one of the apartments in their buildings and he'd never been much of a runner. Weightlifting and fighting had always been more his style.

Mike had run with her once too. When they'd agreed there wasn't any chemistry between them, they'd decided to stay friends. He was fun to talk to and he was a runner. But she hadn't seen him after the one time he'd joined her to run. Only Jack, and occasionally Damon. She wasn't disappointed with Mike not showing up, only in herself because she preferred Jack.

She switched legs, stretching her other calf. A movement out of the corner of her eye caught her attention. Her heart flipped when she saw Jack approaching, but she kept her gaze fixed ahead.

"Morning, Bubbles."

"Morning." She hated the joy that burst in her at his presence. Without waiting for him to stretch, she took off across the street.

She inhaled the crisp October morning air and settled into her stride. It had rained the night before, the scent strong in the air. She jumped over a large puddle, but didn't break stride. A stronger runner than her, Jack wouldn't be far behind. As if on cue, she heard him coming up behind her.

"You're too predictable," he said as he came abreast of her.

"So you've said." Ad nauseam. He was constantly harping on her to change her time and route. But she thrived on routine. It was one of the only things that had gotten her through when he'd walked out on her eight years earlier. She got up, went to class, helped in the restaurant, and studied. Rinse and repeat. Day after day. Until one day the pain receded enough for her to go out with her cousins. And then date.

Her routine had shifted over the years, like when she added running, but not by much. Recently, the only thing that had changed was Jack. But even now he'd become a fixture in her life again. After the first time he showed up in early August, he'd run with her almost every day.

"You ignoring me?" Jack asked, like they were out for a leisurely stroll.

She couldn't even get pleasure from him being out of breath. Damn healthy man.

"I'm running."

Jack huffed a laugh. "Really?"

"I didn't ask you to run with me."

He chuckled again and they both lapsed into silence. Jack had an infuriating habit of matching her stride and accommodating her. He made it too easy to run with him.

As they got to the corner where the path ended, Jack finally spoke. "Let's go to the left instead."

"I like this way." Meredith kept going, running on the sidewalk. She enjoyed running past the small shops and cafes lining the street. A few more blocks and they'd turn again and pick up another path that would take them back to their starting point. During long runs, Meredith added some distance, but most weekday mornings, this five-mile loop was her preferred route.

"Damn it, Mer. You're too predictable. Are you trying to get attacked again?"

"It's a safe neighborhood."

"So is the area surrounding The Magic Plate."

He had a point, but now she didn't want to change her route just to prove a point. She was perfectly safe and had been running for years without him.

Jack didn't stop her, just kept pace beside her. She took a deep breath, hoping to soak in the morning and ignore him. Instead, she caught a whiff of his woodsy scent. She'd always loved it. When Jack first left her, she'd slept with his pillow, soaking in his smell. The first time she washed the pillow case and couldn't smell him anymore, she'd cried.

Now, he was back with his stupid, amazing scent, making it so hard to resist him. Not that she did after the magic session. That had been crazy-good sex. Amazingly good, an entire nineteen days ago. Nineteen long, lust-filled days. Whenever she saw him, she wanted to jump his bones.

Maybe that was her problem. She was just horny. She'd have to get Jack to set her up on some more dates. Or she could ask Mike.

She glanced at Jack before looking back where she was running. On the path again, she picked up her pace. "I'd like another date, Jack."

"I'll take you anywhere you want to go."

She clenched her jaw, then took a long breath. "Not with you. I want you to set me up on another date."

"No."

She glanced at him. "No?"

"No. I set you up on a date. That was the deal. You helped me and I helped you."

"Dates," she said, emphasizing the s. "Plural. Not just one date."

Jack slowed down as they neared the spot where they usually walked to cool off. "Hmm. I don't remember that."

"Selective memory," she hissed under her breath. "Well, I need another date and I don't know any magics."

"Oh damn. You're horny." He let out a large laugh.

She glared at him.

"I know you, Bubbles. You may think you've changed, but you really haven't. Not much. I still remember the first time we slept together. A fond memory, actually. You were insatiable after that. It's like when you've been drinking all night and you finally break the seal, there's no stopping it after."

"That's crude."

"And so true. We broke the seal, so to speak, and now you want more." He crossed in front of her, turned around and walked backward. He spread his arms wide. "I'm here, anytime you want."

She wanted to walk into those open arms and climb him like a monkey. A really horny monkey. But then he'd suck her in and be able to break her heart all over again.

"I'll get someone else to find me a date."

Jack faced forward again. "Come on, Bubbles. Are you ever going to forgive me?"

"I don't know." She wanted to, but if he left her again, he'd more than shatter her, she'd be ruined.

Breaking into a run, she headed for home. She could cool down later.

As she came up to the bench where she usually stretched, a man flashed in front of her, blocking the path.

So startled, she stopped.

He grabbed her arm and the ground disappeared beneath her.

Seconds later, her feet slammed onto the path. She looked up to see Jack land in front of her, his arm outstretched.

Her attacker raised his free arm and aimed his hand at

Jack. But before she had a chance to call out a warning, the ground disappeared again.

After her flashing debacle in the field, Jack had flashed with her in his arms, but not a great distance. He'd said it took an enormous amount of power to flash with someone. Her attacker should weaken soon. She hoped. She had no idea how much power someone had. Could it actually be measured?

Power or no power, she was acting like a helpless damsel. Enough of that. Calling on her magic, she tried to flash.

Nothing happened. She needed to calm herself enough to focus.

She took in a breath, and let it out slowly, hoping to regulate her breathing. The man's grasp on her arm bit into her flesh and once more he took her in a flash. With only a second to prepare, she tightened her body in anticipation of her feet touching the ground.

When her running shoes made contact, she jerked her body forward.

The man didn't let go but fell forward with her. Meredith's knees hit the hard-packed dirt, sending pain shooting through both legs. She sucked in a breath and used all her strength to roll to the side, hoping to dislodge the man.

She twisted to look at his face as a fist crashed into her cheek. Pain exploded through her and the world vanished with another flash.

When she landed again, her hip smashed into pavement, pulling a cry from her. He'd thrown her to the ground. Garbage lay strewn around, soaked from the rain. They were in an alley between some buildings, a dumpster covered in graffiti sat a short distance away. The stench of rotting food filled her nostrils.

The man reached for her again.

Meredith rolled, sliding through a puddle, and jumped to her feet. She faced her attacker and for the first time, got a good look at him. "You're Copeland."

The man smirked and his skin shimmered, as if coming in and out of focus.

"Meredith!"

"The dumpster!" Meredith yelled, turning toward Jack's call.

"Not happening," Copeland said as he swung at her again, but this time she was ready.

She ducked as his fist hit the dumpster. The sound startled her and she turned to look, wasting precious seconds.

He grasped her shirt and pulled her backward. Her arms flailed out to catch herself but her head hit solid metal. Stars swam in her vision as she fell sideways.

CHAPTER NINETEEN

When Meredith bolted, Jack trailed at a slower pace. She'd panicked, but eventually she would forgive him. He wouldn't accept anything else. She was meant to be his. And he hers. He'd had to resist while she'd been spellbound, but now he just had to win her over.

The moment Copeland stepped in front of Meredith, Jack flashed to her. He landed with his hands out, ready to grab her, but hit only air. She was gone too fast.

He whipped his head around, searching until he saw her and Copeland about thirty yards away, landing from a flash.

Copeland wouldn't be able to sustain the flashes with Meredith for long, but he didn't need long to hurt her.

Jack blurred his image with a quick spell and flashed after them. Just as he closed the gap she was gone again.

Usually he wouldn't flash into a place he didn't know. It was too easy to land in a dangerous situation, like oncoming traffic. But for Meredith, he'd do anything. In the past few months, she'd been in more danger than she'd been in for years. All because he'd come back to her.

"Fuck!" Jack's low curse blistered the air as he flashed,

following the signature. When his feet touched down, Meredith and Copeland were only about twenty yards ahead of him now. Either he was gaining on them or Copeland was tiring from the energy drain of flashing with another person, especially one who was fighting back.

Jack had the advantage here. Closing in on the distance, he picked up his speed. With his focus on Meredith, he saw the moment she pitched herself forward, taking Copeland with her. But she never saw the man's fist coming.

Jack was truly gaining on them now. Only a few feet away, Copeland raised his arm and a dagger appeared in his hand. He launched it toward Jack.

Jack veered left, the dagger whistling past his shoulder. But the move slammed him into a building. He stumbled forward. Only losing seconds to right himself, Jack scooped up the dagger from the ground as he ran forward. While running, he conjured a holster around his waist, sheathing the blade before picking up his speed.

His shoes pounded into the pavement and his breathing sped up. The sun was only just rising, the street almost deserted. A small blessing.

He was almost on them when Copeland disappeared into an alley. Jack followed, turning the corner. Seeing his former teacher standing near a dumpster, Jack stopped.

"Meredith!" he yelled, searching for her.

"The dumpster!" At Meredith's shout, Jack ran toward them while he pulled on his magic from deep within and directed a shot of energy toward Copeland. Not fast enough.

Copeland pulled another dagger out of the air and lunged toward him. Jack turned his body, making himself a thinner target, and sidestepped. Copeland missed but lunged again.

They were only a few feet apart now. Jack turned once more and took aim at Copeland. At the last moment, the older man ducked. Jack's magic shot went wide, striking the side of the building. The backlash forced him to turn back toward Copeland.

"You're not going to win this one, Jack. You were always weak."

"Beat you, didn't I?" Jack taunted. Never one to tolerate insolence, his comment would rankle Copeland.

He didn't take his eyes off his former instructor, and that's when he caught it. So subtle. Copeland's face shimmered. Whatever power he'd been using to maintain his façade was fading.

He realized too late that Copeland had likely allowed his image to slip on purpose. The split-second distraction gave Copeland the chance he needed. He lunged forward into Jack, knocking them both to the ground.

Jack landed on his back, a grunt forcing the air from his lungs as he hit the ground. Copeland's weight pushed Jack into the wet concrete as Copeland rose above him, a dagger clenched in his fist.

Jack reached for his magic, trying to flash, but Copeland drove the dagger down before he could vanish. It caught Jack in the shoulder, piercing through his flesh to anchor him to the ground.

Pain engulfed him, like fire shooting down his arm, knocking the breath from his lungs. Stunned, he lay pinned like an insect to a board, amid the filth and the garbage on the ground.

Drawing in a breath, he turned his head to look for Copeland, but the dagger locked him in place. He was forced to breathe through the agony in short pants.

Jack struggled to keep his eyes open, squinting up at his former teacher.

He hovered over Jack. "I've waited years for this. You'll never know when I'm going to attack. Or how. Then, just when you give up, I'll rip her away from you. You'll suffer like I did. You'll lose the love of your life. Poof." He made a gesture with his hand like something was blowing up. "There one moment, gone the next."

"Fuck you." Jack heard Meredith's voice. Lifting his head as much as he could, he watched her swing a piece of wood with protruding nails at Copeland. Meredith missed the man when he flashed away.

Jack lowered his head to the ground and closed his eyes, taking small breaths. Using his magic, he did an internal scan. Something coursed through his system—a poison or drug that Copeland had coated the blade with. It was charting a quick path through his system. He guessed he didn't have long. The pain was intensifying, his vision starting to blur.

"Jack!" He heard Meredith scream his name and struggled to open his eyes.

Meredith knelt by his side, and he turned his head to look at her. The small movement was almost too much. Unbearable pain tore through him. He squeezed his eyes closed against the pain, continuing to pant.

When he opened them again, there were patches in front of his vision. His sight snapped in and out of focus.

He was running out of time. His breaths were choppy now, the torment consuming him. "Mer, call Ben."

"I did, but he didn't answer. I called Damon and Frank and my mom and Fiona. Someone will come."

Jack must have lost track of time for Meredith to have already called so many. "Don't have long." He wasn't sure he had spoken loud enough for Meredith to hear him. "Poison," Jack said through a gasp.

It was getting harder and harder to breathe. A burning sensation unlike anything he'd ever felt before raced inside him. It forged a path of scorching hot fire through his limbs and core.

"Oh my god, I... I didn't know it was this bad. Maybe I should call someone again. I... I don't know how to heal you!"

"S'right." Jack could hear the panic in Meredith's voice and wanted to reassure her, but his eyes felt too heavy to open.

"Jack, your phone is ringing. I need to get it out of your pocket."

He felt a pull on his pants pocket where his weight had pinned it closed. Meredith continued to struggle, and after several moments, she pushed his hip to the side, prying the phone free.

The movement wrenched a groan from him as it jarred his entire torso. Shockwaves of pain tore through his shoulder where the dagger still pinned him to the wet ground.

"Shit, Jack. Sorry. So sorry."

He heard Meredith's panic rise. Time was running out and he didn't have time for panic.

"Shhhh, s'okay," he forced out, not sure if his words were clear.

Ben's voice boomed through the phone's speaker. "Jack. Sitrep."

Jack couldn't open his mouth. He couldn't give a situational report.

"Hurry. Jack said it's poison."

"Meredith, where are you?"

Jack couldn't hear the voices anymore. They'd faded away.

He'd never dwelled on how he was going to die. But he never thought it would be like this.

Without Meredith's forgiveness. Without her love.

Love? What was he thinking?

The pain.

It snaked throughout his entire body, like knives playing a stabbing game with his nerves.

Then it faded.

The pain was disappearing.

Was he getting better?

Would someone come?

What was happening?

The poison, the dagger.

Right. He was dying.

Without Meredith's love.

That's it. He needed to tell her he loved her.

Tell her something before the darkness took him.

Stay awake.

CHAPTER TWENTY

"*B*ubbles."

Meredith startled at the sound of Jack's voice. He'd been sleeping on and off for twenty-four hours, only awake for brief periods of time. During it all she'd barely left his side, choosing to stay curled in the chair beside his bed.

He held out his hand. "Come here."

She crossed to the bed, gingerly sitting on the edge. "I don't want to hurt you."

"You won't. I'm healed, just tired."

"I-I was so scared." More than she'd ever been in her life. She hadn't admitted it earlier during one of the times he'd been awake because until she knew he was going to be okay, she hadn't wanted to shift the focus away from him being treated. Her fears were nothing compared to ensuring Jack would be alright. But when he went slack in the alley, a bolt of pure terror shot through her, and all she could think was that he was gone. Even now, just remembering, sent a shiver of fear down her spine.

He sat up, leaned against the headboard and took her

hand in his to stop her trembling. "I know. I should have expected Copeland to attack again. Your habits are too predictable, it was—"

She put her finger on his lips to halt him. "I get it now. He knew exactly where I was going to be. I'll be better."

"He won't stop. Copeland was always a determined bastard."

She'd already been chastised by every member of her family, as well as Damon's, and Ben's. She didn't want another lecture. "I'm more worried about you."

"I'm fine. The Emissary removed all the poison. I'm just bloody tired."

Meredith felt a strange prickling sensation course through her hand, up her arm, and into her forehead. It wasn't quite pain, but she wouldn't volunteer to feel it again if she didn't have to. "Are you scanning me or healing me?"

"Both, and I'm done." Jack pulled her over onto his lap. "Except for the bump on your forehead and the bruises on your arms, all of which I healed, you seem fine. You should have let the Emissary heal you. Or your mom. Or even Ben or Fiona."

"My injuries were minor. I didn't want them wasting energy on me."

He used his finger to tilt her chin up, looking her in the eyes. "I never want you to suffer if you don't have to. You've already suffered enough for several lifetimes."

Not knowing if he was referring to her family members dying or him leaving her, she just nodded.

"The last day is a bit hazy, but I think Ben took the daggers—the one I put in a holster and the one that pinned me," he said, changing the topic. "I'm sure he'll give them to Kate to examine them. She'll see if she can figure out where they came from and what the poison was," Jack explained.

Meredith had known Damon's sister her entire life. She'd

even seen some of Kate's work as a swordsmith, but it hadn't occurred to her Kate might be able to help. "Then what?"

"We keep living. We just have to be more diligent. All of us."

Meredith felt so out of her depth. Besides learning how to use her own magic, there seemed to be a lot she needed to learn about their world as a whole, as well. "Since the Emissary was able to heal you so easily, why can't she heal Reece?"

"He has a spell on him that no one has seen before."

Meredith sprang to her feet. "You mean people can just make up spells willy-nilly that we can't protect ourselves against?"

"Come here." Jack stretched his hand out and pulled her back into his arms, laying them both down on the bed. "No, most people can't make up spells that don't already exist. That's a skill that must have a specific purpose."

"Then why can't anyone identify the spell on Reece?"

"Magics have been around since the beginning of time. There are spells that have been forgotten by most. This is likely one of those. Council members around the world are all looking into it. Someone will figure it out."

"I'm scared, Jack," she said again, resting her head on his shoulder. She'd been so sure he was dying and she hadn't told him she loved him. All because she didn't want to risk her heart again.

Sitting in that filthy alley, terrified for him as she waited for help, she realized her heart had been at risk since the moment he walked back into her life. She had loved him since she was seventeen years old and she'd never stopped. She lifted her head and met his eyes. "I love you, Jack."

"I love you too." He placed a gentle kiss on her lips and she could have sworn his love poured into her. "I never stopped loving you, and I never will."

She rested her head back on his shoulder, her hand lightly stroking his chest, and soaked in his scent and warmth.

They settled into a comfortable silence until she felt Jack pull in a deep breath and let it out slowly. "But, you still don't trust me," he said softly.

"I'm trying." She meant it. Still, the words felt hollow, even to her own ears. Trying didn't stop the fear curling in her chest that he'd make another decision that would crush her. Trying didn't erase eight years of silence. Eight years of wondering what she did wrong and trying to piece her life back together. Of hating him and loving him at the same time.

Jack ran his thumb along the back of her hand, slow and steady. "You don't have to trust me yet, Bubbles. I just need you to let me keep showing up."

Meredith turned her face into his shoulder. "You can't promise you won't leave again."

"I *can*. I'll never walk away from you again."

She didn't answer. Not because she didn't believe him, but because believing him came with consequences. If she let herself believe, she'd start hoping again. And hope had betrayed her before.

The room was quiet except for the sound of their breathing. She wondered if he could feel the way her heart was thudding, uneven and loud. "I didn't think I'd get the chance to say it," she whispered. "That I loved you."

"You almost didn't," he said gently.

She pulled back enough to look at him. "I know." It haunted her how close she'd come to never saying the words. To letting him die with a lie of omission between them. "I kept thinking that I couldn't risk it."

"What changed?"

She laid her head back down and closed her eyes. "I

realized that it was already too late. I'd risked my heart years ago. I've been in love with you since I was seventeen."

"That makes two of us."

They lay in silence again, her body curled against his, his hand absently stroking hers like it was the most natural thing in the world. Maybe it was. Maybe it had always been.

Eventually, Meredith lifted up on an elbow to see his face. He looked rough, pale with dark circles smudged under his eyes. But he was alive. He was here. She ran her finger along his cheekbone, then down the side of his neck, absorbing the feel of his skin, trying to imprint it on herself. "You scared the shit out of me."

He gave her a tired smile. "I scared myself."

She huffed a breath that was almost a laugh. "Don't do that again."

"I'll do my best."

"I thought I'd lost you again. And this time it would've been permanent."

Jack went up on his elbow, mirroring her position, and leaned in, giving her a soft kiss. He wanted to kiss her for the rest of his life. "Meredith, I need to tell you something."

Meredith turned so she could see his eyes. "That doesn't sound good."

"No, it isn't. But when we were together before, I did things because of magic. Now, I need to lay all my cards on the table. I need you to love me and trust me for who I really am." Jack glanced out the bedroom window, looking for a way to tell her what he needed to reveal. "I spoke with Ben and Frank while the Emissary was healing me and you went to get something to eat. I explained about Copeland being able to flash with you."

"He had extra power to do that, right?"

"Yes, and he was also shielding the damage on his face at the same time. That takes a lot of power. There are some people who can do that, mostly council members, but when the North American council fell apart twenty years ago, the extra power was reabsorbed by the leaders of the remaining councils."

"But you thought Copeland was dead. Maybe he kept the power from when he was a council member."

Jack sighed. "It doesn't work like that; the power is immediately taken in by the other leaders when a council is disbanded. That would have happened when my father died because a ceremony to replace him didn't take place. And if Copeland had died, his portion would have disappeared from his body, just like his normal magic. Dead bodies don't retain magic."

A knot in Meredith's stomach began to grow. She knew that she wasn't going to like what was coming next. She felt a sense of foreboding that was becoming all too familiar. "Then how did Copeland get enough magic to flash with me?"

"Ben, Frank, and I believe it's being taken, siphoned from young children. The magic Copeland siphons won't last long, but it will give him a boost for a short while or until he expends it himself, like he did when he flashed with you."

Meredith closed her eyes, but images of him lying pinned to the asphalt materialized behind her lids, and she flung them open. "Why does he want extra magic? Just to get to me?"

"I think that's one reason, but not the only one. I think he's also trying to use the extra magic to find the box."

"There are so many ways that magic can be used." She shook her head. "I don't understand."

"Frank and Ben believe that there's a map to locate the box. And it might need something special to locate it. Like extra power or a spell. No one's really sure."

"If he needs magic for the map, why did he waste so much flashing with me?" Meredith pulled away from Jack and stood. She needed space from him to think. "You think he wants to use me to hurt you."

Jack sat up against the headboard. "Yes, I do. For the last sixteen years, I've thought Copeland was dead, but when he was alive, he hated me. More than that, he loathed me. Now I think he wants revenge against me for my father's death."

"Why would he blame you for that?"

"Because I'm the one who killed him."

JACK WATCHED Meredith's eyes widen with shock as the truth sank in. That he had killed just like his father had. Killed the man they believed had taken the lives of half her family.

He didn't move, just sat back and waited for her reaction. Giving her the truth could destroy any chance they had of finally being together, but they'd both suffered through enough lies and hidden truths to last many lifetimes.

"I'm sorry you lost your parents, but I'm glad you killed your father."

Jack blinked. "That's it?"

Meredith sat beside him again and he didn't have to think about what to do next. He embraced her and held her tight, soaking in her scent. She was right where he'd always wanted her. He just wished he knew what was coming next so they could both prepare.

Still in his arms, she tilted her head back to look him in the eyes. "Your father wasn't a good man, Jack. Even if it can't be proven, my mother and aunts think your father killed my dad and the others."

"I believe it too. It was because of my dad that I made the promise to myself never to compromise who I was. Never to hide or make my children feel anything less than proud of who they are." She opened her mouth to speak, but he leaned down and kissed the words right off her lips. He would listen to her protests later. "I'm healed and I want to be alone with you. But not here where anyone could check on us."

Meredith nodded, and after Jack texted Jo to let her know they'd be at his apartment, they went to his car. It didn't take long to get to Jack's place.

Standing in his living room, she ran her hand along the spines of the books on a shelf and looked around the comfy living space. "We were never at your apartment much. Your old one, I mean. We used to always meet at the restaurant or my house."

"It didn't matter. I just wanted to be with you." He walked toward her and took her into his arms once more. It had only been twenty minutes since the last time, but it was still far too long. "I wanted you here, in my space, when I made love to you."

She smiled and tilted her head up for his kiss. This time it was heated and held an urgency he hadn't known he felt. He lavished her mouth, kissing and nipping at her lip and tongue, taking in everything she gave him.

When he pulled away, he lifted her up and she wrapped her legs around his waist. He walked to his dining room table, a long, sturdy block of old weathered wood, and just the right height for what he had in mind.

His bed would be softer, but it seemed too far away.

Using only his mind, he conjured a soft pad to cover the table, then controlled Meredith's descent to the surface. He stood between her legs and took in the sight of her. "You're beautiful." Her hair flared out around her, a riotous mass of auburn, silky curls. Her face glowed a soft pink and her lips were swollen from his kisses.

He leaned forward, bringing their bodies flush together, and put his hands on either side of her, supporting his weight. Slowly, he lowered his head and captured her lips in a soft kiss, then he moved himself down the table and kissed his way down her body. He'd wanted her for so long that each time he made love to her he wanted to go slow and savor her, but his body was telling him otherwise. His cock was rock hard where it rubbed against her.

"Jack, don't tease, I want more. I want you, now. We can do slow later."

Jack pulled back and used his magic to expose them both. Their clothing lay in neat piles on a chair beside the table. Once more he stood back to take in the sight of Meredith laying like a feast spread out before him. Whisker burns from his three-day-old scruff marked her flushed skin. A possessiveness coursed through him at the sight.

"I waited so long for you, Bubbles. I want to take each time slow." Supporting himself on his elbows as he hovered over her, they barely touched as he cupped her face in his hands and kissed her.

Meredith tilted her hips up and he groaned at the sudden, hard contact. "Slow later. Fuck me now, please!"

Jack chuckled at the filthy word but couldn't refuse her anymore. He held out his hand and grasped the condom pack that appeared in his palm. He sheathed himself, then took her hips in his hands.

Meredith closed her eyes, but he wanted to see everything she was feeling. "Watch me," he whispered and her eyes drifted open, a small smile on her face. "I need to see you when I enter you." Taking himself in one hand, he supported himself with the other and slowly entered her. The feel of her gripping him tight, her heat enveloping him, was almost more than he could bear. He feared he would shoot off like a virgin teenager. Breathing slowly in through his nose, he managed to get a handle on his control. Then he started to move.

"Yes! Faster, Jack."

"No, slow. I want to feel every stroke and savor you."

Jack lifted her hips and changed his angle as he continued the slow, tortuous strokes. The sounds Meredith made were heaven to his ears.

She pushed her hips toward him and he groaned; he wasn't going to last. Unable to hold back any longer, he pushed her knees to her chest, changing the angle again, and drove deep.

"Yes! Please, please!" Meredith repeated the words like a mantra as she gripped his forearms and he drove into her. Sweat dripped down his back, and his ass clenched with each stroke, but he never took his eyes off her.

He felt her core tighten and her legs stiffen. Knowing she was close, he leaned forward, pushed her knees to the sides to open her up, and captured her mouth with his. The kiss was sloppy and wet as he continued to pump into her.

Her nails bit into his skin as her back arched. She pulled her mouth from his and cried out his name, clenching him in a glorious death grip. Jack groaned when she came, closed his eyes, and let her body milk his, sending him over the edge.

Still panting as he came down from his high, he felt her squirm underneath him. Using his magic as an assist, he pulled back into a standing position with Meredith in his arms. He wasn't opposed to snuggling with Meredith and making love to her again, but on something more comfortable.

A few hours later, they were back at her apartment so she could be close to her family.

She was curled in bed beside him and he wanted to believe he could have this forever. That he'd be able to protect Meredith from Copeland and she would trust him to do it.

CHAPTER TWENTY-ONE

For the past five days Meredith wrestled with her conflicted feelings. She was riding a high from all the time she and Jack had been spending together, not to mention the fabulous sex. But she still couldn't quite forgive Jack for walking out on her all those years ago. If she couldn't forgive him and let it go, she couldn't trust him.

The dilemma stayed in the back of her mind like a nagging old wound—never fresh enough to demand immediate attention, but always aching when she least expected it.

Once more, she shoved it aside as she walked into the back door of The Magic Plate. She looked around at the almost deserted kitchen in the middle of what should have been the prep for the dinner rush. Yet her mother stood in the center of the room doing nothing. "Mom, I got your message to come right away. What's wrong?"

"Oh, Meredith." Her mom turned around, her eyes wide. "I didn't hear you come in. The chef had a family emergency, which meant our sous chef did too, so both had to leave.

Then the two line cooks and four out of the six waitstaff that were supposed to be on shift called in sick. They all said they had the flu. I couldn't get a hold of anyone else, either."

Meredith went to the sink to wash her hands. "That's a strange coincidence."

"Too much of a coincidence, but we'll deal for now."

"What about Jo and Rowena?"

"Jo had another meeting with the university to talk about her leave of absence, and I don't know where Rowena is. That worries me but right now I need to get our customers served and then we'll close."

"What do you need me to do?"

Putting her hands on her hips, her mom gave her a serious look. "I need you to keep the two remaining waitstaff out of the kitchen. They can handle the front of the restaurant and you can take the meals out to them."

"What?" Meredith's jaw dropped. "I need to help you back here."

Her mom shook her head. "No, we're going to do things the fast way today." She put her arms up and pulled her body straighter as if drawing in more energy. The aroma of garlic and rosemary drifted in the air.

Meredith whipped around and saw pots and pans with various ingredients cooking on the range. The counter was covered with foods prepared and ready to cook.

Dual feelings warred within Meredith. She was impressed by how her mother had just taken control and gotten everything ready, but sad about all she'd missed out on. She should have been helping her mom and learning at her side for years.

Had her mother and aunts always done this? All those times they said they couldn't find the right chef and they'd worked the kitchen on their own and the customers raved about the food—had they been conjuring it? "That's amazing. I want to learn."

"Thanks." Her mom went to the stove to supervise. "I'd love to teach you. I like to prepare things with magic, but actually cooking the food ensures the scents permeate the air with the expected aromas a restaurant should have. And that's important."

Meredith raised her brow. "You've never thought it was being dishonest?"

"No, of course not. That's naïve thinking. There are magic people and non-magic people, but that doesn't mean we can't use the gifts we were born with." She turned back to the simmering pots.

Meredith felt a slight twinge of anger that she was denied using her own innate gifts, but she let it go. She just had a lot of catching up to do. "Are the chefs magic?"

"Yes, this chef is, and her husband, of course. But we've had non-magic chefs over the years. The line cooks are magic too as the chef recommended them."

"Did you ever second-guess what you did?"

"The spellbinding? At first, a hundred times a day. But then, each day the sun rose and you were safe and I knew I made what I thought was the best decision at the time."

Meredith pulled out plates and worked alongside her mom, like they'd done so many times over the years. As her hands worked from muscle memory, her mom's words, *I knew I made what I thought was the best decision at the time,* kept replaying in her mind. She wished she hadn't lost the twenty years of using her magic, but she'd accepted her mom's decision. Sure, she might get frustrated now and then, but she honestly couldn't say she would have made a different decision.

Then why couldn't she accept that Jack too had made the best decision he could at the time?

She shoved that question aside with the nagging old wound to deal with later, and instead focused on magic. For two decades she didn't know magics existed, let alone that she was one, and now they seemed to be everywhere. Jack, Damon, Ben, and their families. Even Meredith's assistant, Sophie, and the chefs. Maybe there were other magics she associated with every day but didn't know it. "Mom?"

"Hmmm?"

"Are any of our other staff magic?"

"Yes, actually, the four waitstaff who all called in sick are magics. They're all great..." Her mom stopped stirring the pot on the range.

"What?"

"All the staff who had emergencies or are sick are magics. None of our non-magic staff, at least not the ones on shift today, called in sick or had emergencies."

"You think it's not a coincidence?"

"Quick, let's plate these up and get them served. I'm going to close the restaurant for the rest of the night."

"That's a bit extreme, don't you think?"

"No." Elise plated what was on the range and turned the heat off. "Take the dishes to the front while I call Ben. Then you call Jack."

Meredith felt her stomach start to churn at the panic radiating off her mother. It wasn't like her mom to jump to conclusions, but maybe everyone being sick was more than a coincidence.

She put the dishes on a platter and went out into the restaurant, passing the platter off to one of the waitstaff. Three trips later and everyone was served and the restaurant was closed to new patrons, the remaining diners enjoying their meals.

Back in the kitchen, Meredith helped her mom put food

away and clean up. She even managed to use her magic to wipe down the counter.

"I couldn't reach Ben and Stella hasn't heard from him. Did you call Jack?"

"I didn't get a chance yet." Meredith pulled out her phone and called Jack but got his voicemail. "He's not answering."

"I'll try Fiona."

Meredith waited as her mother called Fiona and left a message.

"Mom, what do you want to do?" she asked as she turned to the dishwasher to put in the remaining dishes.

She felt her body jerk like she'd been hit with a cattle prod, her body spasming out of control, but without the pain. Her knees buckled and she reached for the counter.

"Mom!" Panic tore through her as she struggled to stay on her feet, forcing her knees to hold her upright.

"Get out! Run, now!"

Meredith whipped around in time to see her mom wield a sword in one hand, with electricity sparkling on the fingertips of the other. "Shit, Mom. A sword? What's going on?"

"Meredith, leave now!" Her mom moved to the kitchen door and waited, as if scanning the front of the restaurant, like Meredith had seen Jack do.

"Mom, I won't leave you." She couldn't even begin to know how to conjure a sword—let alone use it—but she hadn't gone through everything to save her mother only to lose her now.

Her mom kept her eyes on the door when she spoke. "Yes, you will. You're still a toddler when it comes to your magic, and I will do whatever I need to do to keep you safe!"

"You could get hurt!" Meredith felt her panic rise as adrenaline flooded her system.

Keeping her weapon raised, her mom half-turned toward Meredith. "Sweetheart, you still don't get it. I'd do anything for you. Anything to keep you safe and make you happy."

"But I don't want that for you, Mom. I want you to be safe and happy too."

"You don't get to make that decision for me, sweetheart." Her mom raised her sword again and turned back to the door. "What you felt just now was a huge draw of energy. I only sense eight people out there, so I think a few of the customers must have left. I don't sense any malevolence, so I'm going to check it out." The sword disappeared and Elise's fingers returned to normal.

Meredith took a step forward. "I'll go with you."

"No." Her mom flicked a hand toward the back door that led to a parking lot. "I've put a small protection spell on the door. It's not perfect, but it should protect you while I check out the front. Call Jack and Ben again and then slip out through the side to the residence elevator."

Her mom turned abruptly and pushed through the swinging door to the main part of the restaurant. Meredith was getting sick and tired of feeling useless. She needed to practice her magic more. And she needed to trust—trust her mom, and trust Jack. Holding on to her anger wasn't getting her anywhere.

She pulled out her phone and tried Jack and Ben again. Neither answered. She left messages and hoped they would call soon because she wasn't going to leave her mom.

"Meredith, come out!"

Meredith spun toward the kitchen door at the sound of someone yelling for her.

"No! Meredith, run!"

She had her hand on the door when her mother's scream reached her. If everyone wanted her to trust them with their decisions, then they were going to have to trust Meredith with hers.

Her mom had protected her for decades.Now it was Meredith's turn, regardless of the danger.

Ignoring her mom's order, she pushed through the kitchen door.

CHAPTER TWENTY-TWO

Meredith felt a drop in temperature when she stepped into the restaurant, like someone had turned the air conditioner on full blast.

She didn't see her mom, her attention caught by the four waitstaff talking near the back wall. The four remaining patrons were seated two to a table, but something wasn't right.

The waitstaff didn't turn toward her or stop their conversation when she walked up to them. It was like they were in a room by themselves.

Meredith tentatively reached out and her fingers collided with something invisible, like a see-through wall. It felt like the bubble Jack had surrounded her with when she'd been attacked, but then why couldn't the staff see her?

She walked over to the first couple having dinner and slowly reached out. Once more, her fingers hit something solid but invisible. The couple didn't notice her as they continued to eat their dinner.

A loud bang sounded from the front of the restaurant and Meredith spun toward it.

Louis Copeland stood by the door, Meredith's mother at his feet. She gasped and took a step forward, then hesitated. "Is she alive?" Meredith sucked in a breath to stop the tears that sprang to her eyes.

"Yes, but she has a nasty little problem." Copeland held up a dagger and spun it as if it was a toy. "You remember these, don't you, my dear? How is Jack?"

Meredith looked down at her mother's unmoving form, then looked back at Copeland. "You stabbed her?"

Copeland's gaze followed hers. "Yes, a poison dagger is a very effective method of stopping someone from flashing away." He flapped his hand toward her mom. Her body jerked, then stilled, like the life had been sucked out of her.

Meredith fought the urge to go to her, not wanting to get too close to Copeland. "What did you do?"

"I sent her soul somewhere safe. That's another great thing about the poison dagger—it doesn't prevent a soul jump."

Spinning back around, Meredith ran to the kitchen. She pushed through the kitchen door so hard it flung back and hit the wall, but Meredith didn't stop. Reaching the back door, she twisted the knob. It wouldn't budge.

She remembered her mom had spelled the door. It was supposed to stop people from getting in, but now she couldn't get out. Her mom probably never imagined Meredith would have to escape. To get to the side entrance, she'd have to sneak into the main dining room.

Lunging at the counter, she grabbed a large knife from the butcher block. Fisting it in one hand, she braced herself to plunge it into Copeland. With her other hand, she pulled out her phone.

The phone whipped out of her hand and smashed against the wall, the pieces falling to the ground.

"Oh no, my dear, that won't do. You don't need to call

anyone," Copeland said like he was reassuring a small child. He stood in the kitchen doorway.

Meredith gripped the knife tighter, waiting for him to come closer. "Where did you send my mother?"

"I told you, somewhere safe. And just in case you didn't know this about a soul jump, your mother has only twenty-four hours, maybe less, before her body dies." He leaned against the wall by the kitchen door, his arms crossed like he had all the time in the world for a casual chat.

The unbinding ceremony helped her save her once. Now, she just had to figure out a way to do it again. Her arm ached as she kept the knife raised, but she didn't falter as she stared down Copeland. "Why?"

He chuckled. "Because, my dear, I want you to suffer."

"I've never done anything to you."

"No, but your father and Jack have. If you suffer, Jack will suffer," he said, spitting the words out like they left a bad taste on his tongue. "I've waited sixteen years to exact my revenge. Tomorrow morning you'll receive a note to come and retrieve your mother's soul, and you'll follow the directions exactly. You won't tell Jack or anyone else. If you do, not only will your mother die, I'll make her suffer like Jack did to me."

Copeland's face shimmered, and Meredith recoiled. The illusion peeled away, revealing a grotesque mass of twisted flesh. Scar tissue clung to his skin in thick, uneven clumps, one side of his face warped beyond recognition. His left eye drooped into the melted mess of cheek and lip, like his face had slid off under too much sun.

Copeland jerked a finger toward the left side of his face, his sneer pulling his mouth into a twisted, lopsided grin. "Jack did this to me when he killed his father. If you don't follow my instructions, I'll have no problem doing the same to your mother and then… then taking my time killing her."

He took a step toward Meredith and her arm flew to the side as if it had a mind of its own. The knife flew from her fingers and hit the kitchen wall with a solid *thud*, the blade burying itself several inches deep.

She dropped her arm, stiff with fear, and took a shaky step back.

"To make sure you follow my instructions," Copeland said, closing the distance between them, "I'll give you a little incentive."

Meredith backed up until her butt hit the counter behind her. He loomed over her, his disfigured face inches away from her, his breath hot and thick against her skin.

When he grabbed her upper arm and squeezed, pain radiated around her bicep like fire. She cried out and twisted, trying to wrench free, but his grip only tightened.

Just as suddenly, he let go and stepped back. "That should do the trick."

Meredith gasped and looked down. The sleeve of her shirt was blackened, the fabric burned away in a jagged circle. In the center of her arm, a strange mark marred her skin. Tears welled in her eyes, but she blinked them back and raised her chin. "What did you do?"

He chuckled. "Just left you a little present. Think of it like a tattoo. I'll be able to hear everything you say, and if you tell anyone about the letter you'll receive or that you're coming to me to save your mother, I'll kill her."

"Everyone will see it. I won't be able to hide the tattoo."

Copeland let out a humorless laugh. "Foolish girl. You really should learn more about magic." Then he vanished.

Meredith stared at her arm. The sleeve was whole again, the scorch marks gone like nothing had happened. She yanked up the hem of her shirt and pulled her arm free. The tattoo had vanished, just like Copeland. But when she ran her fingers over the spot, a chill skimmed her skin, like an ice cube trailing along her flesh.

Hurrying, she wrestled her arm back into her sleeve and ran into the front of the restaurant. It was empty, except for her mother. Meredith dropped to her knees and pressed her fingers against her mom's neck, careful not to disturb her body, still and pale, sprawled out on the floor.

Finding a light pulse, Meredith released a breath, then sprang up. She bolted to the restaurant phone, her hand shaking as she punched in Jack's number.

"Hello?"

"Jack, my mom! Copeland came. He soul-jumped her." The line went dead. She took the phone from her ear and stared at it.

"Meredith."

She looked up. Jack stood in front of her, and she ran into his arms. "He took her soul."

A jolt of pain shot through her arm and she jerked back. It was a reminder that Copeland could hear everything she said. She slapped her palm over the tracker and rubbed, but the sensation didn't fade.

Jack grasped her arms right over the tracker. "Bubbles, are you hurt?"

"N-no, no, I'm fine." The lie wanted to stick in her throat, but she forced it out.

He gave her a skeptical look, but didn't press the issue. "I'll get your mom upstairs to Jo's apartment, since Reece is already there. Then we'll figure out what to do."

Meredith already knew what to do.

And no one was going to stop her.

JACK LAID his hand on Meredith's shoulder where she sat beside her mom, Elise's limp hand cradled in hers. "I've stopped the poison's spread and Fiona will be here to do any additional healing needed," he said gently. "Mer, I'll be in the living room. Ben and Frank are here."

She nodded and hugged herself, rubbing her arms, but not looking up.

He conjured a glass of wine and set it on the bedside table. He wasn't sure if wine was what someone needed in a situation like this, but maybe it would offer some comfort.

It had been two hours since he called Ben and got him up to speed. Ben had flashed to the restaurant almost immediately and confirmed that the staff absence had been legitimate. Or at least strategically staged.

Frank had shown up a few minutes ago and both men waited in the living room. Jack didn't see Jo or Rowena, who were likely with Reece in the other bedroom.

Jack dropped onto the couch beside Ben. "What do we know?"

Frank stood, pacing to the far wall where a bookcase sat beside clusters of family photos. Some were recent pictures of Jo and Reece or Jo and her cousins, but most were images of family members who should still be here but weren't. Pictures of parents, siblings, and children. The wall was a collage of loss.

Now Reece and Elise were both fighting for their lives. Only five Williamses remained and Jack was determined to make sure they all lived to see many more years.

"Let's brainstorm," Frank said as he faced the wall. The photos had been removed and neatly stacked on the dining room table, and the shelf pulled aside. A whiteboard film now covered the space. He uncapped a marker and wrote three names: *Copeland, Skalbeck, Sharpe.*

"We know Copeland's involved," Frank said, "but

Skalbeck and Sharpe are still question marks. Someone is tipping Copeland off. Which means we have a mole and we need to figure out who it could be and stop the bastard."

Ben stood and began pacing. "I agree. Let's work backward. Go over the night's events step-by-step."

Jack conjured a mug of coffee and rested it on his knee after a sip. He needed the caffeine to focus, and couldn't afford to let his mind wander, especially not to the haunted look on Meredith's face when they'd brought Elise upstairs.

He forced himself back to the task. "Our task force got a tip at two o'clock this afternoon that more magic children had been taken. We obtained a warrant, and by five we'd breached the building. As you know, five magic kids were recovered, we secured the premises, the children were checked medically and returned to their families. That took us to around eight."

Jack checked his watch. It was ten p.m. But it felt like three in the morning.

Frank marked down the times. "When did Meredith call?"

"Just after eight. I was finishing up paperwork at the office and noticed she'd called me a couple of times before that, but I missed them."

Ben stopped pacing and dropped into a large armchair, a coffee in his hand. "What time do you think Elise was soul-jumped?"

Jack sipped his coffee, thinking through the night's events. "About seven. Which gives us until seven tomorrow night to get Elise back in her body, maybe less."

Frank scribbled a countdown: *21 hours*. "But we can't cut it that close."

Jack vanished his empty mug and leaned forward. "Let's get back to the mole. Copeland—at least I'm guessing it was him—kept my team busy. But how did he isolate the restaurant staff? I don't buy all the staff calling in sick and the chef and her husband having a family emergency at the same time is a coincidence. Not a chance."

Frank twirled the marker in his fingers. "The chef said her mother was pushed while out shopping and fell and broke her hip. The woman is elderly, so the accident isn't suspicious on its own, but the timing? Too perfect."

Jack agreed. It was too convenient. "What about the others?"

Ben stepped up to the whiteboard and circled the number six Frank had written down. "They all went out to dinner last night, claimed they got food poisoning. That's not completely unheard of, but what struck me as strange is that two of the six were supposed to be going on dates and both got canceled."

"This took tremendous planning," Jack said. "And coordination. Could we be looking at more than one mole?"

Frank shook his head. "It's possible, but until we have proof, we'll assume one." He looked at Ben. "They're your people. Thoughts?"

Ben let out a long breath and faced the whiteboard. "Didn't think I'd ever have to do this." He drew a line down the board making two columns. "People we clear will go on the left and those we need to investigate on the right." In the left-hand column, he wrote Jack's name, then added *Simon Hughes*.

Jack had heard of Simon, but Ben kept the man's work private. Only Ben met with him. Jack lifted his brows. "You sure about Simon?"

"As sure as I am about you. Simon's dad was Edward Hughes, a member of the old council and someone Frank and I would have trusted with our lives. That was one of the reasons I personally recruited Simon."

That made Jack even more curious about the elusive

Simon, but now wasn't the time to dwell on that. "And the other reasons?"

Ben didn't flinch. "None of your business."

That was his superior talking, not his pseudo father figure. "Understood." Jack scanned the other names Ben listed in the *cleared* column: Lisa Munroe, Javier Cano, Drew Bartley. All familiar names, all solid.

Jack hated to think that someone he worked closely with could be a mole, but so far Ben's assessment of his agents seemed sound. Jack had worked with Lisa Munroe for years and she was as truth-driven and honest as they came. Javier Cano was a complete straight arrow and that's why Jack had asked him to help train the W's. Drew had a long history with Frank and Ben. They were all good people.

Then Jack turned to the right-hand column and shook his head. The possibility that eight of his co-workers could be working against them was unfathomable. "Are those names in any order?"

Ben disappeared his marker and turned around. "Yes, I put Mike Hendrix and Aleshia Beaumont at the top because they're the newest members of the team and although they checked out when I recruited them, I still don't know them as well as the others."

Jack tried to ignore the twist in his gut, knowing he set Meredith up with Mike and he could be their mole. "What about the others?"

"They've been with us longer and Lisa works with most of them day-to-day. I'll have her dig in deeper."

Frank returned to the couch and conjured a glass of amber liquid, most likely Macallan, Frank's favorite. The Scotch was a quiet tell that Frank was just as frustrated as Jack.

"Jack, work with Lisa and find this mole," Frank said, glancing at Ben for confirmation.

Ben nodded. "I'll ask Stella and Fiona to stay with Meredith because she shouldn't be alone."

Jack rose. "I'll call Lisa. But something's missing. I just know it." He looked between his mentors. "Why soul-jump Elise? If she dies, we'll all suffer, and while it could be Copeland's revenge against Elise's husband, would that be enough for Copeland?"

Ben agreed. "Hurting Elise might not be about her. It's about hurting Meredith and through her, you. I think you're his real target."

"Copeland's nothing if not calculated. I agree he wants to make me suffer, but this still doesn't make sense."

"Then expect another move," Frank warned.

Jack stood. "I'll say goodnight to Meredith, then call Lisa. We'll work through the night if we have to." And hope they'd find the mole in time to save Elise.

CHAPTER TWENTY-THREE

Sitting in the chair by her mother's bedside, Meredith groaned as she untwisted herself from the pretzel position she'd slept in. She stretched her arms above her head and moved her neck from side to side to work out the kinks. The clock on the nightstand showed it was six in the morning, and beside it was a note in Fiona's handwriting saying Jack had no leads yet.

She stood and looked down at her mom. Refusing to think of her as just a body, she rubbed her mother's arm. It was cooler than it had been the night before. She worried they were running out of time. "I'm coming for you, Mom," she whispered in the silence. Meredith grabbed another blanket from the bottom of the bed and draped it over her.

Copeland hadn't sent her anything yet. Would he send a letter? Would he call her or send a text? Meredith headed to the bathroom to brush her teeth and splash water on her face. She feared taking the time for a shower. Maybe he'd write the message in the steam on the bathroom mirror. She choked out a laugh at herself. She was beginning to panic, not knowing when or how Copeland would get word to her.

When she finished in the bathroom, she headed back to her mother's side and stopped. A single piece of paper sat on top of the extra blanket Meredith had placed on her mom.

Meredith's hand shook as she picked it up and read it in the dim light coming in between the break in the curtains.

You have thirty minutes to come to this address or your mother dies.

Meredith recognized the address at the bottom of the page as a new building. She'd been looking at it for comparisons to her condo renovations. Copeland had smashed her phone last night, so no map app, but she guessed it was a twenty-minute drive. Unfortunately, she didn't know when the note arrived. She checked the time on her watch and calculated twenty-five minutes ahead, just in case, then stuck the note in her back pocket and headed to the door. She turned around, went back to the bed, and kissed her mom. "I'm coming, Mom."

Stella and Fiona were talking softly in the kitchen; their voices reached her before she could see them.

"Good morning, Meredith. How are you doing, my sweet girl?" Fiona walked right up to Meredith and engulfed her in a hug. Meredith returned the hug and then backed away. The clock was ticking and she had to get out of there without them knowing why.

She leaned down and gave Stella a hug, so as not to seem out of character. "I'm going to the restaurant to get something to eat."

"Oh, you don't have to do that, I can conjure or make you something," Stella said.

"Ah, thanks, but I think I need to get out for a few minutes."

Fiona reached over and squeezed Meredith's arm. "Honey, I don't think it's safe. Please, let us conjure you something here."

Meredith did her best to hold her panic at bay—she had to get out of there now. "I just need a few minutes alone. I'm sure the restaurant's safe."

Fiona hesitated. "We don't know that for sure. At the very least, let us get Jack or Ben to go with you."

"No, don't bother them. I'll just pop downstairs and I won't be long." Meredith gave them both a smile she hoped looked sincere, and didn't wait for them to protest any more. "See you soon." She walked calmly to the apartment door and as soon as it closed behind her, she bolted for the stairwell.

It felt like it took forever to get to her car. "I'm on my way," she said out loud, hoping Copeland could hear her. "Please don't hurt my mom. I'm coming."

Last night she hadn't thought of another option besides following Copeland's instructions, but now Meredith second-guessed herself. Was she doing the right thing? Her chest felt tight when she thought about how she hadn't been able to forgive Jack, but he'd still been there for her since he'd been back. Too many times to count.

Yet she hadn't trusted him, and now she was walking into a lion's den to save her mom. Meredith felt like the dumb girl following a trail into the forest in the middle of the night. It was too late to turn around now and she couldn't call for help because Copeland would hear her.

She looked at the street sign ahead and saw that she was almost at her destination. The hypothetical dark forest was looming and she was out of options.

The building was in a newly developed part of the city and it looked like a combination of condos and businesses. Exactly the type of building Meredith was working on herself. The irony was that if the circumstances had been different, she would have reached out to the owners for a tour.

Meredith parked in a visitor's spot and decided instead of

being the girl walking into the forest and too stupid to live, she'd be Hansel and Gretel and leave a breadcrumb trail. She was down to four minutes. Closing her eyes, Meredith blocked out all sound and concentrated on the magic in her center. Hoping Jack would hear her, she mentally reached out and gave him the address. Jack had said that only short bursts of information could be sent telepathically and she didn't know how close she had to be for him to receive her message. After three attempts to give him the address, she looked at her watch and realized time was almost up. Only three minutes remained and she still had to get to the front door.

"I'm at the building," she said out loud. Standing at the building's large double doors, she realized she didn't know which unit to go to. The door attendant stood, staring at her suspiciously through the glass, like she didn't belong there as she loitered outside.

Meredith took the paper from her pocket and even though she knew it hadn't listed a condo number, she stared at it anyway, willing something to happen. "What unit?"

She glanced at the door again, the attendant staring at her, with his hands on his hips. Looking down at the paper again, Meredith huffed out a big breath when a number appeared on the paper where it hadn't been a moment ago.

Presenting a confidence she didn't feel, she walked into the building and gave her name to the door attendant, telling him what unit she was heading to. He pointed to the elevators and went back to his station like this happened every day.

Meredith punched the button for the sixteenth floor and stared at the numbers in the glass panel as they moved up. When the doors opened, she let out a gasp. A blond woman was standing right in front of her.

Physically, she was beautiful, but she had a look in her

eyes that said she had lived a hard life. The woman looked to be in her late twenties, was a couple of inches shorter than Meredith, and had long, curly blond hair and blue eyes.

The elevator door started to shut, but the woman flung her arm out and stopped it. "Are you coming or going?" she whispered as her eyes darted around the hallway.

Meredith shook off the shock and stepped out of the elevator. The floor was deserted except for the two of them. "I'm going to 1605."

"You should leave, she's as good as dead."

"What?" Meredith gaped at the blond woman, who stood there silently, her expression blank.

The woman looked over her shoulder before turning back to Meredith. "You should go. The woman you're coming to save is as good as dead, and you will be too if you go in there. It's a trap."

"I have—" Meredith stopped mid-sentence and looked at the door that opened across the hall. Copeland.

"Morgana, come here."

The woman, Morgana, hung her head and walked to Copeland.

"Get inside, I'll deal with you later."

Morgana eased by Copeland, still standing in the doorway, but didn't touch him. Meredith rubbed her arm over the tattoo. Copeland must have heard Morgana's warning.

"Meredith, come see your mother."

He sounded like he was inviting her in for a friendly visit. She tore her gaze from where Morgana had disappeared into the condo and focused on Copeland. He hadn't bothered to cover his face with a glamour spell, or whatever he'd used when she'd first met him. The skin on the left side of his face was stiff and unmoving when he spoke. His left eye, the pupil a murky gray, drooped lower than his right, too close to his upper lip.

Reality came crashing in on Meredith as she stared at Copeland. She wasn't walking into a forest alone, but this was possibly worse. Jack had told her Copeland was ruthless, but she had honestly hoped that if she showed him she would do what he wanted, he'd let her mother go.

Meredith was worse than the dumb woman walking into the forest at night. At least in a forest she could hide and there was no guarantee evil lurked between the trees. She'd been so caught up in grief from something that happened eight years ago that she never listened to Jack and her mother telling her it was all about people's choices. That had been a mistake, and walking into Copeland's place was likely a worse one. But she was doing it to save her mother.

She had to hope that Jack was coming for her and she could keep her and her mom alive until then. She straightened her shoulders and looked Copeland straight in his remaining eye. "I came like you asked. Let my mother go."

JACK STEPPED into Jo's apartment, every part of him aching to hold Meredith. He, Lisa, and Javier had come up empty last night after hours of chasing leads on the mole's identity. They'd finally agreed to get a few hours of sleep, but Jack hadn't been able to go home. Not without seeing Meredith, not without knowing she was okay.

"You look exhausted," Fiona said as she slid off her stool at the kitchen island and pulled him into a hug.

Jack returned the hug and smiled at Stella. "I'm good. Is Meredith with Elise's b—" He caught himself. "With Elise?" He couldn't bring himself to call Elise a body, not around her friends. Not when Meredith might hear him. Fatigue pulled at him but that wasn't an excuse to make that kind of mistake.

Stella conjured a mug of coffee and slid it across the island toward him. "No. She went down to get something to eat a while ago." Stella turned to Fiona. "Shouldn't she be back by now?"

Fiona frowned. "Yes, we should have noticed the time. She wanted some time to herself, but she told us she wouldn't be long."

A chill skated down Jack's spine. Something was wrong.

He flashed to the bedroom to see Elise lying on the bed, completely still, just like she'd been the night before. He flashed back to the kitchen. The rooms weren't far apart, but flashing was faster, and time suddenly felt critical.

"I'll check out the restaurant," he said, and disappeared before either woman could respond.

The kitchen was dark, the air empty of any scents of cooking. The dining area was deserted too.

He pulled out his phone to call Ben, but something stopped him. A sudden ping of energy echoed in his mind. He froze. Someone was trying to reach him telepathically. Numbers peppered his thoughts like someone was sending him a phone number or an address. The voice wasn't clear, but he knew it anyway—Meredith.

Jack gripped the edge of the stainless-steel counter to keep his knees from buckling. If she was trying to contact him this way, something was very wrong. The numbers came again, garbled. Not enough to go on.

He needed to find a way to track her. Jack dialed Ben the moment his brain caught up. "How do I access the cameras at The Magic Plate?" he asked as soon as the call connected.

"I'll be right there."

Seconds later, Ben landed in front of him.

"Meredith's gone and I think she tried to reach me telepathically, but I couldn't make it out. I think she was sending a phone number or maybe an address."

"You want to look for her vehicle?" Ben asked, already moving toward the storage. Jack followed.

"Yes. If we can see which direction her car went, I might be able to follow." Jack lifted his chin toward the recording equipment. "Do you have permissions?"

Ben nodded. "I set it up. How far back do you want to go?"

"Try thirty minutes."

Ben adjusted the time and scrolled slowly through the footage. "There."

Jack leaned in to see Meredith climb into her car. Since she'd parked up against the building, her face was visible. "She's talking."

Ben stopped the footage. "Copeland smashed her phone last night, so unless she borrowed one, she's talking to herself."

"She didn't say anything to Fiona or Stella about going anywhere. Look, she's rubbing her left arm. She did that in the restaurant too and then both arms at one point. My bet is that Copeland put a tracking spell on her."

Ben restarted the footage. "Or something else."

"Like what?"

"Inflict pain, use it to talk to her telepathically. Even surveillance. The possibilities are endless."

"Fuck."

"Exactly." They watched Meredith pull out of the parking lot. "She's headed south."

"I'll head that way. I'll flash a half mile at a time and try to reach her again."

"Jack," Ben warned, "I know you won't wait for backup, but I'll get it in motion."

Jack nodded and flashed, half-mile hops. At each stop, he reached for Meredith telepathically, but got nothing. He wasn't sure how far to go. If he went too far, he could end up further away from her instead of closer. After four more flashes, he stopped. There had to be a better way.

When he flashed back to Jo's apartment, Ben was on the phone. Fiona and Stella looked up, worry etched on their faces.

"You find her?" Fiona asked.

"No, but I know who might help." Jack turned to Ben as he wrapped up his call. "Can you contact the Emissary?"

"What are you thinking?"

"I want the Emissary to perform the council ceremony on me. I need enough power to track Meredith and defeat Copeland." Asking for the ceremony meant making another decision without involving Meredith. But if it saved her life? He'd make it a thousand times over.

Ben frowned. "I don't think the ceremony is a fast thing, but I'll call her."

"She's in the country," Fiona said.

Ben and Jack both turned to her. "How do you know that?" Ben asked.

Fiona shrugged. "I was close with Mary's parents so she always lets me know when she's stateside."

Mary? That seemed too commonplace a name for the Emissary, but Jack let it go. "Can you reach her?"

Fiona was already dialing. "Hi Mary, this is Fiona... yes, thank you. We need your help. Elise was soul jumped... Yes... Thank you." She ended the call and turned to Jack. "She's in LA with her co-lead and the two leaders from South America. They're on their way."

Less than two minutes later, the front door opened and the Emissary walked in with three others. Introductions were brief and Ben brought the visitors up to speed.

"How can I help?" the Emissary asked Jack.

"I need the council ceremony now because I need more power."

She exchanged looks with her companions. "We'll need time to bring the remaining leaders. They're scattered around the world. And we'll need Meredith present."

"We don't have time." Jack barely managed not to snap. "I need the extra power now to find Meredith and Elise."

"We might be able to help you locate them, but we can't interfere. Council leaders are forbidden from getting involved in other councils' matters."

Jack narrowed his eyes. "Yet you soul-jumped Meredith and me."

"There was no intervening because there was no council. But once you go through the ceremony, there will be."

Jack scoffed. "Sounds like semantics, but I don't care. Can you help me now or not?"

The Emissary looked at her companions and waved a hand. The four council members huddled in silence, shielded by a sound barrier.

They looked animated as they spoke. Jack paced back and forth. Meredith was probably terrified and she could be hurt. He knew firsthand what a bastard Copeland could be. The man wouldn't hesitate to hurt another person if it got him what he wanted and Copeland enjoyed seeing other people suffer too.

Jack was about at his wit's end when the leaders finally broke apart. "Will you help me?"

The Emissary stepped forward. "Yes, but it won't be the full ceremony."

"Anything that will enhance my power to be able to defeat him."

"Jack, we're concerned that you won't be facing only Copeland."

One of the South American council leaders put her hand on the Emissary's arm and nodded at her before speaking. "We have heard rumors in Brazil that someone's seeking the magic box and they are working with contacts in the U.S. We do not know who or how many, but it is not just one person. You must be careful."

Jack nodded. "I'll do whatever it takes to get Meredith and Elise back." He'd walk into any situation he had to, no matter how dangerous, and regardless of what could happen to him. Meredith and Elise were worth any risk.

CHAPTER TWENTY-FOUR

"We will help you," the Emissary said. She turned to the council leaders and gestured toward the living room. "Let's move the furniture and conduct the ceremony over there." When Jack looked, the space had already been cleared, the furniture pushed aside, leaving an open area in the center.

Jack hated ceremonies. They always felt like unnecessary theatrics, especially ones steeped in tradition. He'd skipped his high school and university graduations and would've skipped the FBI one if he could have. You put in the work and the certificate showed up in the mail. No ceremony needed.

Too bad he couldn't do some reading and ask for a certificate for this. But this wasn't something he could bypass. He needed the power they'd transfer to him. He just hated that he needed to do it without Meredith.

There wasn't any point in spiraling down a rabbit hole of what-ifs, but he couldn't help thinking that if he'd acted earlier, Meredith would be safe in his arms. He had let his arrogance of needing her to forgive him first dictate his choices.

Jack checked his watch. Meredith had been in Copeland's clutches for at least thirty minutes. The thought alone triggered a surge of adrenaline like a physical itch under his skin. A fight was coming—he could feel it. Copeland wasn't a patient man, which meant Meredith and Elise were running out of time. Just like a ticking clock, time wouldn't stop for anyone or anything, not even a necessary ceremony.

"This is the right choice," Fiona said softly as she came to stand in front of Jack, laying a comforting hand on his arm. "Thank you for this. You'll bring them back. I know it in my heart." Her voice broke on a sob and Jack's own heart felt heavy with her grief. Elise was the sister Fiona never had and Meredith was like a daughter to her. He pulled her into a quick hug, then stepped back.

"You don't have to thank me, Fiona."

She gave him a watery smile and wiped her tears away with a flick of her magic. "We all make choices and if Elise had the chance to do it all over again, I'm not sure she'd choose differently. But Jack, please remember that the choices ahead of you are yours alone. Just as those of people around you are theirs. You can't change that." She gave his arm a squeeze and walked over to where Ben stood with his arms around Stella.

Fiona's words sounded cryptic but Jack had no time to ponder them.

He stepped into the cleared space as instructed. The four council members moved to form a circle around him.

They were shrouded in robes similar to a judge's—plain black, covering them from neck to feet, with long, billowy sleeves. A thin band of color adorned the neckline, identifying the council they led.

Something draped over Jack. He looked down to see a

plain black robe, like the others wore, but his had no trim, and was so dark it seemed to absorb all color around him. He didn't care. He just wanted the ceremony over with so he could find Meredith. Raising his eyes to watch the Emissary, he waited, holding on to his vanishing patience.

The lights in the room extinguished, and candles sprang to life. His first instinct was to scoff. Dramatic much? But then the gravity of the situation overtook him and the seriousness of what he was about to do finally began to sink in.

His father had been in this exact position. Had taken the power given to him and used it for evil. He'd corrupted those around him and attempted to do the same to Jack. He'd resisted, but in doing so he'd made a promise to himself that had shaped the rest of his life. That had made him leave Meredith.

Could he have found another way? Had there been other options without turning Meredith against her mother?

He dragged his attention from the thoughts as his body heated up and sweat ran down his back. Giving his arms a slight shake within the robe's voluminous sleeves, he forced the tension to fall from his shoulders, imagining it hitting the floor.

A resolve settled over him. He felt no fear. No anger. No regret. Only a determination to take whatever steps were necessary to protect the one he loved. He exhaled and relaxed his shoulders. He was ready.

Looking up, he caught the Emissary's gaze, and she nodded once as if understanding the war that had just waged inside him.

Around the room, the candles flared bright, their flames shooting skyward. The room illuminated briefly, as bright as a flash-bang thrown into darkness. At the same time a spell wrapped around Jack like invisible chains.

He tried moving one foot to test the bonds, but his feet were stuck to the hardwood floor. An icy sensation, not cold but paralyzing, shot all the way up to his shoulders until only his head remained mobile.

This didn't bode well for what was to come.

The Emissary turned to the person on her left and nodded. The council member pulled his hands from inside the folds of his robe and held them out. A large ancient-looking spellbook appeared across his palms, the pages flipping quickly before settling on a page somewhere in the middle.

"Quae in Statera. We Bring Balance."

His voice, a deep baritone, resonated throughout the room, demanding the listener hang on to his every word. He spoke first in Latin and then repeated each sentence in English. Jack never did learn Latin and knew he'd be relying on a cheat sheet if he ever had to spout it. He hung on to the English translations like a lifeline.

"We are but a few trusted to guide the many.

Together we guide and protect.

My experience is knowledge.

My mistakes are wisdom.

These I pass on to you.

I welcome you to stand with us.

To guide and protect.

My gift to you is strength.

With this spell I bestow upon you all my knowledge, wisdom, and strength."

The blast hit Jack like a heavyweight ensuring a win, a force that would have taken him to the ground if not for the spell holding him in place. The effort to keep his eyes open became too much and he let them close, concentrating on the new energy swirling within him.

With the strength of a tornado, the energy rippled

throughout his body, creating heat and light that mixed with his own magic and bonded them together. A heady feeling. Not pain, but a similar sharpness. Power and endorphins exploded within him, almost terrifying in their intensity.

Images churned in his mind. Hundreds, no, thousands of memories that weren't his own, knowledge being passed down. Emotions too. Rage, joy, grief, hope—too many emotions to name bombarded him at once. He pushed them all aside before they drowned him.

His body rotated clockwise. Like the numbers on a clock, he now faced the next council member. It didn't matter who had turned him. His only concern was facing the council member in front of him and preparing for the next round. One down, three to go. For now, he wouldn't think about the ten more he'd eventually have to endure to account for the rest of the council members.

As with the first member, the woman in front of him held an ancient spellbook in her hands and her voice resounded through the room.

"We are but a few trusted to guide the many.

Together we guide and protect.

My experience is knowledge.

My mistakes are wisdom.

These I pass on to you.

I welcome you to stand with us.

To guide and protect.

My gift to you is courage.

With this spell I bestow upon you all my knowledge, wisdom, and courage."

Jack let out a long exhale, preparing to absorb the blast, as the council member spoke the last words. He sent a wave of calm throughout his body, forcing himself into a state of relaxation. His Zen-like presence, no matter how contrived, better prepared him to accept the force more quickly this time, but it was no less powerful in its intensity.

An impact hit. A momentary shaking took over his limbs while his body absorbed and adjusted to the new power.

Again, his body rotated clockwise to face the next member in the circle, and he readied himself once more. The next gift was justice.

Jack felt his body vibrating with the new energy and power. Somewhere in his mind, amongst overcrowded images and overwhelming knowledge, he pictured Meredith in Copeland's hands. He needed to finish this ceremony.

"There are two traits left, but they will come as one," the Emissary said. "I will gift them both and one will become your own."

Once more, he felt his body turn. He knew he had come 360 degrees and was back facing the Emissary, but his eyes remained closed. Too overrun with the memories of others and a new all-consuming energy to care about opening his eyes.

Without warning, his head lifted and locked into place and his eyes opened and fixed on the Emissary. She was standing in front of him, closer than the others had.

She looked different than before. A shiny aura of energy glowed around her, subtle, but undeniable light emanating from every pore of her being.

He knew the verse by heart now and waited only for the final words to be spoken.

"… gifts to you are Perseverance and Self-Discipline. With this spell I bestow upon you all my knowledge, wisdom, perseverance, and self-discipline."

The spell came at Jack like a tsunami hitting the shores of a deserted beach. Wave after wave of energy, experiences, and memories hit him, one after the other.

He collapsed, a shaking heap of muscle and bone on the

hardwood floor. Images and thoughts continued to battle it out in his mind, until finally, they began to slow and fade.

A cool breeze permeated his body, starting with his fingers and toes and spreading through his limbs and torso. It soothed the intense heat that each additional spell had brought with it, his body a massive volcano of heat and energy.

He lay still for several minutes as the cool touch worked its way throughout his entire body.

Hushed voices slowly broke through the fog and penetrated his consciousness. With a loud groan, he rolled to his side and hefted himself onto an elbow. Using his other hand and a knee as leverage, he slowly hoisted himself up and stood.

The rest of the ceremony wasn't going to be high on his priority list to complete anytime soon. It would take twice as long and take twice as much energy out of him as this one had—nope, he wasn't looking forward to it.

He squinted and focused, his gaze catching on one of the council members. A faint aura surrounded her. The same as the Emissary. Snapping his head around, he caught sight of the other two council members. Each had a shimmering aura as well.

"Jack, I just—" Fiona started to speak.

"Do you see an aura around the council members?" he asked, interrupting her.

"Umm, no. I take it you can see one?"

"Yes, I can now, but I couldn't before."

Only council members can see them. The thought thrown into his mind came from the Emissary. She smiled as she approached Jack. "We have located Meredith and Elise. They are not far from here. I will gather the others soon to finish the ceremony. Goodbye, Jack."

"What is the..." As the Emissary vanished, the address

appeared in Jack's mind, as clear as a Google Maps image. He turned around and saw that the other council members were gone as well, the living room back to the way it had been before they arrived.

"Jack." He turned to Fiona. "I noticed the thin band of color on your robe is now a rich brown. That makes sense." Fiona's eyes twinkled; she knew something Jack didn't.

"Okay, I'll bite. Why does that make sense?"

"Brown is associated with strength and maturity, and it is the color of self-discipline."

"Really? That's a thing?"

Fiona chuckled. "Yes, Jack, that's a thing."

"Ben!" Stella's shout came from the bedroom.

Jack was in the bedroom in a fraction of a second, faster than he'd ever flashed before. Ben and Fiona came in behind him. "What's wrong?"

Stella gestured to Elise. "Look."

Jack walked over to the bed. The beginnings of a bruise were visible on Elise's left cheek. She also sported a split lip and her left eye was almost swollen shut. "Copeland's beating her. It must have happened while we were doing the council ceremony, within the last half hour."

Stella lightly ran her hand up and down Elise's arm. "I think Copeland did it right now. When I came to check on Elise, the bruise and swelling popped up and her lip split right before my eyes."

"The lines," Fiona gasped.

As they spoke, dark lines appeared on Elise's neck—the same killing marks the unbinding had erased.

Jack didn't understand how it was possible. Elise had been safe and healthy, yet the effects of the spell had her again. The sight hollowed him, but fear for Meredith struck deeper, tightening every muscle in his body.

He turned to Ben and spewed the address the Emissary

had given him, knowing Ben would send a team, then flashed.

"My dear, it's not as easy as just letting you go. Come inside. My patience is wearing thin."

Meredith hesitated, every instinct screaming at her to run, as Copeland filled the doorway, turning his attention inside. A scream tore through the air, followed by a sickening thud.

He met her gaze over his shoulder. "Are you ready to come in now or should I play a bit more?"

She stepped inside without thinking and the door clicked closed behind her.

Heavy curtains choked out the morning light, keeping the room dim. On the far side, the blond woman—Morgana, Copeland had called her—lay crumpled in a heap by the wall, her eyes closed. Meredith turned toward her, but something caught her eye and she snapped her attention to the center of the room.

"Mom!" Meredith rushed to her mother; she sat bound to a chair, her face battered—one eye swollen shut, her lip split.

Tears streaked down her mom's bruised cheek. "Ah, honey. You shouldn't have come."

Meredith gripped the rope bindings, her magic flowing unbidden into her fingers, but ineffective. This was beyond the basic skills she'd learned so far. "They're stuck. Can you push yourself back into your body?" she whispered.

"No need to whisper," Copeland drawled behind her. "I can hear *everything*."

Meredith popped up and turned. In her panic she'd forgotten about his eavesdropping tattoo.

"Elise can't return to her body. The ropes are spelled." Copeland smirked like a naughty boy pleased with himself. "A nice trick I got from siphoning the essence of a teenage girl with a unique speciality. Her sister had a special talent too—rekindling the devastation of old spells, even ones stripped away by your precious unbinding."

"What are you talking about?"

"The magic that was killing her is back."

Meredith whipped back around to her mom and gasped at the lines that covered her neck once more.

"I thought it poetic justice that the binding your mother cast to save you was going to kill her, so I couldn't let it be undone."

They'd saved her mom once, so they could do it again, but first she had to get back to her body. Facing Copeland, she stood her ground. "You have me now; let her go."

He tsked. "No. I need you both here for the show. We're just waiting for our guest star. Jack should arrive any moment."

She shifted subtly, placing herself in front of her mom. "He doesn't know where we are."

"True. That's the fun part—him having to scramble. But you should be honored because I choreographed this with you in mind."

"Up!" he directed to someone behind Meredith and flicked his hand.

She spun to see Morgana jerked up like a marionette yanked by invisible strings, her mouth open in a soundless cry. Pain distorted her features and her feet scraped the floor as she was dragged forward.

"Meredith, let me formally introduce you to Morgana. She's been my favorite pet for years. When you hesitated at the door, she got a taste of my... disappointment. Let's not have any more of that."

"Don't listen to him," Morgana ground out, as if the words cost her.

Copeland waved his hand and she collapsed, a horrific sound of misery pulled from her. She spasmed on the floor unnaturally.

"Now, now, Morgana, don't make me bring out the spiders," he said like he was scolding a two-year-old for having a tantrum.

Meredith lurched forward. "Stop it!"

"I haven't even started yet." He flicked his hand again.

Elise gasped and Meredith ran to her. An unseen force bent her mom's head back, the veins bulging in her neck from the strain of the angle. Her nostrils flared and her mouth hung open, gulping for air.

Meredith cupped her mom's cheeks, trying to ease her head forward, but she couldn't get her to move. "Stop! You're hurting her! I'll do whatever you want!"

Copeland smiled. The force holding her mom vanished and she sagged in the chair. "I thought you'd see it my way."

Meredith dropped to her knees, her hands on her mom's legs. "I can't let him continue to hurt you. You're all I have left."

Her mom's steady gaze met hers. "No, sweetheart, you have our family. And Jack."

"But none of them are you." Her voice cracked on the last word.

"My sweet girl. I want you to live and love deeply. Have children and know the kind of joy only a child can bring—like the joy you've brought me."

Meredith swallowed against the sudden burning in her throat and stopped fighting the tears, letting them fall. "Don't talk like that, Mom. You sound like you're saying goodbye. You have to—"

"Meredith, stop." Her mother's words cut her off but she didn't want to listen.

She opened her mouth to plead again, when a high-pitched buzzing cut through the room.

Copeland smiled, the expression so twisted that Meredith moved closer to her mom. The noise ceased as quickly as it had started. "That, my dear, is the alarm and means my old friend Jack is coming to your rescue."

"Trust me," Elise whispered.

Meredith clutched her mom's legs tighter. "What are you—?"

"Fuck! No!" Copeland stormed across the room and shoved Meredith aside. She hit the ground, her palms jamming into the hardwood.

He loomed over Elise. "What the fuck did you tell him?"

Meredith pushed to her feet, grabbing at Copeland's arm. "Leave her alone!"

He tore his arm away and landed a punch in the middle of her mom's face. Her head whipped back, then fell forward, blood pouring down onto her lips.

"Mom!"

Turning to Meredith, he narrowed his eyes, now appearing black as oil. She took a step backward, but fell, landing on her butt. She crab-walked back, but he was too fast.

He kicked her legs and she fell flat on her back. Fear gripped her, freezing her in place for a second, and that was all it took.

A dagger shimmered into the air above her, only a fraction of an inch above her face.

"Don't move," he said, stepping closer. "You've seen what one of these can do, and I won't hesitate to let it drop."

Meredith stared up. The dagger's sharp tip hovered right above her eye. She pushed out a slow breath as sweat beaded on her skin. But it wouldn't have mattered if it was touching her, she would fight. Even without knowing how to use all her magic, she wasn't helpless.

She focused on pulling in the energy that surrounded her. Magic once more crackled in her fingertips. She didn't know what it would do, but it *was there.*

"Fuck you!" she whispered, then rolled.

The dagger dropped, the edge scraping along her hairline. She hissed in pain but kept moving, rolling again, then sprang to her feet. Not willing to let the pulse of pain in her temple deter her, she faced him.

Copeland laughed. "Your naiveté is adorable." He conjured two more daggers. "Shall we keep playing?"

Turning quickly, he hurled one. It struck Morgana on the shoulder, knocking her backward to the floor.

"Morgana doesn't have much magic—she's pretty useless, so I didn't use poison. Yet. But keep disobeying me and I will. Then it will be their blood on your hands. You couldn't do anything about me twenty years ago and you won't stop me now."

He'd known all along that she'd seen him at the fire, but she didn't react. Her hands trembled and her scalp throbbed, but she refused to show him any more weakness.

"Don't listen to him."

Meredith looked over at Morgana as she struggled to her feet, holding the bloody dagger in her hand as more blood dripped to the floor. She swayed but stayed standing.

"Ah, Morgana, so tough," Copeland taunted her, the remaining dagger at his side.

Meredith acted. She lunged, tackling him from behind. They hit the floor hard and she realized too late that she hadn't used her magic to give herself a boost.

"Enough!" he roared before twisting out from underneath

her. He flung his arms to the side—one toward Meredith and the other in Morgana's direction.

She flew backward, slamming into the wall. Her skull rang like a bell as her world tilted. Sucking in a breath to steady herself, she pushed to her hands and knees.

"Now, where were we?" Copeland asked as though the last few minutes had only been a movie intermission. "Oh yes, I remember now."

Invisible pressure wrapped around her, dragging her body down with the feel of hands yanking at her legs. She clawed at the air for purchase but the pull dragged her across the floor until more pressure slammed her flat, arms pinned tight to her sides.

"Now, don't move," Copeland said.

A dagger appeared an inch above her left eye. Squeezing her eyes shut, she fought against the hopelessness that threatened to slip free.

Copeland paced, his heavy footsteps vibrating the floor beneath her, while muttering about his obsession with Jack. He lived in the past, feeding on it, and for the first time she wondered if she'd been stuck there too.

Her mother's words from months ago came back to her: *"I want you to know that whether or not what my sisters and I did was right, we had our reasons, made our choice, and accepted it. That's all we can do. Make a choice that seems right for us and keep going. You can't change the choices others make, you just have to accept that they tried to make the right one."*

Her mom and aunts had believed they were saving their children. Jack had believed he was protecting them both. And Meredith—she'd done nothing. She hadn't fought for Jack. For eight years she'd pretended to move on, and find love, but the truth was she couldn't. Because she'd already found it —with Jack—and never stopped loving him.

She couldn't wrap her life in neat, ordered boxes, like

she'd always wanted. Life was messy and you made the best choices you could with what you had. That's what her mom and aunts had done. Even while dealing with their grief, they'd tried to make the right choice.

Jack had tried to tell her that, but she'd refused to listen. She hadn't even listened to her own heart telling her she loved him. She'd loved him since she was five years old. Now, she would die, and never get to experience life—the ups and the downs—with him by her side.

Helpless, she clenched her eyes tighter, but more tears slid free.

"It's going to be okay," her mom whispered. Moving only her eyes, Meredith looked over at her. Blood still dripped from her mom's nose, slower now, falling over her lips and down her chin.

Meredith could just make out Morgana sprawled nearby, her hair fanned across the floor, blood darkening her shoulder. Lifeless or just barely hanging on, she didn't know.

Meredith's chest ached, and not from a dagger. She didn't know if any of them would walk out of this condo, or if it would be their final resting place.

CHAPTER TWENTY-FIVE

*N*o *guards.* Elise's words entered Jack's mind.

He didn't respond. Conversing mentally was too risky—Copeland might detect it. Jack had already triggered one magic alarm when he neared the building, he wouldn't take any unnecessary risks.

Before the ceremony, he would have missed tripping a perimeter alarm. Now he could feel it. The power hummed through him, sharp and electric. His senses were beyond anything he'd known. He no longer just felt his magic—he *was* the magic. The rush eclipsed every tale he'd heard, everything he'd seen his father do.

Jack flashed into the condo building without a second thought. Most magics wouldn't flash into the unknown, but Jack wasn't like most magics anymore. Power coursed through him and he trusted it to help guide him.

He flashed to the sixteenth floor and time slowed down mid-jump. Two doors, dim lighting, and a dark gray carpet from end to end appeared in an empty hallway below him. He hung there, imperceptible for a heartbeat—suspended over the carpet like a raindrop about to fall—then touched his feet down light and silent, visible once more.

Everything matched the snapshot he'd seen while flashing. He would need time to adjust to his new capabilities, but for now, he'd let instinct drive him.

He pushed energy to his ears to enhance his hearing and the surge of sound nearly dropped him to his knees. It took him several breaths to pull back on the power and right himself. Then he heard it—Copeland cursing and the sound of flesh hitting flesh.

I'm going in. Jack sent the thought to Ben with no guarantee of a delivery over this distance, but his new power hadn't failed him yet.

Jack flashed into the apartment.

He landed in an open-concept condo and took in the chaos in a single slice of time. Copeland stood like a ringmaster in the center of his own circus, commanding daggers. One hovered an inch above Meredith's eye, daring her to move from where she lay on the floor. A blond woman lay on the other side of the room, and Elise—bruised and bleeding—sat strapped to a chair between them.

Everything in Jack screamed *Meredith first*, but his training kicked in. He flashed to Elise, his power telling him to lay a hand on each of the ropes holding her. They dissolved at his touch. Another surprise from the ceremony, but no time to dwell on it as he directed Elise, "Push back into your body."

"No." She struggled to her feet. "I'm not leaving you all."

"You're here," Copeland interrupted, sounding amused.

Jack faced the instructor he'd failed to kill sixteen years ago. "And you're still alive. I guess you suck as a teacher."

Copeland's expression tightened, distorting his face even further. Jack hadn't dared talk back while he'd been under the man's tutelage, but he wasn't that scared teenager anymore.

His old tutor looked almost the same—except for the hideous scars Jack had gifted him during their last encounter. But the rest of him remained unchanged: thick hair, blade-sharp jaw, immaculately tailored suit, same cold eyes.

Although he never took his eyes off Copeland, Jack remained aware of his surroundings. Observing the man's stance, he recognized something was different.

At first glance, he thought it was a trick of the light, but his new knowledge told him Copeland had an aura. It was thick and black—like tar around a frame—not the golden light sported by Jack and the other council members. Dark and thick closest to his body, it became grayer and thinner as it fanned out.

Copeland had been a council member for two years before Jack killed his father, and it didn't take a genius to figure out why Copeland's aura was dark—it came from the repeated use of magic for evil intent, and hadn't left him when the council magic had because it had soaked too deep, becoming a part of him.

Jack felt a presence at his side but kept his gaze locked on Copeland.

"Don't kill him yet," the blond woman rasped. "There are more kids, he knows where."

"Ah, Morgana, you do care," Copeland said with a laugh.

Jack ignored the comment, but continued to hold his stare as he spoke. "We found all the missing children."

"No, you haven't." Morgana's tone held a fierceness that belied her weakened state.

Copeland grinned. "And he never will. You're such a small thinker, Jack. You always were, and it seems that the FBI hasn't changed that. Now I get to do what your father should have done decades ago." His lips curved up, his left eye hitching up in a grotesque imitation of a smile. "I'll be doing magics a favor when I kill you, but first, I'm going to make you suffer."

"You're still a blowhard. You never could shut up," Elise spit out, coming up on Jack's other side. "You won't win."

"I already have. Still have those scarves and turtlenecks, Elise? You're going to need them, but not for long," Copeland taunted.

Again, Jack kept silent. Listening to Copeland disgusted him, but reacting would only feed the man's ego. He saw his former teacher for what he was now—a man desperate to reclaim control, not a master of it. Regardless of how pathetic he was, Jack wanted to rip the man's heart out for everything he'd done—for all the people he'd hurt. But then Jack would be no different than him and his father.

Remember that the choices ahead of you are yours alone. Just as those of people around you are theirs. You can't change that. Fiona's words played in his head; he knew she was right.

In spite of the choice Elise made not to tell Meredith about the binding all those years ago, Jack could have. He could have fought for Meredith and found a way to be together, not walked away. As for not compromising? That's where he went wrong. He should have done everything for the woman he loved. As for his children—he would have made sure they were true to themselves. As would Meredith.

He glanced at her. She hadn't moved, the dagger still hovered just above her face—too close, but her eyes were open and alert. Jack would do anything for her, including whatever it took to be with her. That meant making decisions with her, not for her. He just needed a plan.

Jack flared his senses outward—the raw intensity of his new power still an adjustment—but he didn't question what he could do. His magic took over and pulsed in a ripple, like sonar as it bounced off the walls and threaded through the apartment, before feeling the depth of Copeland's power. Although dark and depraved, he wasn't weak, his magic boosted by the life he'd stolen from others. He wouldn't be easy to defeat, but he was still just a man.

When Jack stared down Copeland and remained silent, the former instructor became impatient. "You think you're all powerful now, Jack? That you can best me?" Copeland hissed. "You think I don't have a plan?" His aura flared around him, thick and oily and swirling like smoke, shadow tendrils creeping out across the floor.

Jack watched in horror as those tendrils curled along Meredith's legs and arms like snakes, clamping down on her wrists and ankles. More slithered around Morgana and snapped closed, yanking her to the floor beside Meredith.

The women cried out as they struggled. Jack saw it now—the way Copeland's black, tar-like aura leached the color from their skin, brightness from their eyes. They weren't just shackles holding them in place—they *drained*. Copeland was siphoning from them, absorbing power into himself like charging a battery. But not only taking their power, like the binding had done. He was draining them of their essence.

"You think you're strong now," Copeland gloated, grinning at Jack. "But I've had years to learn. I'm more than a man. I've evolved. Watch."

Meredith and Morgana were snatched upright by an unseen force, their feet dangling inches above the ground. They cried out in pain and clawed against an invisible enemy, ripping into their own skin trying to escape.

Somehow, Jack would get Meredith free, but she needed to trust him. "I love you, Bubbles. I was wrong for walking away. I thought I was doing the right thing, but I should have fought for you."

Meredith's lips moved, but no sound came out. He didn't

need to hear the words she was trying to say to know what she wanted to tell him. "I know. Together," he promised. "We're going to get out of this, but you need to fight with me."

"How touching, Jack, but fighting is useless. I've already beat you." Copeland laughed.

I forgive you. I love you. Meredith spoke the words into his mind and he felt whole for the first time in eight years.

Fight, he told her. He sent the same message to Morgana, and realized he could keep a channel open with them both, and Elise. His telepathy was no longer all or nothing when communicating with several people.

Jack spoke into Elise's mind. *Distract him.*

Without acknowledging him, Elise took a step forward. "Louis, let them go. You've got Jack and me, the women are innocent."

Before Elise finished speaking, Jack was on the move. He flashed once, twice, three times in rapid succession around Copeland and the women. With each pass he closed in, building a rolling surge of energy to tear the siphoning bonds apart.

Copeland screamed in frustration as the bonds fractured. Meredith and Morgana dropped to the ground like dead weights.

Just as Jack stepped toward Meredith, Copeland snarled, lashing out at Elise. She didn't have a chance to react as his magic slammed her backward, her body twisting mid-air. She crashed into the wall with a sickening crack. Her soul shimmered before solidifying once more.

"No!" Meredith screamed.

Distracted by Elise, Jack turned back to Meredith too late.

Copeland stood with one hand wrapped around Meredith's throat and the other around Morgana's, their feet once more dangling off the ground, and the siphoning cuffs back in place.

Blood seeped from Copeland's fingers as the women tore at his flesh with their nails. It didn't faze him. His grip was loose enough that they were still breathing, but that wouldn't last long—he would want to demonstrate his superior strength. And make Jack suffer. That had always been Copeland's objective, and he hadn't needed a reason.

Meredith stopped struggling, one hand dropping to her side.

Jack feared what he would have to do to save her.

SEND YOUR POWER THROUGH ME.

Elise's voice penetrated Jack's mind, more resolute than she'd been before. He didn't want to look at her—didn't want to acknowledge what he feared she was proposing. She stood off to Copeland's side, swaying slightly on her feet. Drywall dust coated her hair and clothing—a stark contrast to the black lines coiling down her neck.

Jack kept his gaze on Meredith, searching his new memories for a better plan, while he answered Elise. *Why?*

The lines on me? Copeland revived the effects of the binding spell. I feel it sucking me in. With your power I can bind Copeland to me.

No. It will kill you. Jack threw the thought back at Elise with force.

It was always meant to. My sisters and I knew there was no going back.

There has to be another way.

There isn't, Jack. This is my choice, not yours.

"Coming up with a plan?" Copeland asked, obviously

sensing the flow of power between them they hadn't bothered to disguise. "It doesn't matter what you think up; you won't win," Copeland continued, his tone condescending, clearly intended to goad. "Your husband thought he could beat me and look what happened. You couldn't save him, either."

Meredith let out a low moan, barely audible. Jack's heart clenched. She and Morgana were running out of time. *How?* Jack asked Elise, although he couldn't believe he was even having this conversation. He didn't want Elise's death on his hands, but he'd do anything to save Meredith. As would Elise.

If you give me enough power, I'll be able to break through the siphoning bond and grab Copeland. The binding spell that's pulling at me will see to the rest.

"Fucking stop talking!" Copeland yelled, the smooth side of his face turning red with his anger. "Look at me, Jack! Don't you see what I'm doing?"

Ignoring Copeland, Jack looked at Meredith and knew he had to make a choice. She was running out of time. Her lips moved and she looked down. Jack followed her line of sight to see her fingers moving, magic still sparking from her fingertips.

She's still fighting, Elise said.

It always came down to choices and now he had to make the hardest one yet—Meredith's life or her mother's. He knew which choice Meredith would make, but this was Jack's choice, and Elise's.

Jack nodded once, more to himself than anyone else. *Once I send it to you, give me a count of two to reach Meredith and Morgana. I have to stop them from being sucked in with Copeland.*

Elise nodded.

Be ready, he told her, then directed his instructions to Meredith and Morgana. *I'm going to pull you toward me.*

Now! he yelled into the minds of all three women. Jack pulled in more energy than would have been possible only hours before, and pivoted. Directing the power into Elise, he threw himself forward, wrapping one arm around Meredith and the other around Morgana. Using another surge of magic, he threw himself backward, taking the women with him, just as Elise's soul lit up, light bursting from every part of her like a star going nova. The binding spell, aided by the power of Jack's magic, flared to life. It wasn't visible to the eye, but Jack *felt* it.

As soon as Jack hit the back wall, Meredith and Morgana still in his arms, Elise let the energy loose. The waves of energy hit him like a tsunami, deafening in their force.

Copeland sensed it too late. He spun, eyes wide. "No—"

Elise grasped onto him as the energy engulfed them both in a golden flame.

Copeland pushed back on Elise's form as it wavered. Jack feared Elise wouldn't be strong enough to hold him. Before he could help, Meredith tore from his hold. She stood and lifted her hands toward her mom.

Jack jumped to his feet to hold Meredith back, but her next words stopped him. "Help me, Jack," she yelled over the percussion of energy vibrating in the room. "She needs more power."

Jack directed more of his magic toward Elise, and it flowed in the conduit of Meredith's power. The energy in the room grew stronger and louder, then surged. Elise pulled it in, surrounding herself and Copeland in a whirlpool of magic.

Copeland opened his mouth, but no sound emerged. Elise gave Jack another small nod and then the world around them exploded.

Jack and Meredith were once more thrown back. He cushioned her fall with his body as a hush fell over the room.

Jack looked over to where Elise and Copeland had stood. The space was empty.

Elise had pulled Copeland to his death with her.

His throat tightened and he swallowed, closing his eyes. He blinked back tears at the thought of her sacrifice and bent forward, kissing Meredith softly on the forehead.

"You came," Meredith whispered.

He tilted his head to see into her eyes. "I love you, Bubbles. I'm so sorry I didn't fight for you."

"That's in the past. I love you." Meredith kissed him, a light touch of the lips, and pulled back, turning around. "Where's my mom?"

Jack swallowed again. "She wasn't really here. It was only her soul."

"She pushed her soul back to her body?" Meredith stood and took a step away. He saw the exact moment she realized what had happened. "No… no… we were helping her… we gave her more power. That was supposed to save her, right?" she asked, her voice unsteady.

Jack could lie. Reaching for her, he tried to pull her into his arms, but she side-stepped him.

"No!" she yelled and flashed away.

eredith almost tripped over her own feet as she landed in the entrance to Jo's apartment. She stumbled forward, heading for the bedroom where she'd left her mom, dread gripping her heart.

It couldn't be true. Jack had to be wrong.

Just before she reached the bedroom, she stopped with her hand on the outside of the doorframe.

Each breath scraped her throat, sharper than the agony of Copeland siphoning her magic.

The door gaped halfway, as if whoever left it that way hadn't decided whether they should invite her in. What if she didn't go inside? If she didn't cross the threshold, maybe it wouldn't be real.

She shook the thought off and placed her hand on the door. Her hand shook when she pushed it against the wood to open it fully.

"Meredith," Fiona said, her voice sounding choked with tears.

"No." Meredith shook her head and hesitated at the

threshold. Stella sat in the same chair Meredith had abandoned only a couple of hours earlier.

Oh god. Had it really only been a couple of hours? It felt like a lifetime ago.

Fiona sat in a blue chair—it hadn't been there earlier. Meredith's gaze landed on the chair and she couldn't make herself look away. Someone must have conjured it. It seemed easier to concentrate on a chair and not look over at the bed.

How long could she stand there and not move? Could she avoid the inevitable? She wasn't ready to face the truth.

She caught sight of Stella out of the corner of her eye. Her mom's friend rose and stepped toward Meredith. The movement awoke something in her and she pulled her gaze from the chair. She held up her hand and Stella stopped.

Meredith's feet felt bolted to the floor. She hadn't moved from the doorway. The sight on the bed beckoned to her, but she couldn't look. Not yet.

No.

Her mom was the only one she had left.

And now she was dead.

No.

She couldn't be dead.

Forcing herself to look, she glanced at the bed.

Her mom lay where she'd left her earlier.

Taking one step, and then another and another, Meredith made it to the bed. She took a deep breath and squeezed her eyes shut. When she opened them, she eased herself onto the edge of the bed carefully, not wanting to disturb her.

Her mom looked even paler than before.

Lifting her mom's hand, she held it in both of hers and rubbed it, trying to give her warmth. Her mom's hands were always cold; now they felt icy.

She summoned her last scrap of energy and poured

warmth into her mom's hand. "You're magic, Mom. You'll be alright."

Bending down, she placed a kiss on her mom's hand. "I need you, Mom. You can't leave—" Her throat cinched, stealing all the room's oxygen. Her tears splashed onto her mom's skin; she wiped them away with her thumb.

This couldn't be real. Her mom had to be here to teach her more about magic. She'd wanted Meredith to find love and have babies she'd then spoil. "My babies will need a grandma, just like I need a mom," she whispered.

"Bubbles."

She looked up as Jack reached for her, and she scrambled off the bed, backing away. "No! Don't touch me, Jack." She spun and pointed at her mother lying on the bed. "Heal my mom!"

He took a step toward her, his hand extended, but she backed up further. Her butt hit the dresser.

She felt trapped. There was nowhere to go to escape the pain.

"You're powerful, Jack! Do something!" she screamed at him as the taste of her tears slipped into her mouth.

Pushing Jack aside, she spun and faced the others in the room.

"There has to be something one of you can do! You're all fucking magic. Heal her!"

Meredith couldn't breathe. It felt like Copeland was strangling her all over again.

She gasped, each breath knifing her throat.

"You have to—" She choked on her words as sobs consumed her and tears obscured her vision.

Stumbling back to the bed, she draped herself over her mom's body as shudders racked her own.

"Bubbles."

Jack lifted her away from the bed, and she thrashed

against his hold. Grabbing at the blankets, she twisted out of his arms until he had to tear her away. "No, no…"

He didn't let go. Just held her tighter.

"I can't… I can't breathe, Jack. It hurts."

"I know." She felt him kiss her forehead as he settled in a chair with her sitting sideways in his lap.

Meredith looked back at her mom's lifeless body. "We undid the spell so she would live. She was supposed—"

Jack didn't say anything and held her as she felt like her heart had broken into a million pieces.

Sometime later, Jack carried her to a bed. He spooned behind her, pulling her into his warmth as she shivered. She wondered if she'd ever be warm again.

IN THE TWO days since her mom died Meredith hadn't left her apartment. Jack had forced her to eat something the day before. Then he'd put her in the shower and she'd just stood there.

They hadn't spoken as he'd put shampoo in her hair and washed it. He added conditioner and ran his fingers through the strands as he rinsed it out. They still didn't speak as she cried and the water washed her tears away.

Afterward, he'd dried her off, carried her to the couch, and held her in his lap.

It reminded her of the time she'd laid out swatches of fabric on the tables in the restaurant after closing. Her mom had helped her pick out the material for the couches that would be in the furnished apartments. They'd laughed at some of the hideous patterns.

Her mom wouldn't be around to see all the buildings finished. Or be there for any more weekly family dinners.

There'd be no more cooking sessions. Or helping Meredith perfect her magic.

Her mom would miss her wedding and she'd never get to hold her grandchildren. Thoughts of what her mom wouldn't experience bombarded her. It felt like the million pieces of her heart would never come together again.

She didn't know how long they'd sat there with Jack holding her. She could only think of more things her mom would miss.

Some time later, Jack moved her off his lap and conjured some soup.

Just the thought of food made her stomach want to revolt. She'd looked up at him with a refusal on her lips, but his expression stopped her. Her tears started all over again.

He was hurting, just like she was. Both of them were now orphans, like her cousins.

They'd eaten the soup and talked quietly about what had happened in Copeland's condo. Jack told her what her mom had done and how she'd sacrificed herself for Meredith.

He said he'd been second-guessing his actions over and over again, wondering if he could have done something different. *"I killed your mom,"* he'd whispered and then buried his face in her neck.

They'd cried together while they held each other. Then she told Jack what her mom had said about choices. It had been her choice to help defeat Copeland.

A short while later, he'd carried her to bed and held her all night. This morning, he'd woken her up with kisses and a latte.

In the two hours since he'd left for work, she'd managed to get dressed and eat some fruit.

Now she was sitting at her kitchen island with her laptop open, staring out the window at the sunshine streaming in.

She hadn't seen her cousins since the day her mom died

and they'd given her space. Of course, they understood why she needed to be alone. They'd lost their moms too.

A piece of paper appeared in the air, pulling her gaze from the window. The paper floated down, landing softly on the kitchen island.

Six months ago, seeing something materialize in mid-air would have freaked her out, but she'd learned to accept a lot in the last several months.

Block letters spelled out six words on the paper.

Meet in the kitchen's back room.

She turned the paper over, but the other side was blank. There was no name or time to meet. The cryptic note stirred Meredith's curiosity. Because the apartment layouts she'd designed had not included back rooms, she guessed the note meant The Magic Plate's kitchen.

The clock on her laptop showed that it was almost lunch time. Maybe the note meant Jack had a surprise for her. She folded the piece of paper and stuffed it in the back pocket of her jeans.

At the door of her apartment, she hesitated, her hand on the doorknob. When she'd flashed from Copeland's condo, it had been the first time she'd flashed since the day in the field.

Instinct had driven her out of the apartment—she hadn't even thought about it. Should she flash now? Could she end up in the middle of a wall? Stuck between the joists?

There was only one way to find out.

Closing her eyes, she pictured where she wanted to go and flashed.

When she opened her eyes, she laughed to herself as she saw she was exactly where she wanted to be.

Walking into the kitchen from the back stairwell, she waved at the kitchen staff and headed for the back room. The door was ajar so she pushed it open and stared into the room at Rowena and Jo.

"What are you two doing here?"

"Good question," Jo said before waving her hand at the door. The soft click echoed in the small room behind Meredith.

"Take a seat, sweetie," Rowena said, gesturing to a chair as she and Jo pulled out chairs and sat.

"I… I'm…" Meredith swallowed and tried again. "I'm sorry for staying away for the past couple of days."

Rowena pulled her into a hug. "We understand."

"I wish you didn't," Meredith whispered as her throat tightened again. She hugged Rowena back. They clung to each other longer than usual.

"This calls for wine," Jo said.

Meredith laughed as she and Rowena separated and looked over at Jo. Three glasses of wine already stood on the table.

Meredith raised her glass in thanks before taking a sip. "Mmm, good. You've come a long way."

Jo flashed her pearly whites. "I know."

"Did you get a piece of paper?" Rowena asked.

"Oh my god, I forgot all about the note." Meredith pulled the paper from her back pocket and put it on the table. Rowena and Jo pulled out identical ones.

Jo picked up all three pieces, examining them, before looking up at her cousins. "Did yours just pop out of thin air too?"

"Yes. And I've got to say, it's kind of scary that I wasn't even freaked out," Meredith said and grinned at her cousins. "I've come a long way too."

Rowena laughed. "We all have. And yes, the paper just appeared in the air."

"Now what?" Meredith asked.

As soon as the words left her mouth, an envelope appeared on the table. It was plain white—just a regular, number-ten envelope. Something she used all the time at work.

The same block lettering spelled their three names across the envelope.

A chill ran through Meredith and she cupped her wine glass in both hands so she wouldn't be tempted to reach for it. "I'm not sure I want to know what's inside."

"I think it's too coincidental that the notes and this envelope arrive right after Aunt Elise died. She's the last of the three sisters. They were always trying to teach us something and for some reason I wouldn't be surprised if they're still trying to. You're thinking it's from our mothers, aren't you?" Jo asked.

"Yes," she and Rowena both said at the same time.

They chuckled and then Meredith glanced at the letter.

"Whenever I close my eyes," she said softly, "I see my mom tied to a chair in Copeland's place, her face battered and bloody. Or I see her lying on the bed, her skin pale, showing signs of death."

Meredith reached out, one hand to Rowena and one to Jo. Her cousins grasped on as if they needed the lifeline as much as she did. "I'm learning to push those images out of my mind and scroll through my memories for happier ones. Like the one of her teaching me how to cook. Or of us having tea together. There are so many to choose from; I just have to pick."

She blinked away her tears and looked over at Rowena, whose own eyes were rimmed. Then at Jo who never cried but Meredith knew in her heart Jo felt the same.

Giving her cousins' hands a small squeeze, she pulled back and picked up her glass, taking a large gulp for courage. "And that's what it all came down to—choices. I think it always comes down to that. Our moms made choices that affected us. Then and now. My mom—" Meredith's throat tightened again like it had so often in the last few days.

"She loved you. She loved all of us," Rowena whispered, as if the moment was too special to speak above a whisper. "Our moms loved us and no matter what's in that letter, we have to remember that."

Meredith blinked rapidly, trying to hold off her tears, and nodded at Rowena to open the envelope. Jo did the same.

Rowena picked up the letter and turned it over, looking at the back before she slipped her finger under the flap. She pulled out a single sheet of paper and began to read.

Dear Rowena, Meredith, and Josephine,

We've spelled this letter and the notes to arrive two days after the last one of us has left this earth, but only if you are unbound. You might be wondering why two days and not two weeks or two months or even longer. We chose two days because we didn't want you to have to wait any longer for us to remind you how much we love you and to give you time to start to grieve.

At the time of writing this letter, Lillian is sick, and we know there's nothing we can do to save her. It's been five years and four months since the fire, and we've thought so often about what we want to explain to each of you.

We chose to write this together because of how close the three of you are, as are the three of us, and we know you'll support each other after we're gone.

The love of a mother for a daughter is neither greater nor less than a love for a son, yet it is still different. Reece will be fine and know that he is loved. We know he'll grieve and then embrace his magic with everything that he is, as he does with all things in life.

It is you three we worry about.

We had hoped to live to old age and see you all grow up and fall in love and have children of your own. As vain as it may sound, we know that if we got the chance, we would be the best grandmothers.

If you've only just learned about your magic, we want you to know why we made the decisions we did. We're writing this in case none of us are around to explain it to you in person.

Rowena, as the oldest, we know you will shoulder much of the responsibility of making sure everyone has what they need. Already we expect that you'll follow in your mom's footsteps and become a psychologist because you are a nurturer and want to make sure everyone is happy. Please remember, sweet girl, that it is okay to lean on others and you don't have to be the strong one all the time.

Rowena choked on the last words and handed the letter to Meredith. Expecting what was coming next, Meredith took a deep breath and began to read.

Meredith, we expect you will take this the hardest. We robbed you of a precious gift you carried from birth and gave you no say. Even as a new teenager, you're a planner, always looking to the future. We expect that having magic blindside you will make you second-guess everything you know. Please understand that it wasn't our intention to confuse you and that we made our decisions out of love.

When her tears obscured her vision too much to continue reading, Meredith passed the letter off to Jo.

Rowena tossed a used tissue on the growing pile in front of her and plucked a clean one off the stack she'd conjured, passing it to her. Meredith smiled through her tears and dabbed her eyes before nodding at Jo to read the rest of the letter.

Lastly, but never least, Josephine, our Jo. We expect you are angry. We lied—something that even as a small child you deplored. We know it won't be easy and expect it will take something monumental for you to understand why we bound you and lied to you. But, in time, we hope you'll forgive us.

We love you all with everything that we are. Every day since we bound you, we've second-guessed our decisions, but ultimately, we always come back to the same conclusion. We made the right decision at the time... because it was what we knew would best keep you safe.

If there ever comes a time when one of us needs to choose between ourselves and you, we will choose you. Every. Single. Time.

There will be many times in your lives you'll face tough choices. And if you are lucky enough to become mothers, you will wonder every day if you're doing right by your children.

Even with magic and seers, there is no way to know for sure whether every decision is the right one. Make sure your intentions are good and you love with all your heart—that is all any of us can do.

All our love,

Your moms

Jo folded the letter and put it back in the envelope. None of them spoke as their mothers had said it all.

CHAPTER TWENTY-SEVEN

Jack lay on his back with Meredith half-draped over him, her soft breaths tickling his chest as the first rays of dawn peeked through the curtains. He traced his hands up and down her soft skin.

It had been a week since Elise's death. That first night when he'd held Meredith, he'd felt like his own heart had cracked. Watching the woman he loved suffer, and unable to do anything about it, tortured him.

They'd buried Elise yesterday. Fiona and Stella had offered to deal with the funeral arrangements, and after some heavy persuasion Meredith had consented.

Jack had been afraid Meredith would completely shut down, but he should have known better. She was so strong. She'd grieve—maybe forever—but the letter from her mom had helped. And also knowing Elise wanted her to keep living, so that's what she was going to do.

They'd gone for runs and she'd helped in the restaurant and had decided to hire a full-time manager.

Between those times, she had moments she broke down

in tears, but every time Meredith picked herself back up and continued on. She left him in awe.

Jack had talked to Ben and Frank about Copeland, but they still hadn't figured out who the FBI mole was.

Only minutes after Copeland died, Ben had arrived at the scene and taken over. He'd had the foresight to bring a healer who often worked with the FBI's magic task force. While Jack had gone after Meredith, the healer treated Morgana on the spot.

The cousins settled Morgana in a furnished apartment in the Williams's building but so far she kept to herself. Jack and Ben could find no record of a Morgana Smith.

Morgana didn't even know where she'd come from, saying Copeland and others had held her for years, but other than that she knew nothing about herself. Fiona and Stella had offered to watch over Morgana, but eventually Jack would question her.

For now, his focus was on Meredith and helping her heal. Each night he tucked her into bed and pulled her tight against his body, letting her soak in his warmth. They didn't need to say the words to know that they both needed the feel of each other to ground them.

Every time he closed his eyes, he still saw Copeland gripping Meredith in his fist, her feet swinging above the ground as he siphoned her magic. Jack couldn't imagine what life would be like if he'd lost her. He'd waited so long to be with her again—she was his other half.

He thought back to what she said to him the night before as she was falling asleep. She'd looked up at him and he'd felt like she held his heart in her hands. All she had to do was squeeze.

"I've learned faster than most that life can be taken away from you at a moment's notice, and we need to hang on to all that is good in our lives. So, I'm going to hang on to you, Jack. I love you."

He'd leaned down and kissed her, knowing he would never get enough of her, but he would take what he could get for the rest of his life.

That morning he lay with Meredith in his arms, content to wait for the day to come to life.

"Good morning." Sleep still clung to her voice, music to him. They were words he wanted to hear from her every morning until he took his last breath.

Shifting her so she was flat on her back, he moved over her, bracing himself on his arms. "Good morning to you too." He leaned down and kissed her, teasing her mouth and trailing kisses over her face and neck.

"Mmm… minty fresh. I still need to figure out how to use my magic to clean my breath, but I appreciate you doing it for us. I'm just not a morning breath type of person."

"I know," he said as he kissed down her throat.

"Anything else you want to help me with?"

"Hmmm, let me see," he said, welcoming the teasing. They needed some lightness, especially after yesterday, and she seemed to want it too. There would be more grieving later. "You seem cold. I could warm you up."

"I'm not…" Her words cut off when he drifted a cool breeze over her breasts. She shivered, and her nipples hardened instantly. She flashed him a sly smile as he stayed balanced above her, waiting for her response.

He'd dealt with a lot of sorrow in his life; there had been little room for laughter. He liked how she brought it out of him. Serious Jack felt normal, like it was his natural state. Teasing Jack didn't come out often, but he wanted to show her this side of him, every part of him.

"Yes, I think you need to warm me up."

"I can do that." He heard her intake of breath as he lowered the bottom half of his body, making it flush with hers. His erection dragged along her thigh as he moved down her body, kissing and nipping at her cool flesh. "I think you're really cold, right here."

A chill followed his words right before he cupped her breasts in his hands and suckled one nipple into his mouth. He grazed her with his teeth before moving to the other. His mouth nipped and sucked while his hands kneaded and teased.

He groaned as Meredith's breathing picked up and she thrust her lower body up to his. Her skin against his felt like pure heaven. His cock became harder, almost painfully so. The need to be inside her warmth pressed on him, as he matched her rhythm with his own, but he didn't want to rush this.

He summoned patience—and a touch of magic—to cool his skin pressed against her heat.

"Oh god, that feels so good. What did you just do?" Her words were breathless as she reached up, trying to bring his body closer to hers.

"I cooled myself off. I don't want to rush this."

"No, please rush this. It's been too long. Please, Jack, I want you inside me. We can go slow later."

He chuckled. "You say that every time. Shush, woman. I'm busy."

"Okay, please continue," she said as she laughed softly at the fake scowl he aimed her way.

No more words were needed as he worked further down her body, kissing and nipping his way to her core, trailing kisses along her stomach. Lifting her up by her waist, he moved her up the bed, then nestled himself between her legs. Pushing her legs open wider, he slid his arms under her thighs, cradling her so he could bring her forward.

The sound of her gasp as he brought his mouth to the heat of her core for his first lick drove his movements. He took advantage of the stimulating contrasts between his smooth mouth and the several days' growth of whiskers on his face to heighten the sensations.

So attuned to her, his magic told him when the conflicting touches flooded her already feverish skin. He relished the fact that he could make her instantly wet.

Her hands found their way to his head, threading her fingers through his hair and gripping tight. Ignoring how her tug on his scalp made him harder, he used it as a tell when he sucked or licked her just right.

His mouth continued to assault her in the most delicious way while he kneaded the flesh of her ass. He flicked his tongue over her clit and bit down lightly, then sunk a finger into her depths. She would have come off the bed if he hadn't been holding her down.

Meredith's breathing sped up even more and the soft groans she made spurred him on. With everything he was, he wanted to please this woman, not just now, or even just today, but forever.

Her legs stiffened as she started to reach her climax; he added another finger and bit down gently on her clit. The orgasm exploded throughout her body, and she bucked in his arms as she called out his name.

When her high subsided, he crawled up her body and once again braced himself on either side as he hovered over her. She opened her eyes and grinned at him.

"That was okay." The teasing glint in her eyes was beautiful.

"Just okay, was it?"

"Hmmm, yes, I think so, but before you improve on that, I'd like to help you with something."

"Oh, really, and what is that?"

"I think you need some attention and maybe it will give you some incentive to do better next time. But I'm feeling too good to move, so I think I'll just reach waaaaaaaay down here."

He sucked in a breath as her hand wrapped around his length, sure and possessive. She stroked him for several minutes, her thumb using his precum as lubricant. And when she guided him to the edge of her inner warmth, he didn't think he'd be able to hold off much longer.

Locking his gaze with hers, he brought his body closer to hers and sunk into her with one long, slow stroke. They both groaned at the heady sensation of once more being joined.

Dropping his body so their lengths were flush with each other, he captured her mouth with his. Their mouths were the only parts of them moving as their lower bodies remained locked together and still. His mouth made love to hers, showering her with all the emotion that had been ratcheting up inside of him for months.

When they finally came up for air, he started to move again, slowly at first, still braced on his arms above her.

"More, Jack. I want to feel you so deep inside me that the rest of the world falls away and there's only us."

He didn't say anything; the time for teasing was over. Moving onto his knees, he pulled her hips toward him, increasing his strokes, thrusting into her over and over, wanting to be so deep they were one.

Without giving her a warning, he pulled out, gripped her around the hips, and flipped her over in one move. She went onto her knees without a word and dropped her chest to the sheets, giving him an amazing view of her ass. He ran his hands over her butt cheeks and back and then gripped her hips and eased into her, loving the clench of her inner muscles squeezing around his cock.

She rolled her hips, drawing him deeper, eliciting a groan from them both.

As much as he loved seeing her face when she came, this

view was fucking amazing. "Rub yourself. I'm not going to last, and I want you to come with me."

She reached between her legs and it wasn't long before her muscles clenched and spasmed around him, sucking him in as she breathed out his name while she came. The feel of her coming around him was his undoing and he followed her over the precipice. A glorious fall.

A few minutes later they lay in each other's arms, their breathing steady again. For the first time he could recall, peace filled him.

"I want a memorial tattoo for my mom, a magic one. Like you have for your mom and Charlie."

Jack sat up against the headboard and conjured a black coffee for himself and a latte just the way Meredith liked it. He waited until she'd pulled herself up and passed her the latte. "Do you know of what?"

"No, but I want it on the inside of my wrist so I'll see it all the time."

"I think your mom would like that. She loved you so much." Jack's throat tightened. He'd never forget the moment he realized that Elise was going to sacrifice herself to save her daughter. But he would forever be grateful she chose to save Meredith and he would make sure he gave Meredith the best life he could.

When she was quiet for a moment, he looked down and saw tears streaming down her cheeks. He used his magic to dry them and leaned over to kiss her hair before settling back against the headboard. "I'm sure you'll think of the perfect tattoo."

They drank their coffees in silence for several minutes before Meredith sat forward.

"Oh."

"What?" He leaned forward to see her face and then she sat back.

"We didn't use a condom. I'm not sure I know exactly what day it is, but I think we're okay."

He levitated the cups to the side-table and drew her over him. Her body blanketed him as he looked in her eyes. "Would it be awful if you were pregnant?"

"You still want kids?"

"I've always wanted kids with you. You did too." He huffed out a laugh. "I suppose we should have revisited this topic earlier, but better late than never."

"Yes, I still want kids and I want them to grow up surrounded by family… aunts, uncles, and cousins." He knew the words that she left unsaid. There wouldn't be any biological grandparents, but they had Fiona, Stella, Ben, and his brothers Joel and Frank.

"I love you, Jack."

He leaned over and kissed her. "I love you too, Bubbles." He didn't expect life would be easy, and they still hadn't discussed the magic council, but Jack was okay with it all now that he had Meredith by his side.

Four months later...

"Is she coming down?" Meredith asked Jo as she joined them at their usual table in the back of the restaurant. The Magic Plate was quiet tonight due to an early spring snowfall. Only a few stragglers remained from the dinner crowd. The waitstaff had them covered and would soon head home, leaving the large group on their own.

She scanned the tables and smiled at the sight of Fiona and Stella, the unspoken matriarchs of their new cobbled-together family, along with Ben, Frank, and Joel, the patriarchs.

It was bittersweet to be carrying on her mother's weekly tradition of gathering whoever was around. But knowing that they were bringing together different generations, as well as people who didn't have any loved ones nearby, like Jack's FBI colleagues Lisa, Javier, and Drew, helped with her grief.

Mary, the Emissary, caught her gaze and shared a smile. In the month since Meredith had gone through the council ceremony, she and Mary had become friends, bonding over both losing their parents far too soon.

"No. Morgana has another headache," Jo said, pulling Meredith out of her reverie. "But Damon said he'd take something to eat up to her." Jo reached for the bottle of wine on the table to refill their glasses.

"Did the healer make any progress this week?" Morgana's magic was almost non-existent and she often had debilitating headaches, but no one knew what to do.

"No, no progress."

"What about Reece?" she asked Jo while her eyes traveled to her only male cousin sitting at the end of the long table.

Jo shook her head. "He hasn't improved. He's still really weak and can't use his magic. But he hasn't deteriorated either. The healer thinks he just needs more time."

The sadness over the loss of her mother and aunt and all they'd suffered still pulled at Meredith most days. She looked across the table and gave Jo a small smile. "Yes, time."

The chatter of her family—those by blood and those bonded by grief, love, and friendship—warmed her heart. Several conversations were happening around her, but she was content to sit and watch.

Everyone gravitated to their own kind: agents with agents and business people with business people, the others floating in between. They were just like the cliques that formed in high school. But unlike school, there was a bond between them all. A bond that had grown stronger over the months, through their grief and their fight to continue the battle they'd started.

So far, none of the children Morgana said were kidnapped had been identified, and they still didn't know who the FBI mole was. Copeland said he hadn't been working alone, but whoever he'd been working with was still a mystery. Jack and his team wouldn't give up looking.

Rubbing her forearm, she looked down at the tattoo she'd gotten the week after she buried her mother. Jack had reached out to an old friend of his, Isaac, who was one of only a handful of magics who could create memorial tattoos.

As a favor to Jack and for a change in scenery, Isaac had flown to Blue Mountain to do Meredith's tattoo and he had fallen in love with the city. He decided to stay and rent one of Meredith's new business spaces and was now a regular at the weekly dinners.

She loved her tattoo, a small compass with blue and red watercolors swirling around it. Her mother had been her true north and she'd passed the torch to Jack, so it seemed fitting. Meredith ran her hand over the compass and could feel warmth, her fingers tingling with the memory of her mother's laughter.

Jo and Rowena had gotten similar tattoos in memory of their own mothers. The tattoos were just one more thing they had in common. It was poignant having their mothers' laughter with them at all times while knowing they would never hear it come directly from them again.

"Bubbles." Meredith looked up at Jack standing beside her. He held out his hand. "Come on, I want to take you somewhere."

"You don't want to wait for dinner?" Each week several people took turns bringing out all the dishes that had been made earlier in the day, and she'd just seen Rowena and Javier walk into the kitchen to get the food.

"No, we don't need to."

Jack gripped Meredith's hand a little tighter and pulled her up. "Follow me."

They'd learned last month, when they were experimenting with their new abilities, that they were now powerful enough to flash with another person. They could also direct each other in a flash. It had taken her awhile to get over the fear that she'd flash into a tree again, but with Jack's love and reassurance, she could now laugh about that experience.

Meredith's feet softly touched down on the grass and she knew immediately where they were—the meadow where the Emissary had first taken her and Jack. It was also where she'd first learned magic. In the waning light, the meadow felt magical.

Jack stepped to the side and Meredith gasped. A large blanket lay on a patch of lush green grass amidst the field of snow. A picnic basket sat on top. Jack had ringed the blanket with soft lights and heaters, adding to the romantic ambience. "It's beautiful, Jack."

"I wanted to bring you here because this is where it all started for us. The Emissary brought us here in a soul jump, but I think I first fell in love with you in a field just like this. I was ten years old when you asked me to make you bubbles and even though I didn't really understand love back then, you touched me in a way no one else has."

He knelt down on one knee and opened his palm. Her hands flew to her face, covering her mouth as her eyes widened. Tears slid down her cheeks, but she didn't care. They were tears of happiness.

"I made a choice that doomed me to a life of darkness, but you showed me the light. It sounds cheesy and isn't overly romantic, but Bubbles, you saved me. You showed me what it's like to truly love. Showed me the light I have inside me and how to share it. I love you more than I ever thought possible and I want to wake up with you every morning, fall asleep with you in my arms. Raise a family together, and grow old by your side. Will you marry me?"

"Yes! Yes, yes." She threw herself into his arms as more tears fell down her cheeks. Jack kissed her long and hard before pulling back and reaching for her left hand.

"Wait, Jack."

He raised his eyebrows and smirked at her as she took a big steadying breath. "I've already said yes, but I need to say one more thing."

He chuckled as he stood and pulled her up with him. "I wouldn't expect anything less."

She rolled her eyes, then grew serious. "For years I looked for love and didn't find it because I'd already had it. You owned my heart—even when you weren't with me. I was too caught up in the past and wallowing in my own misery that I didn't fight for what I needed—you. You saved me too, and not just physically. You saved my heart and soul and they'll always be yours." Her throat constricted and she swallowed against the lump. "I love you, Jack."

He slid a beautiful white-gold solitaire ring onto her finger. "I love you too. I wanted this time with you," he gestured to the blanket, "before we celebrate with our family. They're waiting back at the restaurant with champagne and cake."

Meredith chuckled. "Of course they are. But us first."

"Always you first, Bubbles." Jack kissed her again, and she felt all his love in that touch. It was quite a while before they made it back to the restaurant, but no one seemed surprised.

Jo LOCKED her brother's apartment door and flashed up one floor to hers. Flashing was her favorite thing about magic. Lately, she'd made herself walk every other trip, banking some exercise for all the flashing she enjoyed.

Inside her own apartment, she sat on her couch and conjured a glass of wine, not bothering to turn on a light. In the dark she could pretend that things were like they used to be. That her mother and aunt were still alive and her brother wasn't slowly wasting away.

The week before, the night Meredith got engaged, Jo hadn't lied about her brother's health. The healer said he wasn't deteriorating, but Jo could see Reece slipping away in subtle ways. His physical weakness was chewing away at his spirit.

Reece didn't joke like he used to and he kept to himself more and more. Most days now he slipped into his beloved bakery before anyone else arrived, baked the day's goods, then left it for his staff to run.

Jo only knew because she now made several quick check-ins on him every day. She'd already lost her parents and one brother; she wouldn't lose Reece too.

A knock on the door pulled Jo out of her morbid thoughts. "Come in," she yelled, not moving off the couch. Only family could ride the elevator or get through the protections to the apartment floors without being buzzed up.

She looked over her shoulder and saw Jack walk in. Oddly, Meredith wasn't with him.

"Jo, I wanted to talk to you about something."

"Sure, can I conjure you a scotch?" She gave Jack a grin. "I'm getting better."

"Sure, but let me be the judge of your prowess."

Jo laughed at him. He'd definitely loosened up since Meredith forgave him. That was funny in itself as Meredith was the uptight one of the four cousins. Jo put her wine on the side table and concentrated. A tumbler of dark amber liquid with three chips of ice appeared in her hand.

Jack took the drink and swirled it around before breathing in the peaty aroma and taking a sip. "Not bad. You are improving."

Jo picked up her wine and settled back on the couch as Jack took a seat across from her. "What's up?"

"I need you to do something for me. For the council."

"I thought the council members were selected, you said you aren't allowed to pick them."

"True, and we don't know how long that will take. This can't wait."

"You have me intrigued. Or should I be worried?"

"Meredith mentioned that you've extended your leave of absence from the university."

"Yes." Jo didn't know where Jack was going with this. Being a professor at the university teaching young minds about history and leading field work every summer was a dream come true, but her family was more important right now. "I'm staying here for as long as Reece needs me."

"Good, because I need you to look for an ancient book. Reece needs it."

"I'll do anything for my brother, you know that. But give me details. You're not making sense." It didn't matter what Jack was asking. If it would help Reece, she'd do it.

"Meredith and I had a recent training session with a couple of the European council members and they told us about some ancient magic books. They believe there are seven of them, one for each council in the world. They believe the books are all the same and contain some information about the magic box that Copeland was looking for. It might also contain a spell that will help Reece."

Jo disappeared her wine glass and sat forward. "Holy shit! Where do I find one of these books?"

"That's the problem. We don't know. My dad had one and gave it to your mother and aunts to spell bind you, but the moment they finished the binding, the book disappeared. I'm not sure if it went back to my dad or returned to its original owner. None of the ancient books from dad's estate went to auction. So if it returned to him, I don't know where he put it."

"Then how do you know it still exists?"

"I don't, but it did at one time. Plus, the other council leaders are sure all the books still exist."

For the first time in months Jo felt some hope for her brother. If a book existed to help him, she'd find it. "I assume you want me to look for it because it won't be suspicious if a historian is researching or looking for old texts?"

"Exactly. And you'll probably be the best choice for following any clues."

Jo blew out a breath to push her bangs out of her eyes and gave herself a little shake to contain her excitement. It didn't matter that it was late in the evening, she wanted to get started right away. "Where do I start?"

"You're familiar with the Blue Mountain Public Library?"

"Of course. It has more than twenty million items, making it the fifth largest library in the country. I've spent more than my fair share of hours researching there."

"Viktor Szabo is in charge of all the magic books in the library. It's a massive collection."

"Viktor is a legend, but I've never met him personally. He's the good-looking old Hungarian guy, right?"

Jack chuckled. "I've never heard him described as good-looking, but yes, I believe he's Hungarian. I think he's in his late fifties or early sixties."

"Hey, that's just what I've heard. Anyway, if Viktor runs the place, wouldn't he know if the book is there?"

Jack sighed. "Unfortunately, no. Magic book, means… well… magic. The book has vanished, and rumor says that when the right person follows the clues it will reveal itself."

Jo nodded in understanding. "I'm in. When can I start?"

"There's something else, Jo. We're not the only ones who want the book. There's been talk from some agents at the office that the people Copeland was working with are looking for it too. Ben has sent an agent in undercover, but I don't know who the agent is. Hence, undercover. You'll just have to be careful and keep me updated. I'll help where I can."

"Like I said, I'm in. When can I start?"

Jack disappeared his tumbler and stood. "Viktor will expect you in two days."

They said their goodbyes and Jack vanished. Jo took her time getting ready for bed, going over everything she'd need to do before she started her new task.

She'd find the book. Nothing and no one would stand in her way.

BEN FLASHED into the narrow service lane behind the Maplewood Market, finding it empty. A single security camera covered the loading bay area. He waved his hand, erasing the last several minutes of footage and the red recording light winked out. After confirming he wasn't seen, he made his way to the front door.

He grabbed one of the scarred green baskets and made a slow circuit of the outside aisles. Perusing the baked goods, he chose a carrot-cake and placed it in his basket. Playing the casual shopper, he meandered down an inside aisle and forced his shoulders to loosen. This wasn't an op. Just a mentor checking on an undercover agent. Ben had sent the agent—someone he considered almost a son—into a sticky situation nine months ago. And hadn't heard from him in over a month.

He grabbed a box of tea off a shelf and added it to his basket. At row six, he walked halfway down the aisle, as the message had instructed. There were plenty of displays to block them from sight and no cameras.

Ben placed his basket on the floor, picked up two jars of peanut butter and pretended to compare labels. He wasn't alone for long.

A tall man in a gray T-shirt and faded jeans turned the corner, pushing a cart with an easy slouch that said he didn't have a care in the world. Moss-green eyes, messy dark hair, and a few days of stubble, the man offered a nod. As usual, the agent arrived as himself, leaving his arrogant blond persona behind.

"Morning," Ben said casually.

"Morning." The younger man parked his cart nose-to-nose with Ben's basket, the groceries forming a little barricade. To anyone looking they appeared to be two friendly shoppers chatting about the pros and cons of different types of nut butters.

"No salt. No preservatives. Plain and simple." Ben waved his hand toward the shelves as if gesturing to the different products. "A barrier's in place. I had started to worry by the time I got your message."

"Yeah, sorry about that. I didn't want to call until I knew I'd be able to change identities without being seen."

"Have they been keeping close tabs on you?"

"I think so. At least at the family gallery. I've been tailed a few times."

Ben put the jar of peanut butter back on the shelf and picked up another. He looked down at the label. No one could hear them, though they were visible to anyone walking past. "Don't underestimate these guys. Copeland could have been spewing bullshit, but Jack said he sounded damn confident about the people he worked with."

"I'm careful. It's just that it's been three weeks since my contact's last text. I'd been expecting something to happen by now." He sighed. "I've been working this case for seven months."

The agent had always prided himself on patience, but that many empty months would test anyone. Ben cocked an eyebrow. "Slow burn, remember? You're still in their orbit. That means you're doing something right."

"Feels like I'm doing nothing. I know more about art than anyone in the gallery I'm supposed to be running, but apparently my alter ego hadn't given a shit. I made a purchase for the gallery last week and by the reactions you would have thought I gave away the family fortune."

Ben chuckled. "Oh, some of the joys of undercover work."

"I've lost track of the number of charity functions I've attended. The more I'm around his mother, the better chance for a slip."

"You'll be fine. You've done this before." Ben returned the peanut butter. "How's Catherine?"

The agent's expression softened. "She's a wonderful woman, but lonely. Her son was a real bastard. Every time she calls me son, I think about what will happen when she finds out the truth."

Compassion pinched Ben's chest. The agent was a good man. Living with your dead mark's mother would twist any soul—especially one who tragically lost his own mother years ago. "You're giving her more kindness than her real son ever did. That counts for something."

"Tell that to my nerves. I spend time every day coming up with amusing things to tell her about my day."

A middle-aged shopper nudged past with her cart. Ben nodded his head in greeting and waited until she rounded the corner before speaking again. "Again… patience. And in other news, we haven't learned anything about the mole, but keep your ears open about that."

"You worried?"

"We'll find him. Or her," Ben said, not answering the agent's question. He had enough to worry about on his own without taking on what was now a council problem. "Just don't let that make you rush anything. Remember—predators sense desperation."

"Got it." The agent glanced down the aisle, verifying they were still alone. "Ben… you trust me, right?"

"With my life."

"Then tell the higher-ups to stop hovering. I'll get results if they give me room."

Ben let out a soft laugh and didn't remind the agent he was the impatient one a few moments ago. "The higher-ups? You mean the Magic Task Force's leader, my brother Frank? He agreed to sending me for groceries instead of hauling your ass into the office. Be thankful this is his idea of *hovering*."

That earned a genuine grin. "Understood. I know you hate grocery shopping."

"And lucky for me it's not a common occurrence." Ben picked up his basket. "But I'll do whatever—or go wherever—you need me."

The agent's smile wavered. "Ah… thanks."

In the next aisle over, a child squealed. Ben cleared his throat. "Are you expected back soon?"

The agent checked his watch. "I'm supposed to be getting tea."

"Then, here." Ben transferred his items, including the tea, from his basket to the agent's cart. "You're all set. Head to the check out."

"Thanks." He looked down at the tea and grinned. "I don't know if it's the right brand, but if it's not she won't be surprised that her *son* messed up."

"And if you don't want me *hovering*…" Ben let the sentence hang. The fluorescent hum bled into the silence.

The agent lifted a brow. "Yes?"

Ben vanished the barrier. "You'll check in more often."

He chuckled. "Will do." With that, the agent wheeled away, singing a tune to himself.

Ben watched him disappear around the corner, pride and worry braided tight in his chest. He picked up his empty basket and dropped it into the stand near the door.

Back in the service lane behind the building, Ben pushed some magic toward the alley camera and the recording light flickered back to life.

As with all missions, he worried what an agent would face. But this time was different. Years ago, a seer had predicted something big was coming and Ben feared that time was now. Whatever happened, he would be there for the agent. And if needed, he'd help him find his way out of the dark.

Thanks so much for reading *Hidden in Magic!*
You don't have to say goodbye just yet.
Go to:
https://kjwarawa.com/hidden-in-magic-bonus-scene/
to download a free bonus scene with more of Meredith &
Jack's HEA.

Then find out what happens next when Jo and Simon fight for their Happily Ever After because only one will succeed in their quest and one will lose everything in
Truth in Magic
https://books2read.com/truth-in-magic

ALSO BY KJ WARAWA

IN MAGIC SERIES

Hidden in Magic

Truth in Magic

Found in Magic

Courage in Magic

Love in Magic

Forged in Magic

Forever in Magic

CURSED TO LOVE SERIES

Cursed to Love

Cursed to Dream

Cursed to Wither

Cursed to Suffer

ABOUT KJ WARAWA

Paranormal romance author KJ Warawa had worked every job under the sun, including swimwear seller, switchboard operator, legal secretary, sign language interpreter, soldier, massage therapist, and process improvement advisor, before settling into the career she'd always dreamed about: Author.

She still loves processes and spreadsheets, doesn't love massaging feet, and is currently living out her own love story in Alberta, Canada.

STAY IN TOUCH WITH KJ:
Join KJ's Newsletter at
https://kjwarawa.com/free-book/
to receive a FREE book, exclusive deals, special offers, behind-the-scenes info, and learn about new releases, plus more!
www.kjwarawa.com